ACKNOWLEDGMENT

To Darrell W. Hutton
of the Oregon Liquor Control Commission,
who patiently answered all my questions.

"What do you think you're doing?" Samantha shrieked from the door

The baby remained asleep as Shea cradled him in his arm.

Shea gazed at Samantha with practiced innocence. "I'm taking him with me. Home for Christmas. I thought you understood that."

"No, you're not!"

"Yes, I am." He made himself sound surprised that she didn't understand. "We just agreed. Your lawyer's going to call my lawyer about visitation rights."

"No!" She caught his free arm and tried to stop him. "Shea, you can't take him! I'll have you arrested for kidnapping."

"He's my son, Sam. It wouldn't be kidnapping, because there's no established custody. And a simple test will prove I'm his father."

"I'm his mother. He should be with his mother."

"His mother just lost her job and her house," Shea reminded her. "His father, however, is a partner in a business that's been written up in *Money Magazine*."

"Shea," she pleaded. "Zachary's all I've got."

"Then you'd better pack a bag," he said implacably, "because he's coming with me. At least until after Christmas."

Dear Reader,

No, my cards aren't written, my gifts all purchased or my wrap and ribbons located. But my Christmas book is ready for you!

At last, here is Shea's story, the third in my DELANCEY BROTHERS series, and the one that was the most fun to write. After avoiding his past for the first two books and refusing to discuss the woman in it, Shea is confronted with both and forced to deal with them. What a perfect time of year to learn that everything you thought was lost is just waiting for you to turn around and discover it.

I am unashamedly schmaltzy to my very core, so I give you Christmas lights, a snow-covered winery in a cozy valley, mulled wine, scrumptious food, danger and heroics and—finally—families reunited to celebrate the holidays together.

I wish each and every one of you all the love in this book—and send you my own.

Muriel Jensen

Books by Muriel Jensen

HARLEQUIN SUPERROMANCE
683—HUSBAND IN A HURRY
751—THE FRAUDULENT FIANCÉE
764—THE LITTLE MATCHMAKER
825—FIRST BORN SON (THE DELANCEY BROTHERS)
842—SECOND TO NONE (THE DELANCEY BROTHERS)

THE THIRD WISE MAN

Muriel Jensen

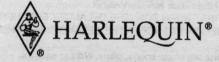

HARLEQUIN®

TORONTO • NEW YORK • LONDON
AMSTERDAM • PARIS • SYDNEY • HAMBURG
STOCKHOLM • ATHENS • TOKYO • MILAN • MADRID
PRAGUE • WARSAW • BUDAPEST • AUCKLAND

ISBN 0-373-70880-7

THE THIRD WISE MAN

Copyright © 1999 by Muriel Jensen.

This edition published by arrangement with Harlequin Books S.A.

® and TM are trademarks of the publisher. Trademarks indicated with ® are registered in the United States Patent and Trademark Office, the Canadian Trade Marks Office and in other countries.

Visit us at www.romance.net

Printed in U.S.A.

CHAPTER ONE

"UNCLE SHEA!" Megan Delancey exclaimed in admiration as Shea pulled the roasting pan out of the oven. "That's the most beautiful Thanksgiving turkey I ever saw."

"Me, too!" Her sister, Katie, closed in on Shea from the other side as he hefted the pan with the twenty-eight-pound bird onto the counter. "You're probably the best cook in the whole world!"

"He's a chef!" Megan, nine, corrected Katie with big-sister superiority. "Daddy says it's better than a cook. Right, Uncle Shea?"

The girls barely gave him elbowroom as he used two meat forks to place the golden, sizzling bird on a platter.

"Not better, necessarily." Shea pulled off the oven mitts and stuck two pans of rolls in the oven. "But a chef has more formal training." He considered how those words would sound to young ears and amended, "He goes to a cooking school and learns to make some pretty fancy stuff. But it doesn't make him better than the cook. Some cooks are very talented and work really hard. Watch the pan, Katie. The drippings are hot."

"Nobody's better than you," Megan said loyally. "Want me to set the timer?"

"Eight minutes," he replied, reaching for the green beans waiting in a colander. He knew he could trust her to set the clock precisely. Her sister loved working in the vineyard with their stepfather, Shea's brother Tate. But Megan spent a lot of her spare time cooking with Shea. "Thanks, Megan. It's not true, but I like the fact that you think it is."

"Well, we know you're the best chef in the compound, at least."

He grinned at her. "I'm the *only* chef in the compound."

"The best cook, then. Daddy says Delancey's got a five-star…" She tried to remember the right word and finally settled for "thingie."

"Rating." He puffed up a little at the memory of *West Coast Magazine*'s rave review. "Yeah. Well, I have some pretty special people cooking with me at the restaurant."

"How come we didn't cook *this* in the restaurant?" Katie asked, resuming her place at his elbow as he put half a pound of bacon in a sauté pan. "Like you did for Uncle Mike and Aunt Veronica's wedding."

He set the heat on low.

"Because one of the best things about cooking a turkey is how great it makes the house smell." He turned the sweet potatoes in the bubbling brown sugar and butter on a back burner and stirred the corn kernels the girls had asked for.

"Anything I can do?" Tate appeared in the doorway, smiling and relaxed, eating a slice of baguette with baked Brie and pecans from the appetizer tray Shea had put on the coffee table in the living room.

Megan and Katie went to Tate, pulled like magnets by his confidence and competence. He'd been their father for a brief five months, but they had accepted him wholeheartedly. When Shea thought about what he and his brothers had undertaken almost eleven months ago, he was more amazed that they'd tried it than that they'd succeeded.

But Tate had been so certain they could take the decrepit winery they'd inherited and bring it back to life. That they could then add a restaurant and a bed-and-breakfast and make those pay, too.

Shea and Mike had been drawn in by Tate's faith in their ability to work together, by his conviction that their combined talents could pay off in a big way. So they'd given their all—financially, physically, emotionally.

Shea's financial "all" at that time had been pretty pathetic, but they hadn't bothered to count one another's contributions; they'd just worked as hard as they could.

"I appreciate your wanting to help," Shea said, handing Tate a cup. "But what can you do? Design a skyscraper that'll withstand fire, flood, earthquake and celestial debris? That's not going to help a lot in the kitchen."

"He can peel potatoes," Megan said, her arms wrapped around Tate's right one.

"No, he can't," Katie corrected, holding on to his left hand. "Mommy says he takes too much peel and makes them too small."

"He makes good coffee."

"That's not cooking," Katie objected. "The coffee-pot does that."

Tate held up the cup in his right hand. "Actually, my skills lie in the area of testing. If you put a little dressing in this, I'll rate it for you."

Shea made a scornful face. "My dressing is excellent. But I thought you might want to test the mulled wine." He pointed to the corner of the counter.

"Now you're talking."

"I'll do it, Daddy." Megan took the cup from him, carefully ladled the spicy mixture into it and brought it back to him.

Tate took a sip, closed his eyes and nodded his approval. "I hate to admit how good you are at this, Shea. No wonder Sullivan said our tasting room deserved five stars, too."

"Didn't you say he was the best chef in the world, Daddy?" Katie prodded.

"I don't think so." Tate helped himself to a spoonful of cranberry relish from a nearby bowl. "Doesn't sound like me. Who told you that?"

"You did!" Katie laughed, knowing he was teasing her. "You were telling Mommy how good the restaurant was doing and you said it was because your little brother was the best chef in the world."

"Ah." Tate leaned against the counter and took another sip from his cup. "I meant Uncle Mike."

Both girls were now giggling.

"Uncle Mike doesn't cook," Megan pointed out.

"Yes, I do." Mike strode into the room, smiling and relaxed. There was always an edge of awareness to him that bespoke long years as a cop, but his new bride had mellowed him considerably. "Remember when your mom and dad went to Seattle for the weekend and you stayed with Aunt Veronica and me? I made peanut-butter sandwiches."

"That's not cooking!" Katie screeched, delighted in her exasperation with her father and her uncle. "For it to be cooking, it has to go on the stove and you have to put things in it and stir it and stuff. Or you have to bake it.''

Mike frowned at Shea. "Is that true?"

Shea separated the strips of bacon as they began to warm. "Pretty much."

"Why are you frying bacon?" Mike asked.

"For the green beans."

"Aren't you going to put in mushroom soup and those fried onions out of a can?" Mike asked expectantly. "I like that."

Shea gave him a pitying look. "No, I'm not. Soup is not sauce, I don't care what your *Cooking from a Can Cookbook* says. You'll like this better."

Mike rolled his eyes. "The five stars you got are in a tourist magazine, not on your shoulder. You still don't outrank us. You'll always be the kid brother." He frowned suddenly at the contents of Tate's cup. "Mulled wine? Where'd you get that?"

Shea handed Megan another cup, and she filled it and handed it to Mike. Then Shea passed Tate a potato masher and pushed Mike toward the cupboard at the far end of the kitchen. "Would you get four serving bowls off the top shelf? Katie, you want to get your dad the butter and the milk from the fridge, please? Megan, the pickles and olives and peppers are on the table. Will you put them into that divided bowl for me?"

His kitchen staff pressed into service, Shea turned and found a small redhead and a tall brunette in the kitchen doorway. He experienced a warm sense of happiness at the knowledge that the redhead belonged to Tate and the brunette to Mike. But it also left him with a strange sense of loss he really didn't want to think about.

"People come in here," Colette, Tate's wife, said as she approached to look over Shea's shoulder, "and they don't come out again. Are Veronica and I missing out on samples?" She snatched a green bean from the colander and took a dainty bite.

Veronica leaned a forearm on his shoulder and pointed to the turkey. "That looks marvelous! Are you susceptible to bribes for one of the legs?"

"Tate and Mike have already claimed one each. You'll have to negotiate with them."

Colette laughed and exchanged a knowing look with Veronica. "This is going to be so easy. We control their 'dessert.'"

Shea smiled, knowing they weren't talking apple pie.

SHEA CALCULATED that he could have had the final dinner preparations done in half the time his willing assistants required, but the cozy closeness of seven people bumping shoulders and elbows in the confines of the old kitchen was an experience he wouldn't have missed.

Armand and Rachel Beauchamp also joined them at the table. Armand was Colette's father, and Rachel, his new bride, had lived on the compound when Shea and his brothers inherited it.

"Somebody has to say grace," Megan declared. "'Cause Thanksgiving is about being thankful."

Everyone looked to Armand, since he was the senior member of the family. He shook his head and pointed to Tate. "You do it. You're in charge of Delancey Vineyards."

Shea pointed to Veronica. "You're the ex-nun."

She deferred to Shea. "It's your house and your dinner."

"All right." He reached out for a hand on either side of him—Megan's and Rachel's—and everyone around the table joined hands. He could almost hear the energy humming in the circle. He thought about what the last year had meant to him. "Thank You for this food," he said, "mercifully free of canned mushroom soup and fried onions." He met Mike's upbraiding glance across the table. "Thank You for the blessings the last year has brought us—specifically, all the ladies at this table. Thank You for lending us Armand's wisdom, for bringing us even more success than we'd hoped for, for keeping us safe and bringing us peace. Amen."

Rachel patted his shoulder. "Well put," she said. "I've never seen a family like this one, which skates from one traumatic event to the next miraculously unscathed. What a gift."

"Hopefully all traumatic events are behind us for a while," Colette said, putting a dollop of mashed potatoes on her plate and passing the bowl to Megan. "We're coming into the Christmas season and we're all going to be so busy personally and with compound business that we don't need any distractions."

"Let's enjoy Thanksgiving," Tate said, helping himself to the relish tray, "before we start worrying about Christmas."

"Are your daughters coming from Paris?" Rachel asked. She split a flaky roll in half and buttered it.

"That was the plan." Tate held the relish plate while Colette considered it, fork poised over it. "But my ex and her husband are going to Gstaad for the holidays. Susan and Sarah might find that just too much fun to pass up. I'm waiting to hear."

"More fun than *us?*" Mike asked. "There's no such

thing. Okay, I'm going to give these green beans a try. They'd better be as good as the green-bean bake you maligned during grace."

Mike put a small portion on his plate, then tasted it cautiously, his expression unrevealing. He smiled reluctantly and helped himself to another overflowing spoonful. "Okay, it's better than the green-bean bake, but don't get cocky."

"Patrons are now having to make reservations for dinner at Delancey's six weeks ahead." Colette took the bowl from him. "He *can* be cocky—" she smiled across the table at Shea "—because he's brilliant."

"Don't tell him that," Tate teased. "When the three of us decided to make a go of the winery instead of selling it, he was the one who'd lost his last dime. Now his restaurant is keeping the rest of the place afloat until we can sell our wine. He'll get a big head."

Shea was relieved when everyone finally settled down to eat. He was used to being the object of his brothers' teasing; he'd had a lifetime of it. But their praise was something new, and after his failures in San Francisco, he wasn't comfortable with it. When the police had closed down his restaurant pending an investigation into the illegal dealings of his partner, he'd used the last of his savings to pay his employees. Then the notice arrived from his uncle's attorney, informing him he'd inherited one-third of a winery, and he'd headed north to try to renew himself in the company of his brothers and figure out how to repay all the creditors he'd left behind.

He'd been sure his brothers intended to sell the winery left to them by their missing uncle, Jack Delancey, who'd finally been declared dead after seven years.

He discovered that first night in this house that each

of them was at a crossroads and had to make tough choices. Tate had abandoned a lucrative partnership in an architectural firm in Boston; Mike, a shattered career with the Dallas police department.

But he was the only one who'd left a weeping woman behind. He knew the tears had come from anger and not just grief over her separation from him, but the image of her, gray eyes pooling, pink mouth quivering, had lived with him for the past eleven months.

He'd done the right thing by leaving her; he was sure of it. But he was beginning to think he'd never forget her.

Shea made cold turkey and dressing sandwiches with cranberry relish for dinner. There were barely enough leftovers to save, except for a cup of green beans, which Mike warmed for himself in the microwave.

Shea did up cappuccinos for the adults and hot chocolate for the girls and served them with pumpkin pie as they all settled down to watch the evening news. Then the lead story destroyed for Shea the peace he'd given thanks for earlier that evening.

"Adam Haskell was nowhere to be found today," a somber male reporter said, "when his empire crumbled in the face of Oliver Owens's takeover of Haskell Media. It's suspected that Haskell's much-publicized affair with Wendy Merriweather, a twenty-two-year-old showgirl in Las Vegas, contributed to his financial demise. He apparently was so distracted by this liaison he failed to notice that the stockmarket 'correction' of August '98 left his corporation vulnerable to the ravenous Owens. Haskell could not be reached for comment."

The reporter's grave face was suddenly replaced by

what appeared to be a mob scene in front of the Haskell Media building on California Street in San Francisco.

"Reporters," the voice went on, "caught Haskell's daughter and vice president in charge of print media leaving the building after a farewell meeting with the staff. KPIZ's Jeremy Johnston asked her about the day's events."

A tall, slender woman broke free of the crowd and tried to reach a limousine where the liveried driver held open the back door. She wore a red suit with gold x-shaped buttons, and carried an armful of papers. On her shoulder was the small square black purse that was her trademark. She never carried much, she'd insisted, because she didn't need much.

A reporter got between her and the limo and there was a closeup of her face—gray eyes pooling with tears, pink mouth quivering.

Shea put his cup on the coffee table before he dropped it.

"How does it feel, Ms. Haskell," the reporter asked, "to lose your status as vice president of your father's company and probably much of your inheritance?"

"Good Lord!" Shea heard Colette exclaim as he stared at the screen. "There has to be a special place in hell for reporters who ask such stupid questions!"

"Really," Veronica said. "I hope she belts him."

The woman firmed her lips, however, and gave a defiant toss of the silver blond hair that fell in a straight veil to her shoulders.

"The money never defined me," she said, the tears glistening in her eyes but not falling. "You win some and you lose some. The Haskells will be back. Watch for us."

She pushed the reporter aside and climbed into the limousine.

"But what about your infant son?" the reporter shouted through the tinted glass of the limo's rear window. "How will you provide for him?"

The limousine moved away, leaving the reporter's question unanswered.

Shea missed the speculation that followed over Adam Haskell's future. He was busy dealing with the sudden increase in his blood pressure the reporter's last question had brought about.

Infant son? Sam had an infant son? He calculated backward. He'd left San Francisco at the end of the previous January. The last time he'd made love to Samantha Haskell had been just weeks before that on New Year's Eve.

A feeling that was weirdly hot and cold ricocheted inside him until he felt as though it might beat him to death.

Samantha Haskell's infant son was…his.

CHAPTER TWO

SHEA EXCUSED HIMSELF and went into the kitchen, trying to think.

Maybe the baby *wasn't* his.

Maybe Samantha had met someone after he'd left.

That was impossible. If the baby was an "infant," that meant it could only be a few months old. And Shea *had* been her lover as recently as the end of last year.

He loaded the dishwasher frantically, as though clearing the kitchen could somehow clear his mind.

"So *that's* her," Tate said, walking into the kitchen with the tray of sandwich plates that had been left on the table when they'd retreated to the living room.

Shea hadn't talked about Samantha to his brothers, knowing there was nothing to be gained by it. The relationship had broken and couldn't be fixed. Yet Tate and Mike would have tried to help. Shea guessed that his shocked expression during the news story and his withdrawal to the kitchen had tipped his hand.

"You have good taste," Mike said, placing the glasses he'd collected in the living room on the counter. "She's beautiful *and* gracious in the face of ruin."

"What happened between you?" Tate asked. He pulled down a bottle of brandy from the cupboard and filled the bottom of a snifter. "Here. You're the color of your mashed potatoes."

Shea closed the dishwasher door, then took a swig from the glass, trying to answer the question. But his brain kept telling him, she had your son! She had your son!

Mike pushed him gently toward the breakfast nook that angled off the kitchen. They'd plotted the course of their lives there several times over the past year. Now they sat—Shea on one side, Tate and Mike on the other.

It was always like that, Shea thought. Them against him. Not *against* him precisely, but allied to watch out for him. At thirty-three, he'd stopped resenting it, yet didn't know how to change things so that he was one of them.

Still, that wasn't the problem now. Sam had his son! And she hadn't told him!

"She was a patron at Chez Shea," he said. "She came back into the kitchen one night with her compliments for the chef." She'd been wearing something black and silky that had clung to every curve, and she'd looked like the ice princess in every adolescent's dream. He remembered that he'd felt hot and clumsy, but she hadn't seemed to notice. "She asked me out."

Mike huffed in exasperation, "How come those things never happened to me?"

"You were armed," Tate replied. "You traveled in a vehicle with sirens and rotating lights. Some women like subtlety. Go on, Shea."

Shea downed the last of the brandy. "We dated for a while. Seven, eight months. But she had everything, and before long I *lost* everything...." He spread his hands in a there-you-have-it gesture, sure the rest was obvious.

Tate and Mike stared at him.

"What?" he demanded. "Like, either one of you would have stayed with a woman who had to support *you?* She wanted to pay off my debts and help me set up another restaurant."

"The witch," Mike said.

Shea pinned him with a look. "You'd never have let a woman do that for you."

Mike held the look, then admitted with a brief nod, "Maybe not. But did that have to end it?"

Shea pitied his innocence. "You fell in love with a reasonable woman. My 'beautiful and gracious woman', as you called her, is used to wielding power and having her own way. And it isn't pretty when she doesn't get it."

Mike's eyes widened. "You think Veronica is *reasonable?* You've got to be kidding."

Tate shook his head. "No woman is reasonable when you're the man who has to live with her. But what did Samantha Haskell do that was so *un*reasonable?"

Shea remembered the night they'd met at his place, supposedly to resolve everything, and instead had said goodbye.

"Since I wouldn't let her pay my debts and set me up again in business, she wanted me to take a job as chef in the executive dining room at Haskell Media." He said the words with the disdain he'd felt when she'd offered him the position.

Again Tate and Mike stared at him as though waiting for him to explain the problem that presented.

"She wanted me to work for her father," he clarified.

They continued to stare.

He closed his eyes and shook his head. "That meant

she was just fitting me into the life she already had—
and at a salary. We weren't making a new life together.''

Tate, ever the businessman, didn't see the logic.
"You'd lost everything. It was an opportunity to do
what you like to do.''

"You know, you have this pride problem..." Mike
began.

"Of course I do! I'm not going to be supported by
my heiress fiancée's father.''

"It was a job.''

"I got a job! I was breakfast cook at a little diner
near my place, then did the dinner rush at a place that
catered to the theater crowd. But that didn't leave us
much time together and she didn't want to wait it
through to better times.''

"Which might have been some time away," Tate
guessed.

"Yeah. We'd been talking about getting married on
Valentine's Day, but I wanted to push the wedding
back until I was out of debt.''

"Why?" Mike asked. "I mean, even if you hadn't
lost the restaurant, no matter what you were bringing
in, she'd have always had more money than you. You
must have made some kind of peace with that when
you asked her to marry you.''

Shea wasn't sure he had. "At least when the restaurant was doing well and we were getting good reviews,
I knew I was operating at the top of my form. I tried
not to think about the money issue because...''

He hesitated, unwilling to utter the words, knowing
they would hurt. "Because...?" Tate prodded.

He sighed and made himself say it. "Because I loved
her.''

"And the infant son the reporter mentioned…"

"Is mine," Shea said. "I'm sure."

"She might have met someone after you left," Mike suggested.

Shea shook his head. "He's mine," he insisted. "The timing's right. And I feel it." He rubbed a spot on his chest where a burning sensation had erupted the moment he'd realized Sam had had a child. He was feeling possession. "I have a son."

He pushed his brandy snifter aside and made his position clear. "I'm going to be gone for a couple of days. Don't worry about Delancey's. I'm sure Charlie will be fine without me. I'm bringing her back."

Tate and Mike looked at each other, then back at him.

"Uh…we're fine with that, of course," Tate said, "But are you sure *she'll* be?"

"She has to be."

"Why?"

"Because she has my son."

"Shea, her life's just fallen apart." Mike pointed toward the television in the living room. "You go barging in there demanding…"

Shea raised his hands in a gesture that said stop, and to his complete surprise, Mike stopped. "I'm going to San Francisco," he said emphatically. "And I'm bringing her back."

Tate and Mike exchanged another look, then both smiled. They were the superior smiles he'd been subjected to all his life. We've been there, the smiles said. And we know you're going to get creamed. And we're going to enjoy it.

"Good luck," Tate said.

"You want me to teach you a few self-defense moves before you go?" Mike asked.

SAMANTHA HASKELL FED eight-week-old Zachary in the old Boston rocker that had been her grandmother's and watched in grim disbelief as the unsavory events of the past few years of her parents' lives were reeled out and discussed on *The Money News.* She would have changed the channel, but she'd left the remote control on the coffee table. She'd been up all night with the baby and she didn't have the energy to stand.

"It's incredible, Margo," a bald, bespectacled man in a pin-striped suit said to a woman who sat across a table from him in a prim white blouse, "that a man of Haskell's fiscal savvy would have let this happen."

"Oh, John," Margo replied with a regretful air that was completely phony, "you see it happen all the time in other walks of life. You just don't expect to see it among big board players of Haskell's stature. Marital discord leads to reckless behavior and pretty soon no one's minding the store."

"I don't suppose it's helped that Audrey Haskell made the cover of the *Enquirer* frolicking in the Trevi fountain in Rome with that Arab prince."

That sympathetic smile again from Margo. "It looks as though a powerful financial empire was brought down to some extent by the antics of a menopausal woman."

Samantha swore at the television, held the baby to her and got up to turn it off.

Zachary whined and stirred. "I'm sorry, baby." Samantha paced in the socks and bathrobe she'd been wearing since 3:00 a.m. It was now almost noon. "I didn't mean to ignore you." She patted Zachary's back and walked across the living room of the old mansion she'd bought with her first bonus check. She'd just put the house back on the market two days ago.

The baby rooted at her neck and she pressed her cheek to his warm, fuzzy head. "I know the first eight weeks of your life have been pretty traumatic, what with undergoing a last-minute cesarean, having to stay an extra week in the hospital, and seeing your grandparents' splattered all over the national news. Not to mention losing most of your inheritance. I know you're probably wishing this trip came with a return ticket, but you're here to stay, Zack. I'm going to make things better, though, I promise. We're going to find a little newspaper somewhere that needs a good reporter, and you and I are going to be fine. Just fine."

Zachary punctuated her declaration with a belch.

"Good boy."

By the time Samantha walked from the fireplace to the window and back again, Zachary was asleep. The one good thing about all this, she told herself, was that she no longer had to leave Zachary with a baby-sitter so she could go to work.

Tomorrow she'd think of a solution, she told herself as she walked into her office in the solarium, but today she would just enjoy being home with her son and try to get her head together. She placed the sleeping baby in the bassinet by her desk and simply stared at him for a moment. Her life was in shambles and she knew her situation was desperate, but she found it impossible to despair when she had something so magical.

She turned up the baby monitor and went into the kitchen for a cup of coffee, but stopped abruptly in the middle of the white-tiled floor, threatened by a wave of sorrow despite her new maternal bliss.

Coffee. Coffee always made her think of Shea and
the cappuccinos no one else in the world could make
with quite the same perfection.

Then rage rose up to banish the sense of loss. Certainly the absence of good coffee was preferable to the
presence of stupid male pride and reverse snobbery.

She drained the coffee carafe into a cup bearing the
Haskell Media logo and went to the kitchen table,
where she'd left the morning paper. She should try to
call her father again, but she was tired of talking to his
answering machine. He'd called in a message two days
ago, warning her of impending doom and asking her
to talk to the staff. And he'd been out of touch ever
since. He'd probably gone off to Barbados with Legs.

She was tempted to call her mother, just to hear a
familiar voice, but her mother wasn't speaking to her,
thinking she'd taken her father's side in their dispute.
And she had no idea where she was now, anyway. She
skipped her usual morning perusal of the NASDAQ,
was afraid to check her horoscope and went straight to
the comics.

Dilbert was too insightful to be funny, considering
her current circumstances, and she scanned the page
for *Hagar the Horrible.* The naive Viking had real appeal for her at the moment. She'd love to get a longboat
and two dozen good men and raid the headquarters of
the Oliver Owens Network. Now, *that* was doing business.

She raised her head as the doorbell chimed. Her father? she wondered. Prospective buyers for the house?
It was more likely some disgruntled employee out to
exact revenge on her for letting his livelihood go down
the tubes. Owens had retained the working staff but
eliminated many executive positions.

She hurried to answer it so that whoever it was wouldn't ring a second time and wake the baby.

She pulled the door open—and stood face-to-face with Shea Delancey.

All manner of feelings she couldn't control raced through her, one after another—love, delight, relief. And just as she would have leapt into his arms, she felt remembered grief, abject disappointment, fury.

She doubled her fist and drew back her arm.

SHEA LOOKED INTO Samantha's gray eyes and didn't notice for a moment that they were bleary. He saw only the spirit that always lit them, the energy alive in them. And for the first time in almost a year he felt a little warmth where his memories were. They hadn't been all bad. He and Sam had had some pretty good—

He credited the time spent with Mike, who was always tense, always alert, for seeing the punch coming. The thrust behind it developed in her eyes, tightened the line of her mouth, bunched her pointed little chin, then headed for him like a line drive aimed at his jaw. He reacted quickly to block the blow and catch her wrist. "Hello, Sam," he said.

And then he noticed that her eyes were soupy, her face pale and her hair, although tied back, bedraggled. She wore a pink chenille robe with white stars on it and a pair of long white socks. She was a wreck.

He couldn't help but stare. In the months he'd known her, he'd never seen her anything but perfect. Even when she was at home, even tangled in the bedcovers, her hair always appeared artfully mussed, her makeup dewy and fresh.

"Take a good look," she said, pulling against his

hand, "and consider yourself lucky that you left when you did."

"I'm back," he said, using the hand he held to push her into the house.

"No, you're not!" she said in an angry undertone as she was forced to take several steps away. "You may be here, but you're not *back*. And I don't know why you are here, but you'll save yourself a lot of grief if you just turn around and go home to your grapes."

She was five-seven, but she seemed smaller than that in the robe and socks. She was obviously exhausted. He didn't want to fight with her.

"I couldn't take your father's job," he said gently as he closed the door behind him. "And I couldn't take your money. We don't really have to go over that again, do we?"

She pulled against him again and he let her go. "We don't have to go over anything," she said, rubbing her wrist. Bleak humor filled her eyes. "But you should have taken the money while I had it. Now I couldn't afford to retain an attorney to make you pay it back."

He looked around the French-country living room he knew she'd lovingly decorated with some very expensive new pieces, as well as secondhand pieces she'd restored herself. "At least you have the house," he said.

She cinched her robe tighter and folded her arms. "No. I have to sell it to help pay the debts."

"Aren't your personal possessions exempt from the corporation's fiscal obligations?"

She nodded. "But not from my own sense of obligation. I'll be fine in something much smaller."

Shea couldn't believe Adam would let her sell the house. "What does your father say about that?"

"Nothing," she replied. "I haven't been able to reach him. Anyway, it's my decision. He's never run my life, though you've always thought his money had some kind of hold over me."

"Not his money," Shea corrected, "but the things it's given you. Don't you remember the weekend that truck backed into your Audi in the parking lot? You didn't have time to wait for the insurance to pay off because you had an interview with Gingrich at the airport and he wouldn't do it with anyone but you. You went out and bought another one that afternoon. Your average working stiff couldn't have done that."

"I know. But I was able to. You always made me feel the privileges I enjoyed diminished me somehow."

"I'm sorry. I never intended that. But I think you don't understand what real life is like for most people."

It was an old argument. He wasn't surprised when she spread both arms in exasperation. "What do you want, Delancey? I have things to do."

He remembered the baby, and quickly recovered the self-righteous indignation he'd come to the door with. "I'm sure you do. Motherhood takes a lot of time." He looked around the living room, then went through the dining room to the kitchen beyond. "Where is he?"

He heard her small sound of distress but kept moving. Remembering that her office was off the kitchen, he crossed the room—and stopped in the office doorway as he spotted the bassinet.

"He's been up most of the night," Samantha whispered from behind him, "and just fell asleep. Don't…"

Shea leaned over the ruffled white lace bassinet trimmed with light blue ribbon, but all he could see was blanket. He reached in to carefully pull the patterned fabric and found spikes of punk-rocker hair. A lot of it.

The face beneath the blanket was plump and round, full cheeks rosy, little Cupid's-bow mouth working, so that the tip of a tiny tongue protruded. A hand with minuscule fingernails was curled on the pillow beside him. He was easily the most beautiful thing Shea had ever seen. That possessive feeling in his chest now had the power of a backflash.

He rested his hands on his knees and just stared.

SAMANTHA WAS A BUNDLE of nerves. She stood in the doorway and watched her baby's father take in their child's beauty. She struggled against any reaction to the touching wonder in Shea's face.

Zachary would be that handsome one day, she thought. Dark brown hair with a tendency to curl cut short and side-parted. Expressive brown eyes over a strong, straight, cover-model nose. Square chin. Rangy body with the strength to toss around hundred-pound bags of potatoes, while still retaining the grace to rumba like some Cuban playboy.

Samantha brought herself back from the past by mentally listing her grievances against Shea.

His absolute refusal ever to see anything her way.

His refusal to come to the telephone when she'd called him at the winery the day before she delivered Zachary.

Twenty-two hours of labor endured alone because she'd been a week early and her best friend and Lamaze coach was at a spa in the Seychelles, her father was attending Legs's new show in Vegas and her mother was bathing in the Trevi fountain.

Only four hours of sleep every night since because

she had no one to hand off to when she felt too tired to cope.

Raging mastitis that had finally made it impossible for her to breast-feed.

She was just working up a good head of steam when Shea turned his head in her direction and gave her the grin she'd fallen in love with a year and a half ago. "Tell me this hair is pasted on," he said.

She went toward him, her grievances nudged aside by his obvious delight in the baby who so delighted her.

"The hair is your contribution." She reached into the bassinet and tugged the blanket down to waist level. "He has your coloring."

"And he's all right?" Shea asked with sudden gravity. "He has no problems of any kind?"

"He's perfect," she was proud to reply. "Except for wanting to socialize at 3:00 a.m. That's probably also your contribution. You were always wide-awake after you'd closed the restaurant and prepared for the next day."

He nodded.

She wondered if he remembered that she'd sometimes pick him up at the restaurant and they'd go dancing until the wee hours of the morning, then come back here and lie in front of the fire and plan their future. She'd focused on her memories of that time to get her through labor.

But those memories made the months without Shea that followed the baby's birth that much more bleak.

Shea pushed the blanket back up to Zachary's shoulders, then straightened and faced her. "Why didn't you tell me?" he asked, his tone half injured, half angry.

That question clarified the situation for her. He didn't remember anything. He never remembered anything.

She turned and marched into the kitchen, waiting for him in the middle of the room.

He pulled the office door partially closed and came toward her, hands on his hips, clearly ready for a confrontation.

"WHY DIDN'T I *TELL* YOU!" Samantha demanded, rising on her stocking-clad tiptoes in her anger. "When did you ever, *ever,* consider anything I told you? How many different plans did I come up with for us to stay together? Huh? How many?"

Shea wasn't sure what this had to do with his question, but he'd argued with her enough times in the past to know that her methods weren't always logical. "They all involved either working for your father or accepting your money."

She jabbed a finger at him. "At least I was trying to find a solution! But all you could think about was that you'd lost everything and that meant I had to get lost, too!"

"Sammie, be honest!" he implored. "You wear haute couture clothes, you call the deli to deliver pâté at midnight, you have lunch with supermodels! You couldn't be married to a guy who was broke."

"Don't tell me what I can and cannot do! What peat bog were you scooped out of, anyway? We had a relationship, and my half of it was just as important as your half."

"I never questioned that. I told you I was going to Oregon to find out about the inheritance and I asked you to wait until I had hard facts. You told me—let's see if I can remember the words…" He didn't have to

think long. They'd been embossed on his brain since
she'd said them. "'You're a jerk and a bastard, Shea
Delancey. I won't wait for you one minute longer, and
I don't care if I ever see you again.' That makes it
pretty clear how important my half of the relationship
was to you."

"We were engaged!" she shouted at him. "And you
thought you could go off for an indefinite period to
'get yourself back on your feet.'"

"It was for both of us!" he shouted back impatiently.

"It was for *you!* I had money for us to live on, but
it wasn't good enough for you because it was mine."

He drew a breath to quell his temper. "Sam, it was
important to me to know that I could come back from
failure without a handout."

He saw the anger in her morph into something that
put her even further out of reach. "I wasn't offering
a handout. I was offering my love. It just happened
to come with liquid cash." She smiled thinly and
shrugged. "But...neither one of those things exists any
longer, Shea. So what are we fighting about?"

Guilt prodded him. He remembered how desperate
she'd been to find a solution for them, but he'd dismissed her efforts out of hand because he'd thought
about them as financial help from her family rather than
manifestations of her love.

She'd still called him a bastard, he reminded himself.
She'd said she wouldn't wait for him. She'd sent back
his ring. She'd had his baby without telling him! He
pulled out the kitchen chair beside her. She looked
about ready to colapse. "As I recall, I asked why you
hadn't told me you were pregnant, and you launched
into all this old stuff. Sit."

He drew another chair out at a right angle to hers. She remained stiffly standing. So did he.

She wore that look from the television close-up, her gray eyes brimming with tears, her mouth quivering.

She picked up a coffee cup that sat in the middle of the table on top of an outspread copy of the newspaper and took a long sip. When she grimaced, he guessed the coffee had gotten cold since he'd arrived.

She put it down again and sat. "You don't remember a telephone call one day at your place in Oregon at the end of September?" She gazed at him, hurt and resentment on her face. "You wouldn't come to the phone."

He remembered that very well. The family had gathered at the house for pizzas after an incident at Veronica's day care and he'd been feeling justified in his decision to join his brothers in French River. He'd been afraid that if he even heard Samantha's voice, he might be tempted to abandon his plan and go back to her.

"First I kept the baby from you as a way to hurt you," she admitted, one tear spilling over. "But there's something about having a life growing inside you that eventually leaves no more room for grudges. Especially when that life is half of someone you once held... dear." She swallowed, cleared her throat and swiped a hand across her eyes. "Anyway, the night I called I knew I was going to deliver in a week or so, and I was packing a bag for the hospital and trying to organize my life. So I thought I'd let you know that you were about to have a child. I was going to promise to send pictures, to tell you you could visit if you wanted to. But..."

He wouldn't come to the phone. Guilt now raced through him like a virus, taking over his system so that for one long moment that was all he was—one pulsing mass of excruciating guilt.

"I'm sorry" was so inadequate, but he was compelled to say the words, anyway.

"Doesn't matter now," she said.

Like hell.

SAMANTHA DIDN'T KNOW what to make of Shea suddenly striding across the kitchen to the wall phone over the chopping block. He stabbed out a lengthy number, punched in a few more, probably in response to voice-mail directions, then leaned a hip on the block and waited.

"Tate, it's me," he said after several seconds. "Yeah, I'm here. Look, can you do me a favor? Great. Will you call the travel agent you got my tickets through and ask him to add another adult and an infant to my return ticket?"

She was on her feet and marching toward him while he was still talking. "We are *not* going with you!" she said, standing on tiptoe to shout into the receiver. "No! No tickets! No!"

He fended her off, still talking to Tate, whom she knew to be one of his brothers, then he laughed mirthlessly. "Tell me about it," he said. "Yeah. He's beautiful. Wait till you see him. Uh…yeah, that'd be good. I'm not sure. Hold on." Shea put the phone to his chest. "You have a car seat for Zachary, don't you?"

"We are *not*…" she began to reply.

He raised the phone to his ear. "Ask Mike to put one in the Blazer. I'll pay him back when I get home. Yeah. Good. The number's…" He read the telephone number on the dial. "Okay. I'll be here. Thanks, Tate."

"You made the decision to leave me," she said the

moment he hung up the phone, "but that is the last decision you get to make that affects me. I don't love you anymore. You made it clear that you don't love me. I'm not going anywhere with you."

"You have my son," he said calmly, walking around her to peer into the office. Apparently satisfied that Zachary still slept, he pulled the door partially closed again. "You've lost everything and you have to find somewhere else to live. It's almost December. We'll spend the holidays together in French River and decide what to do about the baby."

She didn't know which emotion she felt most deeply—anger that he thought he could manipulate her life like this or terror that he might try to make claims on the baby.

"There is nothing to decide," she said, carefully concealing her fear. "You wouldn't stay with me. He's mine."

"You didn't tell me about him," he retorted, going to the coffeepot. He knew where she kept the coffee and the filters and proceeded to start another pot. "I have legal claims as his father and could file charges against you for keeping him from me."

She watched him in disbelief. "I never kept him from you."

"You never told me you were pregnant."

"If you had cared about the state of my body," she said, her voice rising with her panic, "you could have come and checked!"

He slid the basket with its filter and four scoops of some rich dark blend into the coffeemaker. "I'm here now," he said, turning to her, "and I won't give you any trouble about this if you don't give me any. Come home with me for the holidays and—"

"Give *you* any trouble?" She stopped to gasp in complete exasperation. "I just put my house up for sale, my father is nowhere to be found, the office staff—"

He wasn't moved by her attempt to convince him of her desperate situation. He turned on the coffeemaker. "Your real-estate agent will handle the house, your father's business can be handled by his attorneys and the staff are now someone else's responsibility. All you have to worry about is you. I'm only asking for a month. Time for me to get to know Zachary and for you and me to talk about custody."

She didn't want to do either of those things, so she repeated the only clear thought in her mind. "I'm not going with you."

He frowned at her in consternation, then said with an easiness that made her suspicious, "All right, Sam. Have it your way."

He walked off through the dining room to the living room, where he'd left his coat—an old woolen peacoat she remembered from their days together. She watched, pleasantly surprised, as he pulled it on. He was leaving.

"It wouldn't work, Shea," she said, her tone slightly conciliatory. "Even for just a month."

He buttoned it. "You're probably right."

"We can work something out about visitations over the phone."

"All right."

Buoyed by his cooperation, she went on, a little giddy with relief. "I'll ask Albie Biggs to call you." Albert Biggs was her personal lawyer.

He pulled car keys out of a pocket. "My attorney is Lloyd Reynolds in French River."

"Good. I'll tell Albie." She went to the door and
opened it. "I appreciate your com— Hey!"

SHE'D PROBABLY BEEN RIGHT to call him a bastard,
Shea thought as he marched back toward her office.
What he was doing was extreme and, in dealing with
her, probably even dangerous, but he had to make her
come with him. She looked as though she needed help
desperately, and she wouldn't take it from him unless
she was forced to.

In the office he went to the bassinet, reached in to
scoop up the baby, careful to keep the blanket wrapped
around him.

"What do you think you're doing!" she shrieked at
him from the door of the office.

The baby remained asleep as Shea cradled him in
the crook of his arm. Delicate sooty eyelashes fluttered
on his pudgy cheeks. He really was the most beautiful
thing.

Shea gazed at Sam with practiced innocence. "I'm
taking him with me. I thought you understood that."

"No, you're not!" She barred the door with her arms
to the molding, looking heroic and determined despite
the bathrobe and socks. But there was panic in her
eyes.

"Yes, I am." He made himself sound surprised that
she didn't understand. "We just agreed. Your lawyer's
going to call my lawyer to set your visitation rights."
And while he had her shocked by what she considered
his complete misunderstanding of the plan, he pulled
one of her hands from the doorway and walked past
her.

"No!" She caught his free arm and tried to stop him,
but he made himself keep going, through the kitchen

and the dining room, halfway across the living room. "Shea, you can't take him! I'll have you arrested for kidnapping!"

He stopped. "He's my son, Sam. It wouldn't be kidnapping because there's no established custody." He wasn't sure that was a legal fact, but he was hoping she didn't know, either. "And a simple test will prove I'm his father."

"I'm his mother. He should be with his mother!"

"His mother just lost everything," Shea reminded her brutally, disliking himself but determined to make her listen to reason. "His father, however, is a partner in a business that's been written up in *West Coast Magazine, Wine Spectator* and *Money Magazine.*" The article in *Money Magazine* had been a profile on Tate as a successful mid-life career change. He and Mike had merely been mentioned, but she didn't have to know that.

"Shea." She was on the brink of tears. He steeled himself against them, noticing she looked less sure of herself and more mistrustful of him. That was good. He had to get her home to the compound. "I can't just leave."

"I'm sorry," he said. "I can."

He headed for the door. She ran around him to stand in front of it. "Shea," she pleaded. "Zachary's all I've got."

"Then you'd better pack a bag," he said implacably, "because he's coming with me."

CHAPTER THREE

SAMANTHA RESISTED the temptation to leap on him in a rage and unleash all the pain she'd suffered in the past eleven months. But he held Zachary, so she shouted at him, instead. "Delancey, you are *so* rotten! If you take me to court, how do you think a judge would feel about a man who uses his infant son as blackmail?"

"I don't know," he replied. "Are you saying you'd like to go ahead with legal proceedings for custody of Zack and find out?"

She was so angry and upset she couldn't think logically. She sputtered, searching her mind for a threat that would defuse his. But she couldn't think of anything.

"All I'm asking you to do," he said mildly, "is to come and spend the holidays with me in a beautiful spot filled with nice people so that I can get to know my son and we'll have time to decide how to share him."

She made a scornful face. "Beautiful spot. I hear it rains all the time in Oregon."

He nodded. "Not all the time, a lot. But that makes everything green and the air so clean that when the wind blows I swear you can smell the tropics. And everywhere the trees, the hills and the sky look like an artist placed them for his perfect landscape."

"I love the big city," she insisted stubbornly. "The business and the news..."

"The daily pictures of yourself on television?" he asked. "The headlines about your father, and the vulture lists of all your losses?"

He was right. She hated that part. But everyone else had run out on her and she didn't want anyone to think she was beaten. She might be, but she didn't want anyone to think so.

"I'm not a quitter," she said, then wished she hadn't. It sounded theatrically heroic.

She waited for Shea to laugh, yet he didn't. He simply put Zack to his shoulder when the baby started to fuss. "Who said anything about quitting? I'm talking about a break, a holiday vacation. When you're refreshed, you'll be better able to plot your comeback."

"If you recall," she said, "I once made a similar offer to you to help you out of a bad situation, and you threw it back in my face."

She expected denial or a smart remark in return, but he simply met her rebuking gaze and replied quietly, "Well, let's hope you're smarter than I was."

She stared at him a moment, struggling to sustain her need to argue.

She leaned her head back against the door. If she closed her eyes, she knew she could fall asleep—she was that tired. Spending a little time far away from the bad soap opera her life had become held definite appeal.

"Just for the holidays," she said.

He nodded. "Right."

"I have your word you won't try to keep me there a moment longer?" she asked.

He patted Zack's back, his movements awkward but charming in their earnestness. "You have my word."

She straightened away from the door and looked him in the eye. "I'm not sleeping with you."

"You always hogged the bed and the covers, anyway," he said absently, his attention on the baby.

Samantha bristled, a little annoyed at being dismissed so easily when she'd once felt as though she turned his world. But she wasn't entirely surprised. Her parents were proof positive that even the love in a thirty-year marriage wasn't safe from destruction.

"I would have to make a few phone calls."

"Of course. Zack and I'll sit right here." He went to the big upholstered chair near the window and sat down. Zack had quieted and stared at Shea with wide eyes, his little mouth shaped into an O. "Is he hungry or something?"

"He just ate." She brought Shea the pillow from the sofa and propped it under the arm in which he held the baby. "He was sleeping when you came. He just wants to study you. You're something new."

Shea looked up, his eyes upbraiding her. "I should be familiar to him by now. I should have been one of the first things he focused on."

"Next time," she said, refusing to accept the blame for the fact that he wasn't, "you should take your phone calls. I'll be upstairs."

Again, Samantha left a message for her father, then she left a message with her attorney's secretary, telling them where she was going.

Then she called her real-estate agent, who was also out of the office, and began to wonder if everyone she knew or did business with had fallen off the face of the earth. The agent had the key, and Samantha was aware that even if she sold the house tomorrow, the deal wouldn't close for several weeks and the owner wouldn't take possession until a week or two after that, so she didn't have to worry about moving her things.

A housekeeping service came regularly, so they would attend to the rubble of the past few days.

Samantha dialed her best friend at home.

"Sam!" Hannah Moore said with flattering excitement in her voice. She and Samantha had been interns together in the *Chronicle*'s newsroom right after college. Then Hannah had grown less enchanted with reporting and more enchanted with the words themselves and quit to write mysteries.

She now had a lucrative career and lived two blocks away.

"When's your next TV appearance?" Hannah teased. "You looked wonderful in that suit. Donna Karan?"

"Armani. Han, I'm going to be gone for a while and I wondered if you could pick up my mail." She laughed mirthlessly. "I've canceled the paper, since I don't run it anymore, anyway."

Hannah missed the joke. "Gone where?" she asked worriedly. "I thought you sold the place in Aspen to pay the broadcast-news-division salaries."

"I did," Samantha replied briskly. "I'm going to Oregon for the holidays."

"There was a moment's silence. "Where?"

"Oregon."

"Why?"

She answered quickly and confidently. "To spend a couple of weeks with Shea."

"What!" Hannah shrieked. Samantha could imagine her rocketing to her feet in the poison-green sweats that were her work uniform. "You mean he called and you're going to run to him? After what he did to you?"

"No, he came here," Samantha said. "And I'm just going with him to give him a little time to get acquainted with Zack. It has nothing to do with him and me."

"You *hate* him."

"Yes, I do."

"Is he at your house now?"

"Hannah…"

"I'll be right there." Before Samantha could protest, Hannah had hung up.

Great. Add to her current list of problems the imminent meeting of gasoline and matches in her living room.

"Hannah's coming over," Samantha announced to Shea as she handed him a cup of coffee and placed a small table on the side of his free hand.

He held her gaze for a moment, fatalistically amused. "You can't upset me, because I've just discovered my son and he's so beautiful. But if you could, that would do it."

There was an authoritative rap on the front door.

Shea turned his attention to Zack as Samantha opened it.

Hannah pushed her way past Samantha into the living room.

Shea got to his feet without jostling the baby. Samantha noticed that already he looked a little more comfortable holding him. "Hello, Hannah," he said politely. "Good to see you again."

"I *hate* seeing you again," Hannah replied, standing pugnaciously in front of him. She was five feet two inches tall with a severe Napoleonic complex. It made her a good mystery writer. She was willing to take on anyone, as the diminutive heroine in her books always did. "You hurt my friend and ruined her life and I wish you'd stay the hell out of it." She then turned to Samantha with a defensive tilt of her chin. "I couldn't have counted myself any kind of a friend if I hadn't said what I thought."

"Thank you." Shea remained polite. "Now will you go?"

"No." She put a gentle fingertip to Zachary's tiny hand protruding from the blanket. "I'm going to stay and see if I can talk Samantha out of going with you."

"Why don't you mind your own business," he said. "Or do you even know how to do that?"

"My friend is my business."

"And my son and his mother are mine."

Samantha caught Hannah's arm. "Come and help me pack."

"Pack," Hannah said with a scornful glance at Shea as she allowed herself to be led up the stairs. "What does one wear to Oregon? A Hefty bag with eyeholes in it so that you at least stay dry? Samantha, no one goes to Oregon in the winter. In fact, I think no one but men who wear plaid flannel ever go to Oregon at all."

"Hannah, please." Samantha led her into a room with small-floral-print wallpaper and light oak furniture. "Don't make this harder than it has to be. I appreciate your concern, but don't hassle me, okay?"

"I'm not hassling." Hannah sat dispiritedly on the edge of the bed as Samantha pulled a suitcase out from under it and placed it on the pink-and-green coverlet. "I'm just reminding you of what you've been telling me since you found out you were pregnant. You don't need him. You can do this on your own. You're better off without a man who has so much pride he has to decimate yours to keep his afloat.''

"I'm holding to all that," Samantha insisted. "But one of the things I *didn't* say all those months was how guilty I felt not telling him he was going to be a father. So I'll let him have the holidays with his son, we'll work out a visitation plan for Zachary and I'll be back January 2 to figure out what to do with the rest of my life." She pointed to the five-drawer bureau. "Will you put my undies from the first drawer into this, please, while I pack a bag for the baby?"

Hannah looked belligerent. "I don't think I should be any part of this because I just know you'll live to regret it. But I'll do it, only because you've always supported me when I've gone a little crazy."

Samantha smiled at her over her shoulder as she pulled baby things out of the shelves in her wardrobe. "At least I never ran away with the circus."

Hannah went to the bureau and opened the top drawer. "I ran away with the catcher in the trapeze act. That's different." She carried an armload of cotton and silk back to the suitcase. "He had the strongest biceps," she said wistfully. "But the experience taught me that things that *feel* right, aren't necessarily the best thing for you."

"Yeah, well. This feels right for Zachary, not for me."

"You're involved, too, you know. I don't think you should sacrifice yourself so your eight-week-old son can spend a month with his father. Is he going to remember him when he's eight and needs someone to play catch with and Shea Delancey is off somewhere else proving himself again?"

"He wants to be a part of Zack's life."

Hannah let the armload of clothes fall into the case. "Good luck with that. If he's a part of Zack's life, you won't be able to keep him out of yours."

Samantha draped the baby outfits over her arm and reached into the bottom of the closet for the unopened package of disposable diapers, the blue vinyl duffel that had carried her things back and forth to school in the old days. She dropped everything on the bed. "Shea and I can be civil in the interest of Zack's comfortable future."

Hannah focused on her worriedly over the top of the suitcase. "Are you doing this because you're afraid you'll need child support given what's happened? You know I can lend you..."

Samantha frowned at her friend as she fitted the diapers into a corner of the duffel. "No, I'm not. I'm doing it because he came, because I feel guilty, because I think it's the right thing for Zachary, because..." She sat down suddenly beside the duffel, more tired than she ever remembered being. "Because...everything's gone, Hannah. My job, my investments in the company, and apparently my father and my mother."

Hannah came around the bed to sit beside her and put an arm around her. "I'm sorry, Sam. It must be awful. You're so uncomplaining I forget how much you've lost."

Samantha sighed wearily. "It's really not the money," she said. "I had fun with it, but I can do without it as long as I can support Zack and me. But I miss the work, you know. I loved the people and the excitement. And when we uncovered a scam or solved a crime, it was a great feeling." She paused, her gaze unfocused. "I loved working with my father, even after my mother left and stopped talking to me because I stayed. He's the best at what he does, Han. He knows everybody, finds out everything, sticks his neck out for the truth.''

The words brought her mind and her gaze back into focus. She patted Hannah's knee. "At least, he used to be fearless. I don't know what happened. He called to tell me about the takeover, asked me to explain to the staff, and I haven't seen him since.''

"He probably took off with the dancer.''

"Yeah.''

"Men are no damn good, you know.''

Samantha stood and turned on Hannah in exasperation. "Hannah, you've got to stop thinking that way. Some men are rats, and unfortunately for you, you've known more than your fair share. But some men are great.''

Hannah stood, too. "Oh, yeah. Look over the specimens in our lives. My father—gone when I was eight. Your father—gone when you needed him most. My husband—left me because I spent too much time writing, then called to borrow money when I made my first sale. Shea Delancey—doesn't give a rip about what you want out of life and goes his selfish way, leaving you high and dry, and now that you have something he wants, he's dragging you off to that godforsaken—''

Samantha put a hand over her friend's mouth. "I didn't say we knew any," she amended, retreating gracefully. "I just said that some men were great. There are a couple of sweaters in the middle drawer I'll probably need.''

Samantha and Hannah packed four bags—one for Zachary that also contained toys and blankets, and one with his formula, extra bottles, extra pacifiers and the mobile over his crib.

Then suddenly it all began to seem too impossible. She couldn't go. What about Zack's bassinet? What about his…? His…?

Trusting Hannah to search through her coats for something appropriate for the Northwest, Samantha ran downstairs and found Shea on a cell phone in the chair where she'd left him, Zack asleep in his arm.

"…them how much I appreciate that," he was saying. "I can't believe she thought of that and put it all together so quickly. Right. Men should have such an efficient network. And you got the tickets handled?" He listened for a moment, then laughed. "Great. If our flight comes in at seven, we should see you about nine or so. Hey, thanks again. I owe you big-time. Bye, Tate."

Shea turned off the phone and put it aside, then noticed Samantha standing over him, her expression concerned.

"We forgot a few important things," she accused, her tone suggesting that *he'd* forgotten them.

He tried not to panic at the possibility that something really was going to prevent him from having this month with his son. He felt so connected to him already he didn't think he could accept anything getting in his way.

"And those are?" he asked calmly.

"What about his bassinet?" she asked, seeming pleased to put roadblocks in his path. "His bouncer? His stroller?"

"Bouncer?"

"It's a swing. He loves it."

So that was all? He was careful not to let his self-satisfaction show.

"Well, we may have forgotten," he said. "But fortunately for us I have two very clever sisters-in-law who even as we speak are moving a crib, a stroller, a playpen and some kind of musical swing thing into the house."

She appeared speechless for a moment, the wind taken out of her sails with every problem solved.

"*They* have babies?" she finally asked.

He shook his head. "Tate and Colette's girls are eight and nine, and Mike and Veronica don't have any kids yet, but she has a day care on the compound. They put out the word when I called earlier to tell them you were coming, and a mother of one of Veronica's kids brought over the playpen and the swing. Colette still had a crib, and we have a priest friend whose house-keeper donated the stroller."

Her mouth fell open. "Well," she said finally. "That was very nice of everyone. But they don't even know me."

He couldn't help the grin. The baby made him feel as though it had taken up permanent residence inside him and would now light everything in his life. "I'm the little brother. My brothers take care of me out of habit, and now that they're married, their wives do the same thing."

"That's lucky." She reached over him to stroke the baby's head. "I'd have loved to have a sister or a brother. Sometimes I feel..."

He caught a whiff of something herbal, probably soap, and watched her slender, graceful fingers stroke the punk-rocker hair. He could remember them on him, tender, gentle, teasing, then artfully competent when she got down to business.

A thrum of long-forgotten, but still-familiar, passion played through him. He waited until it subsided, then cleared his throat and asked, "You feel…?"

"All alone," she said with a sigh as she straightened away from him. "I don't know what I'd have done this past week without Hannah."

"Once you meet my family," he said, "you'll find yourself praying for time alone. They're wonderful, but they all think they're radio psychiatrists—full of advice and solutions to your problems."

"Ha. I'd like to see them handle my problems."

"I promise you, someone will try."

She noticed his empty coffee cup and took off to the kitchen with it. She returned in a moment with the steaming cup and placed it on the table.

"Thank you," he said in some surprise.

"I remember that you have to have a coffee cup at hand at all times—" she frowned down at him as though she didn't want that memory "—or you lose your ability to function, even in the kitchen. Your staff at Chez Shea were always threatening to get you an IV pole for the dinner rush and hang a bag of coffee on it."

He laughed, remembering that, too. Had that only been a year ago? His life had changed so much since then.

"Those were good times," he said.

"Yes," she admitted, her tone grudging. "They were." Then she turned to the stairs. "But they're gone forever and I have to finish packing."

He glanced at his watch. It was just after three. "If

we leave by five, we should have plenty of time. We can eat at the airport."

"All right. I'll be ready."

"Hannah hasn't talked you out of it?" he asked. He wouldn't have let her, but he wondered why she hadn't.

"No," she replied simply. "It's right for Zachary, and that's all my life is about now."

Hannah came downstairs a short time later, carrying an overfilled duffel. She put it down at the bottom of the stairs and came to take the baby from him. "I'll hold Zack if you'll bring down the other bags."

"Sure." He carefully transferred the child. "I'm sorry your mission here was unsuccessful." He couldn't resist the needling. When he and Samantha had been engaged, Hannah's harassment of him had been friendly, but it had taken a decidedly wicked turn when he'd refused Adam Haskell's offer of a job.

"I hope I've planted a seed of doubt," she said.

He excused himself and loped up the stairs two at a time. He'd spotted the bags on the floor beside the bed and was deciding how best to distribute the weight, when Samantha walked out of the bathroom wrapped in a light green towel. Her hair was piled loosely on top of her head, damp tendrils hanging over one ear and down her neck.

She stopped short when she saw him, her hand going instinctively to the spot where the towel was tucked in on itself.

He didn't know where to look first, hadn't realized how starved he was for the sight of her. His wandering gaze drank in smooth white shoulders, slender arms, long shapely legs he couldn't see without remembering them entangled in his own—treasures masked by the towel he knew better than to recall.

She raised an eyebrow. "I always hog the bed and the covers, remember? So don't stare at me like that."

He picked up the bags, hoping that would balance his shaken equilibrium. "Keep reminding me," he said, and went sideways through the door as quickly as possible.

He put the bags in the car he'd rented, then just sat behind the wheel for a few minutes, thinking that he'd be wise to make a plan if he intended to get through the next month.

He'd set out from French River on simple instinct when he'd learned he had a son, his primary purpose to spend time with him. He'd thought if he could convince Samantha to allow that, things would be perfect. He and she had so hurt each other that what they'd shared had been destroyed.

Or so he'd thought.

But he'd discovered this afternoon that his feelings for her were very much alive—physically and emotionally. She'd shown great courage as a mother and as a businesswoman, and despite the hell she'd put him through, he had to admire that.

And that glimpse of her bare limbs had made him recall how delicious lovemaking was when hearts were entwined as well as bodies.

She still hated him, however, and he guessed they wouldn't be entwining anything in the foreseeable future. She was coming with him for Zachary's sake, and that was all. It would be futile for him to try to revive something she no longer believed in.

The trouble was, the past year had given him a new lease on faith. He'd arrived at French River feeling demoralized and defeated, but Tate's plan for the winery had provided him with something to work for, and

Mike's struggle with his past and his final victory over it had convinced him that nothing was impossible.

The winery was thriving and Mike had his life back. Now it was time for Shea to reclaim his.

This was going to require subtlety—something he wasn't usually good at. But word around town was that the Delanceys were invincible. If he could behave as though all he wanted out of this holiday season was a relationship with his son and visitation rights, then Samantha might relax sufficiently to let the vineyard and its people work their magic on her.

Because he didn't think he could leave her again. Or let her leave him.

CHAPTER FOUR

SHEA LEARNED THE DOWNSIDE to fatherhood on the brief flight to Portland. Zachary screamed from gate to gate, and nothing Samantha did would appease him.

Shea took him from her halfway through the flight, confident that because he'd kept the baby quiet all the time Samantha was packing, he could probably work his paternal magic again.

Zachary disabused him of that notion within five minutes when he grew even more agitated and turned purple in his rage at his parents' incompetence.

"Do you think he's sick?" Shea asked Samantha as she took him back.

She shook her head, putting Zachary to her shoulder and rocking him in the tight confines of her seat. "I don't think so. The doctor saw him yesterday. Sometimes he's just fussy. And I suppose the cabin pressure feels different, and he probably senses my..." She lifted her free shoulder, as if embarrassed by what she was about to admit.

"Your what?"

"My nervousness."

"Over flying?"

"No." Zachary's screaming quieted somewhat but continued relentlessly. "Over meeting your family."

"My family's great. They got all that stuff together for us when they heard you were coming."

She nodded, smiling apologetically at the woman across the aisle, who looked over her magazine at them and winced at the noise. "I know. I'm sure they'll be very polite, but all they know about me is that you left me. They'll think there's something wrong with me."

"There is," he said, keeping a straight face. "You're hardheaded, hard-nosed and generally difficult to get along with. But they also know that I dropped everything to come and get you."

She looked into his eyes. "You dropped everything to come and get your son. Let's be honest about this. You'd have left me behind in a heartbeat."

"And yet you're here."

"Because I threw myself in front of the door."

Shea gave Samantha a knowing look that annoyed her. "I suspect it was because you wanted to come."

"You flatter yourself, Delancey," she replied. "If I wanted to come at all it was for Zachary and not for me."

She'd have sworn his eyes indicated he didn't believe her, but he turned his attention to the baby and said as he stroked Zachary's head, "I'm sure it's not helping him to feel the tension in you. Try to relax, believe that this month is going to be good for all of us and that you and Zachary will enjoy my family and the holidays."

A flight attendant stopped beside them with a sympathetic smile and asked if she could do anything.

Samantha thanked her but declined. "I'm sorry we're so noisy, but I'm new at this and I don't always understand the problem. I just know he's fed and dry and healthy."

The attendant laughed. "I have a three-month-old, and when this happens to me, I put her in her baby seat and drive around until she falls asleep."

She added with a grin, "Don't worry. We've all been there."

The flight attendant excused herself to respond to a hail from the forward cabin.

"I think I'll start a book on ways to calm a fussy baby," Samantha said to Shea, transferring Zachary to her other shoulder. "Everyone has a different method, and some of them are really bizarre. Do you suppose babies get together at their day cares and decide to riot like this just to see if they can make us act like idiots?"

Shea shook his head at the baby. "I wouldn't put it past them. I don't know much about babies, but I can bear witness to the fact that children do band together at their day cares and plot mayhem. My sister-in-law Veronica is always on her toes to combat their plots."

Samantha yawned. "I'm so tired I feel as though I could fall asleep in the back of a car myself. Or in a paint mixer, or on a bed of nails, under an air-raid siren…"

Shea handed her the earphones and reclaimed the baby. "Listen to some music and try to doze. You've got about twenty minutes until we land."

"But he's…"

"I know, but I have to learn to deal with him when he's like this as well as when he's happy. Close your eyes. We'll be fine."

Samantha couldn't quite believe he'd said that. Even the most devoted husbands and fathers she knew were happy to give a screaming baby to his mother, let her find a solution to the crisis, and fend off the stares of disapproving passersby. This instance was even worse because there was nowhere to go to remove herself from the stares.

But she selfishly put on the earphones and closed her eyes.

She was astonished to discover half an hour later that she'd dozed off, the plane had landed and many passengers were removing carry-ons from overhead compartments, while others lined up behind them waited patiently to move out. Zachary continued to cry but was wearing down. The sound was a little less desperate.

"Hey. Welcome back." Shea handed her the baby so that he could pull their bags down.

"You were supposed to get him to sleep," she teased, wrapping the blanket more tightly around the baby. "So your family would think he's angelic and delightful."

He put her carry-on in his empty seat, then reached up for the other. "Yeah, right. No one in my family is angelic or delightful, so they wouldn't recognize those qualities if they fell over them. Well, Tate and Colette's girls might be, but that's it. Mike's picking us up. He used to be a cop. He has a high tolerance for trouble."

"Good. As long as he doesn't arrest us for disturbing the peace."

Shea brought the other bag down, then stepped in front of the seat to let the passengers in the aisle move past him. "He *used* to be a cop. Now he does the winery's PR and runs the bed-and-breakfast."

She nodded, remembering something from the days when she'd first known Shea. He'd been worried about Mike then. "He's the one who was a hostage negotiator and had…that incident when we first met."

"Right."

"Did he ever resolve it for himself?"

Shea smiled. "He's a changed man."

Samantha led the way through the arrival gate with the baby, and Shea followed her with the bags. A man who looked very much like Shea stepped out of the crowd and opened his arms to her. He was about an inch shorter than Shea and more thickly built.

"Mike?" she asked.

"Sam," he said. "Welcome to Oregon."

She wrapped her free arm around him as he enfolded her and the baby.

He freed her, then bent over the baby, who wearily wept his displeasure. Mike took him from her. "Dude!" he said, holding the baby's face to his. "Oh, I know. It's a rotten world, isn't it? Cold and demanding *and* they give you Shea for a father. How's a guy supposed to have a fighting chance?"

"Hey," Shea complained, "he likes me, so don't talk him out of it."

"Did he cry like this all the way here?"

Samantha rolled her eyes. "The other passengers would have voted to throw us out over southern Oregon, but we had an understanding flight attendant. We're hoping he'll go to sleep in the car."

"He should," Mike predicted. "Shea usually bores everyone. Come on. Let's find your luggage."

ZACHARY WAS ASLEEP before they left the airport. Samantha sat beside him in the Blazer's second seat and felt the quiet like a balm on her entire body. Shea had offered her the front seat beside Mike, but she declined, afraid the baby would need her.

"Thank you for picking up the car seat," she said as she tucked Zachary's blanket around him. "I heard Shea ask you to get it."

Mike shook his head. "No problem. Consider it a tardy baby gift from Veronica and me."

She opened her mouth to insist that that wasn't necessary, but he raised his right hand to forestall any argument. "Please. I get enough of that from Shea."

"Thank you, Mike," she said. "That's very thoughtful."

"Tate and I are excited to have a nephew. So far, the family is full of little girls."

Mike concentrated on changing lanes and Shea looked over his shoulder to navigate. Samantha stared out at the Portland night, neons signs and headlights making it appear like any other city in the darkness. She wondered idly where her father was and what he was doing.

On second thought, if he was with Legs, she didn't want to know. She would not have believed that a man could experience such a virulent case of middle-aged madness if she hadn't seen it herself. She felt lonely for him suddenly—or for the way he used to be.

While she was at it, she wondered what her mother was up to. She couldn't be spending *all* her time in the Trevi fountain. According to the article in the *Enquirer,* she had been spending a lot of her time with the young prince, though.

Samantha had never been quite sure what had happened between her parents. She remembered a happy childhood with them seemingly content in each other's company. She recalled that they'd disagreed about retiring early and moving to the chalet in Switzerland.

Her father had had more and bigger plans for the company. Her mother had taken that in stride, or so it had seemed. Samantha had just graduated from college then and joined the company.

For several years she'd been involved exclusively in her own life, excited by the world of journalism, lost in the discovery that she'd inherited her father's affinity for it and was able to devote every waking hour to it without the thrill fading. She had her own condo, her own friends in the business who also talked nothing but work.

Then her father had called her one Saturday night in February, asking if she knew where her mother was. They'd had a fight, he'd explained, and she'd taken off the previous day.

"The Pink Cloud Spa in the desert somewhere," she'd told him. "She phoned me before she left."

"That's what Bitsy said, too, but she's not there. I tried." Bitsy was the housekeeper.

Samantha had been filled with alarm as she considered the possibilities that could have prevented her mother's arrival at the spa.

Her father had flown down, and he and the police found her the following morning in a compromising position with the young Italian chauffeur. A remarkably swift divorce had ensued, Samantha had been written off by her mother for her disloyalty in remaining at her job at Haskell Media, and her mother had taken off for Europe with half her husband's assets and not been heard from since.

That had all happened shortly after Shea had left for Oregon, and Samantha had felt as though her life had been swept away by a powerful hand—except for her work at the Haskell Media offices. Now that was gone, too.

Of course, Shea was back—temporarily. It was impossible to determine yet whether his company could be considered compensation for any of the other things she'd lost.

Shea looked at her over his shoulder. "You warm enough back there? How's Zack?"

"We're both fine." She covered a yawn. "Maybe I'll just doze until we arrive."

"Veronica put a pillow and a blanket in the third seat for you," Mike said, finding Samantha in the rearview mirror. Passing headlights lit up his smile. "Shea probably told you that my wife works with children."

"He did." Samantha reached over the seat for the blanket. She was warm enough, but nothing helped a nap like a blanket. "She must be one of those women who think of everything."

"She does. She's always armed with tissues, Handi Wipes, an extra pair of mittens, you name it."

"In my case," Samantha said, opening the polarfleece throw over her, "an extra pacifier, an extra diaper and a bottle of formula."

Shea reached over the back of his seat to smooth the blanket where it had bunched up on her knee.

"He looks happy," he said of the baby. "The flight attendant was right about the soothing qualities of the car. There's some research for your book completed already."

"Mmm." Samantha sighed as she felt herself relax.

"Seems to be working on you, too," he observed with a light laugh. "Go to sleep."

That was all the encouragement she needed.

"THANKS FOR COMING FOR ME," Shea said to Mike as they drove on. "I also appreciate your getting the car seat."

"Not a problem. You're going to need it, anyway. I checked to make sure it'd fit the wagon."

Now that the restaurant was doing so well, Shea's days without a car were over. He'd finally bought one—a used Chevy station wagon with room to carry restaurant supplies. But he hadn't wanted to leave it at the airport, where cars were sometimes vandalized. Tate had driven him in this morning.

"Anything happen today that I should know about?" Shea asked. "Any eccentric arrivals at the B and B? The James boys haven't made gunpowder again, have they?"

Veronica cared for a trio of brothers who were intelligent as well as adventurous. As a single force, they were trouble. Allied with the other children at the day care, they required the equivalent of UN troops to maintain order. Fortunately, Veronica was in charge.

"No." Mike frowned. "But that old apartment building that's used for senior housing burned to the ground."

"What!" Shea remembered a woman on the second floor of the building who must have entertained herself by sitting in her window all day and watching the world—or at least the town of French River—go by.

Shea had looked up one morning after coming out of the bank and noticed the woman waving. He'd waved back. Since then, he'd never gone to the bank without looking up, and the woman had always been there to wave.

"Did anyone get hurt?"

"Two cases of smoke inhalation." Mike glanced in the rearview mirror as he slowed to accommodate a pickup packed with furniture. "But they're doing fine. Seventeen old folks homeless, though. Father Wolff's gotten cots into the school auditorium and farmed people who needed closer care to Newberg and McMinnville. The residents pretty much lost everything. Being older they move slowly, so the firemen, with the help of some of the local merchants and onlookers, spent most of the time getting *them* out. There wasn't time to save *things*."

"Jeez. Perfect timing with Christmas right around the corner."

"I know. Felicia called an emergency meeting of the council and anyone who thought they could help. It's going on right now. Tate and Armand went."

"We can donate food," Shea suggested. "I'm ordering tomorrow. I'll just double up on chicken, triple up on soup makings."

"Sounds like a plan." Mike glanced at Shea and smiled. "Zack's a beautiful baby. How did that happen with you half-responsible?"

Shea glanced over his shoulder again, feeling both proprietary and humble. "I'm sure the looks are all Sam's, though he has Delancey coloring. But I'll bet he'll be in the kitchen with me as soon as he can stand."

Mike glanced in the rearview mirror, trying to decide, Shea guessed, whether or not Samantha was truly asleep.

"She's asleep," Shea said, noting her quiet, even breathing. "If she were awake, she'd be fighting with me. Why? What's on your mind?"

"You talked about the baby being in the kitchen with you," Mike said softly. "So…she's staying that long?"

Shea shook his head. "I got her to spend the holidays. After that, I don't know."

Mike was silent, frowning at the road.

"I know it doesn't sound like much, but when you consider how we parted, it's quite a lot. Maybe even enough to see if we can find a common ground again."

Mike nodded. "I know what it's like to cling to a thread of hope where a woman is concerned. Just try to remember that what she wants is as important as what you want—even when you're doing what you think is right for her. When you're involved, it's her life, too. I kept forgetting that."

"I'm not sure she could be happy here, anyway." Shea stared moodily out the window at the dark shapes of trees beside the road. "You wouldn't believe what she's used to. You've only seen it in movies."

"There you go, making judgments for her. How old are you going to be before you start listening to me?"

Shea groaned. "How old am I going to be before you stop thinking I *should* listen to you?"

Mike laughed. "Like that'll happen. I'll haunt you from beyond. Actually, I was just reminding you. If she was the vice president of her father's company and her father was a respected newsman and a financial genius, she's obviously competent and clever. You can trust her to think for herself."

"I know that." Shea let his head fall against the headrest and sighed. "I'm just afraid she'll decide that the competent and clever thing to do with her life is *not* to spend it with me."

SAMANTHA AWOKE TO DARKNESS lit only by an occasional lamp on what appeared to be a narrow road, considering how much Mike had slowed their speed.

Samantha saw that the baby still slept, the wrapped bundle of his little body moving up and down as he breathed. She looked out the window and caught a glimpse of long rows of naked vines in the dim light.

"Is this your vineyard?" she asked, her voice a little froggy with sleep.

"Yes," Mike and Shea replied simultaneously. She heard the pride in their voices.

Shea turned to look at her. "Sleep well?"

She stretched, feeling surprisingly fresh. "Very well. I've learned since Zack was born that even a ten-minute nap can keep you going for a long time."

"From now on," Mike said, "you're going to have lots of baby-sitters available when you need a break."

"That's nice to know. My friend Hannah was eager to help, but I was always afraid she'd diaper Zack's face or something. She's that incompetent with babies."

Two lights in the distance slowly materialized into two carriage lanterns flanking an entrance made of un-cut logs. The lanterns were entwined with vines that met over a carved wooden sign reading Delancey Vineyards. Many cars were parked single file on the right side of the road.

"Why are the cars there?" she asked.

"Parking for the restaurant," Shea explained. "One of our priorities is to put in a lot somewhere. We just don't know where. We're thinking about having one at the bottom of the hill, with a shuttle up and down."

As they drove through what she'd heard Shea refer to as the compound, they passed a large frame building on their left. A light above another wooden sign illuminated the words Delancey's Winery.

"The restaurant," Shea said, pointing to it. A dozen cars were parked in front of it and talking, laughing groups of people moved in and out. "Veronica's day care is the barn back there on your right."

Samantha turned. She saw a light in the distance but could make out no detail. Behind them now was a pretty little cottage with lights in all the windows. Beside it was a fenced area. She caught a glimpse of something she was sure was the product of weariness and mild disorientation.

"Rachel's cottage and animal pen," Mike said.

"Then...I did see a llama?" she asked.

The men laughed. "That's Victoria. Rachel rescued her when some gentlemen farmers moved away a few years ago and abandoned her. Rachel has geese there, raccoons, a deer, cats, dogs..."

"And that's the bed-and-breakfast." Shea pointed through the windshield to a beautiful, brightly lit Victorian house with a curved porch and a cupola. "Tate designed it."

Samantha gasped. "I was hoping you'd say that was your place."

"No, we're not quite that grand," Shea replied as Mike drove up another small slope to a parking area beside an old Victorian house that was much plainer than the bed-and-breakfast. "Tate calls it 'a four-square Victorian'—I suppose because it's just that. No rambling little wings, just the same even floor space up and down. There's a porch in the front, but nothing fancy. Tate and Mike and I lived here together until they got married and abandoned me."

Mike turned off the engine. "You keep telling us how glad you are that we're gone and you have the house to yourself."

"But there's no one to help take out the garbage and do all the other fun chores."

"Don't look at me." Samantha unbuckled the baby from his cocoon within the car seat. "I'm a guest."

Mike laughed as he climbed out of the car.

A stream of women came down the back-porch steps toward the car. Samantha handed Shea the baby, then accepted his hand down from the Blazer. She stood with a cautious smile and an impulse to duck back into the vehicle. Crowds coming at her in the past week had usually involved cameras, tape recorders, and her face all over the six o'clock news.

This group, however, seemed more interested in the baby than in her—at least at first. They clustered around Shea, who showed off Zachary to a tall slender brunette, a beautiful redhead and an older woman in coveralls and a coronet of gray braids.

Then he leaned down so that two little girls, hopping up and down for closer looks, could also see the baby.

"Sam," Mike said, while Shea was occupied, "I'd like you to meet my wife, Veronica." That was the brunette. "Tate's wife, Colette." The redhead. "And this is Rachel. We have no claim on her, but she lets us call her 'aunt'."

Samantha was embraced by the older woman in coveralls. She noted a youthful sparkle in the woman's eyes and a warm smile. "Welcome to the Delancey Vineyards, Samantha," she said, taking her arm and drawing her toward the steps. "Shea's been in this house alone since Mike got married two months ago and moved into Veronica's apartment over the day care, so we've been trying to spruce it up a little for you. He's tidy enough, but he puts in long hours at the restaurant and not much gets done around here."

They climbed the back steps and Rachel opened the

door so that Samantha could pass through first. Everyone followed behind in a long parade.

"How nice of you," Samantha said as they walked into a brightly lit kitchen with tall cupboards and an old speckled Formica countertop. The room was spotless and smelled of something wonderful. "But I'm only visiting."

"Yes, of course, but we want you to be comfortable. Smell that? We snagged two halibut in gooseberry wine sauce from the restaurant. Tate was sure you wouldn't get dinner on the short flight."

They crossed a small hallway into a breakfast nook papered in the ugliest wallpaper she'd ever seen. It had a blue background and large green leaves. But a cozy bench was fitted into a corner and a big window would let in a lot of light during the day.

"When we decided to take over the winery instead of selling it," Shea said, tapping a finger on the table in the nook, "we did a lot of strategizing right here."

As he tapped his finger, a silver-gray tabby leaped onto the tabletop from somewhere underneath. It purred loudly as Shea stroked it.

"This is Sterling. He was a gift to me from Colette and the girls." He pinched the chin of the taller of the two little girls. She had gray eyes in a round freckled face framed in strawberry-blond hair. Her smile was sweet and shy. "This is Megan. She has plans to be a chef when she grows up. And this is Katie." He caught the tip of the smaller girl's pert nose between his knuckles. She had big blue eyes and long, platinum-blond hair. "She's going to run the winery when the rest of us are too old."

There was a loud, indignant meow from the cat. He

placed his forepaws on Shea's arm to sniff the stranger in the blanket, his tail swishing.

"He likes him!" Katie said. "His tail swishes when he likes things or people. He has a brother and a sister. Daddy has the brother. He's black-and-white and Daddy calls him 'Joe Boxer' after his underwear 'cause he was lost one time and that's where Daddy found him. In the drawer where Daddy put it. His underwear, not the cat." The little girl rattled off information, as though she'd been storing it up to share. "And Uncle Mike has Bonnie. She's named after Bonnie...?" She looked to Mike for help.

"Parker," he told her.

"She was a crook with some guy named Clyde. They shot people all over the place. Well, they shot the people just a couple of times, but they did it in a lot of different states. Mommy put flowers in your room. Want to see?"

She took Samantha's hand and led her through a dining room, then a living room painted a warm cream color and furnished with well-used overstuffed furniture. The walls were decorated with old photos and a large grapevine wreath.

Samantha commented on the wreath as Katie led her toward the stairs. "Mommy made it. There's one in your room, too. We painted the bedrooms while Daddy was in Boston. He wasn't our daddy then, though."

"He and Mom got married in the summer." Megan danced ahead of them onto the bottom stair. "We went to Banff on our honeymoon."

"All of you?" Samantha asked.

"Yeah. Me and Katie got to see the Rocky Mountains! In the summer, we run the booth at the Saturday

Market. I'm in charge. We sell wreaths and vine starts and sometimes stuff that Rachel bakes.''

''Samantha,'' Rachel called.

Samantha turned to see that Rachel, Colette and Veronica had followed. Mike and Shea and the baby had stayed behind in the kitchen.

''I'm going to say good-night.'' Rachel waved and smiled. ''I don't do stairs unless I have to. So—welcome again, and I look forward to our spending some time together.''

''We'll do it soon,'' Samantha promised. ''Thank you for all you've done.''

Rachel dismissed that as unnecessary with a shake of her head. ''Don't forget that dinner's in the oven.''

''I won't.''

''Good night, girls.''

There was a chorus of good-nights as Rachel went to the front door. Mike loped toward her. ''Hold up. I'll walk you back to the cottage.'' At the front door, he turned to wave toward the stairs. ''See you tomorrow, Sam.''

''Thanks again for picking us up,'' she called.

''Sure.'' The door closed behind him.

The girls led the way up the stairs, Colette and Veronica following Samantha. The upstairs hall was a colonial blue-gray with moldings painted white.

''This is Uncle Shea's room,'' Megan said, pointing to the room at the top of the stairs. It was the same color as the hallway, with dark-blue-and-red striped curtains and a coordinating bedspread. She smiled. ''Mommy made the bed so you wouldn't think Uncle Shea was messy.''

Colette shook her head at Megan while tugging teasingly at her hair. ''That was our secret.''

Veronica laughed. "There are no secrets around here. And the kids aren't the only squealers. If there's something you don't want known, don't even think it, because Rachel's intuitive, the men are observant and the kids never miss a trick." She pointed to the second bedroom. "This was the best we could do for a nursery in the time alotted us. What do you think?"

This room was the same gray-blue, but yellow curtains with brightly colored circus animals enlivened it. A matching quilt lay in the crib they'd borrowed for Zachary's use.

"This was my toy chest," Megan said, pointing out a red box in one corner. "There were twin beds and an icky dresser in here, but Daddy and Uncle Mike took them up to the attic."

"Mommy rocked us both to sleep in this when we were babies." Katie sat in a Boston rocker by the window and demonstrated the chair's abilities.

Samantha was overwhelmed. For the past week she'd felt that everyone in the world had gone out of their way to hurt her. This shower of friendship was a balm to her wounded spirit.

She turned to Shea's sisters-in-law. "I can't believe you went to all this trouble. Thank you so much."

"Nothing's too much trouble for Shea," Colette said. "He's very important to all of us, and he was so thrilled to learn he had a son."

Samantha felt an instant panic, which she tried very hard not to show. But she knew immediately that both women had caught it. She smiled feebly as she remembered Veronica's caution of a moment ago: If you have something you want to keep secret, don't even think it.

"So it isn't just Rachel who's intuitive or the girls who don't miss a trick," she said, looking from one to the other. "You've been with Tate and Mike long enough to have picked up their powers of observation."

Colette put an arm around her shoulders and led her out of the nursery to the third room. "We're not that good. It's just that panic is easy to identify because Veronica and I have both known it. But don't worry. I didn't mean anything by that—except that Shea was happy about the baby. Girls, why don't you go see if Uncle Shea's doing all right downstairs, or if he needs help with the baby."

Megan and Katie took off, clearly eager to comply.

"This is your room," Veronica said, walking in to smooth the simple white chenille spread on a double bed. Teal-and-white striped curtains hung at the windows. There was a simple slipper chair in one corner, a full and healthy-looking philodendron on one end table and an old lamp on the other.

She put a hand on a French-provincial dresser. "This is known affectionately among the guys as 'the girlie dresser.' When they first moved in, they kept trying to unload it on one another because it's so frilly. It's nice that there's finally someone here who might appreciate it."

She opened the top drawer. "I cleaned it out for you and Colette lined it with paper and dropped in a few sachets. For a while this fall everything around here smelled like wine, including us."

"This is also," Colette said, "where Tate found the letter and photograph that sent the boys on the search for their uncle Jack. Both items were stuck in one of the slats of the top drawer."

Samantha sat on the edge of the bed to test it. "I remember that Shea told me their uncle had been declared dead after having gone missing for so long, and that's how he and his brothers inherited the winery.''

Colette nodded and came to sit beside her. ''The boys spent a lot of time with him when they were kids, and they hated to believe that he was really dead when there was no real proof except his absence.''

Veronica sat on her other side. ''After they found the letter and the photo, they began to wonder if Jack might have disappeared deliberately. So far their investigations have led them to believe they're right about that.''

''Why? What happened?''

''Well, we're not sure. But it seems the woman he loved was killed at the same time he disappeared. Only, she died in a fiery train wreck and there was no body.''

''So...they're thinking she didn't really die?''

Colette shrugged. ''Maybe not. Mike has a private-detective friend who's still working on it.'' Colette smiled and bounced a little on the mattress. ''So, what do you think? Will you be comfortable?''

''Oh, I'm sure I will.''

''We know you're used to much more...elegant surroundings.''

Samantha made a face. ''If you've been watching the news, you also know that I've lost my elegant surroundings. And anyway, I've felt used and abused by the press. Even though news is my business, I like to think Haskell Media followed the facts, not the pain of the people involved.'' She wasn't quite sure why she'd gone into that. The cozy old beauty of this house, she imagined, and the warm welcome of the people inside.

''These surroundings are quite wonderful. Thank you. I'm sure Zachary will think so, too.''

SHEA FOLLOWED THE SOUND of conversation but was
momentarily sidetracked by the nursery created out of
the room Mike had once occupied. It was bright and
cheerful, and he knew it represented a lot of effort and
an expression of love on the part of his sisters-in-law.

It shocked and pleased him anew to think that *his*
child would occupy this room.

Of course, with that pleasure came the reminder that
the baby's presence was only temporary. But he didn't
want to think about that now. He had what he'd set out
to get this morning, and for the time being he would
just enjoy it.

Tomorrow he would worry about how to keep it.

He flipped off the nursery light, then followed the
women's voices to the last bedroom, which had once
been his. He leaned a shoulder in the doorway and
enjoyed the sight.

Samantha sat on the edge of the bed between Colette
and Veronica. They were talking about the house. He
didn't quite hear the words in his distraction over what
a picture they made—a blonde, a brunette and a redhead sitting on his old bed, looking like a gift of some
kind, a beautiful collection of energy, emotion and
charm.

He smiled over the knowledge that a man would get
a lot more than those positive qualities—a woman with
a mind of her own often complicated a man's life.
Though it would probably be worth it—at least Tate
and Mike thought so.

They noticed him suddenly and got to their feet.

"Where's the baby?" Samantha asked worriedly.

"He's fine," he assured her. "Megan and Katie are
holding him in the big chair. They have orders not to
move."

"Is he awake?"

"Yes, but he isn't fussing. He's just staring at them. Katie's telling him all about Rachel's animals."

Samantha hurried past him to see for herself, but he stopped Colette and Veronica in the doorway, taking both of them into his arms. "Thanks for everything, you sweet things. You really went above and beyond the call. It means a lot to me."

Colette kissed his cheek. "Well, you mean a lot to us. If my supply of penuche fizzled, I don't know what I'd do, so it seemed best to keep you happy."

"Yeah," Veronica agreed. "If you have to move to San Francisco to be with her, we'd all lose out on the best chef this side of the Mississippi. So we have to make sure she learns to be happy *here.*"

"Mmm, right." He led them to the top of the stairs. "It's clear that your efforts were entirely self-serving. Dinner on Sunday as usual?"

"Shea, it's Friday. You'll hardly have time to…"

"Sunday," he said. "Same time."

Colette and Veronica looked at each other and nodded. "Okay. We'll be here."

Samantha reclaimed a very wide-eyed Zachary so that the girls could leave with their mother and their aunt. Shea walked them out to the old Jeep Colette always drove.

They met Mike coming back from Rachel's. He had three separate foil-wrapped packages, two of which he distributed to Shea and Colette. "Cookies from Rachel," he said.

The girls scrambled into the back of the Jeep. Colette drove off with a wave and Mike and Veronica headed back to the barn.

Shea stood alone in the dark, quiet end of the compound. Farther down toward the restaurant, patrons were coming and going and he could hear their laughter, the sound of their car doors slamming, the clink of crockery from Delancey's kitchen.

That made him smile. He could remember how quiet it used to be here at night. How he and Tate and Mike had sat on the porch steps and talked about their futures, about women.

He hadn't wanted a woman in his future then; he'd been filled with anger and bitterness over Samantha's unwillingness to see things his way. But now, when he looked into his son's eyes, he couldn't remember any of that. All he could think about was that Zachary deserved parents who occupied the same house.

But he knew that even being able to approach Samantha with that concept without frightening her or making her violent would take time.

He went back into the house and found Samantha at the kitchen table, feeding Zachary. The baby made eager sucking sounds, as though he couldn't get the food in fast enough. His feet kicked in apparent appreciation, and one tiny hand rested on Samantha's on the bottle, tiny fingers splaying and folding as he drank.

"Hungry little guy," Shea said, leaning over her shoulder to look down on the baby.

Zachary followed his movements, staring at him with solemn interest.

She dabbed with a small towel at a collection of milk on the baby's chin. "Your family is pretty wonderful. I can't believe how generous they've been with their things and their time."

He went to the stove to check on dinner. "My brothers are great, but their wives and Colette's girls have brought a new dimension to things that rounds out our life here and warms it up. Can you eat one-handed?''

''Do it all the time.''

''Coffee to drink or wine?''

''Coffee, please.''

Shea laid place mats and silverware on the table and the rolls someone had also put in to warm. Then he served a pair of steaming casseroles. After he poured coffee, he placed the cups well out of the reach of little kicking feet.

He sat across from Samantha and watched in admiration as she managed to hold the bottle in the same hand that held the baby.

''You look very experienced for only eight weeks of motherhood,'' he observed.

She nodded as she chewed a bite of lemon-buttered broccoli. ''You have to get good at it pretty fast because it's very demanding. But already I can't remember what I did without him.''

''So…what are your plans?''

She seemed distracted for a moment. She took another bite of halibut and closed her eyes. When she opened them again, she said with a sigh, ''I haven't had halibut like this since Chez Shea. Nobody has the delicate touch with fish that you have.''

He was pleased and flattered out of all proportion to the simple praise. She was here in his kitchen! With his son!

Then she met his glance, her own disparaging. ''I could almost forgive you for ruining my life.''

''Hey. I'm not the one who let Haskell Media go down the tubes.''

She shook her head. ''That just ruined my career. And only temporarily. You ruined my life.'' She smoothed the baby's brow, drew the nearly empty bottle away and put him to her shoulder. "But I didn't come here to resurrect old injuries. My plans are—"

Zachary interrupted her with a loud burp. "Good boy," she said, continuing to pat him. "My plans are to find a job on a paper or with a station and just keep going. Hannah said we can move in with her until I locate a smaller place."

"Have you heard from your mom?" he asked.

It took her a moment to answer. She resettled the baby in her arm, tucked his blanket around him, studied the remaining ounce of milk in the bottom of the bottle.

"No," she said finally, lightly. "Just through the tabs and the gossip on *Entertainment Evening*."

Adam and Audrey were still together when he'd been with Samantha. She'd taken him to dinner at her parents' place several times, and he'd invited them to Chez Shea on occasion. Had thought they'd all seemed close and comfortable together. He'd been shocked when he'd learned that her parents had divorced.

It was hard for him to believe that her mother hadn't contacted her, considering the circumstances.

She shrugged. "I understand her a little better now than I used to. My father wasn't listening to her and she must have felt pretty desperate."

Shea heard the unspoken implication—that she understood because he had put her through much the same thing.

"I suppose it's hard for a man like your father to slow down," he said. Adam Haskell had always been warm and kind to him, with never a suggestion that he'd been aware of their different social standings. Whatever reluctance Shea had felt about accepting a job from him had been strictly due to his own pride.

"I'm sure his reputation is a result of his constant in-sistences on quality control and his never leaving the details to someone else."

"But work should not have meant more to him than my mother," Samantha argued. Again, she was talking about their situation as well as her parents'.

"You don't know what was in his head," Shea said.

"That's true. I just have to live with the result—and whether or not he intended a better outcome doesn't really matter."

Zachary had drifted off to sleep and she placed him in the carrier on a spare chair. Now free to deal with her dinner with both hands, she reached for a roll and buttered it.

"They're both usually smart, responsible people when they're not engaging in revenge behavior, so I'll just have to trust that they can take care of themselves. Meanwhile, I have to focus on Zachary."

"Good idea." He topped up her coffee. "I'll focus on both of you." Samantha felt those words slide com-fortingly over her but resisted their snare.

"Don't do that," she told him firmly, pointing her roll at him.

He met her glance innocently. "Do what?"

"Pull that protective stuff on me. You were always there with whatever it was I needed—a hand on my shoulder, an attentive ear, a dinner that could make me forget my troubles. But I don't need it anymore. I can trust myself to come through for me."

"Everybody needs someone to look out for them," he challenged.

"I used to think so." She chewed and swallowed a bite of roll, continuing to eat so that he would see her nonchalance. "Until I tried to look out for you and you threw my efforts back in my face. I think this month will go more smoothly if you just look out for yourself and I look out for myself.''

She expected that frank dressing-down to annoy him, but he smiled, instead. "I've learned a lot in a year," he said. "I'd care for you differently today."

"Thank you, but that isn't necessary." She continued to eat, then curiosity got the better of her. "How differently?" she asked finally.

He put his fork down and pushed his plate away, then leaned his forearms on the table. "Mike just told me to remember this truth—that what you want for yourself is as important as what I want for you."

She frowned as she chewed, then nodded. "Mike's a smart man. Good for Veronica."

Shea laughed softly. "But Mike tended to forget that truth when he fell in love with her. An unfortunate male weakness, I think. The urge to protect often goes into play before the need to understand. But he's finally got it down."

She rested her fork on the side of her plate. "You're not going to tell me you've got it down, too?"

"No," he denied instantly. "I don't know if it comes from being the youngest, but I'm also the slowest to learn anything. The last thing I ever wanted to do was take Tate's and Mike's advice, because I wanted to prove I was as smart and strong as they are. Well, I've finally screwed up enough times to reevaluate."

She raised a finely arched eyebrow. "So...*have* you changed?"

"Not completely." He smiled. "But I'm trying to. While working with Tate and Mike this past year, I discovered that all the help they offered—financially, emotionally, whatever—they gave without thought of payback and then even forgot they'd given it. I put such pressure on myself to return it—and all this time..." He shook his head, his eyes momentarily unfocused as he enjoyed the revelation. Then he met her gaze and said in wonder, "It was free."

Though she had no siblings, she understood what he was saying. She'd been the youngest on her father's editorial staff, the green kid everyone wanted to steer in the right direction. And she'd been as receptive to their help as Shea had been to his brothers'.

"My point is," he went on, "that while our relationship is very different from my relationship with my brothers, I'm learning better skills."

That was an admission she found hard to criticize in any way. Which made it difficult to tell him that be that as it may, she had no intention of reestablishing their relationship.

He seemed to read that thought in her eyes.

"It's all right," he said amiably. "I intend to wear you down."

She took her last sip of coffee and pushed herself to her feet. "You've apparently already forgotten everything you've just told me. Wearing me down is what you want. You've never asked me what I want." She picked up the carrier. "Good night, Shea."

Shea watched her leave the room and groaned quietly to Sterling, who leaped up onto the table to investigate the leftovers. "I said I was learning new skills," he told the cat. "I didn't say I'd perfected them."

ZACHARY WAS UP SEVERAL times during the night. Though Samantha responded quickly each time, Shea got up, too, feeling obligated to provide moral support while she fed, changed or walked the baby.

He was surprised, therefore, when he awoke to the ring of the telephone and found daylight filling the room. "Are you up?" Tate inquired cheerfully.

"What time is it?" Shea asked groggily, trying to focus on the clock.

"Eight-thirty," Tate replied. "I'm inviting myself over to see your son and talk to you about plans to raise money for a new home for the seniors. You heard about the fire?"

"Yeah. Mike told me."

"Shall I pick up doughnuts and give you half an hour to get yourself together?"

"Yeah."

"You got it."

Shea climbed out of bed and found both the nursery and Samantha's room empty. But he could hear the stereo downstairs and noises in the kitchen.

He took a quick shower, pulled on jeans and a sweat-shirt and hurried down.

Samantha waltzed around the living room in jeans and a bulky blue sweater, her hair caught up in a casual coil at the back of her head. Zachary, her dance partner, was enfolded in her arms as she turned in graceful circles, singing in slightly off-key harmony to a country-music tune.

Shea gave himself a moment to simply enjoy the sight, then walked into the room. One particularly wild turn brought her and the baby right into his arms. It afforded him a whiff of her fresh sweet scent, which seemed to cling to his clothes when he left her, and the sight of his son's gummy smile over his mother's antics.

"Good morning," she said breathlessly.

He held her until she was steady, then held her a moment longer, using the pretext of greeting Zachary.

"Good morning yourself," he said, taking the baby from her. "How can you be so wide-awake when you got five hours' sleep tops?"

She shrugged and fell into a corner of the sofa. "Getting used to it, I guess. I was just thinking about making breakfast for you."

He looked up from the baby to eye her doubtfully. "Another pattypan squash and olive loaf omelette? I don't think so, but I'm flattered that it occurred to you."

"I only did that once, and just to prove to you that you weren't the only one who could be creative in the kitchen."

"The rule for successful culinary creativity, is that the food has to taste good."

She tucked her legs up beside her. "Well, I've never been one for arbitrary rules. So, then, *you're* cooking?" she asked hopefully.

There were several rhythmic knocks on the door.

"Here's breakfast now." Shea went to admit Tate, who walked into the room with a pink bakery box on the flat of his hand.

"Well, Zachary," Tate said, handing the box to Shea and taking the baby. He held him over his head and brought him down toward his face until he earned the same smile Zachary had given Samantha.

Shea was torn between delight and jealousy.

"Your aunts and your cousins said you were a handsome devil." Tate settled him in the crook of his arm and, his voice several tones higher than his usual bass, heaped praise upon him. "But I had no idea how much a Delancey you really are. No denying those looks. I'm going to be your favorite uncle, you know. Your uncle Mike will tell you that he is, but don't listen. My girls like him, but there's just no accounting for taste. You know women. Just because a guy once wore a uniform, they fall for him."

"He's going to like his father so much," Shea said, "that he's not even going to notice his uncles. Isn't that right, Zack?"

Samantha was completely charmed. She'd never seen men fuss over babies the way the Delanceys did.

Zachary ate up the attention, legs kicking under his blanket, hands flailing as he tried to communicate with Tate.

She got to her feet and went to Tate and him.

Shea put his arm around her. "Sam, I'd like you to meet Tate, my *oldest* brother." He teasingly emphasized the adjective. "Tate, Samantha."

Tate socked him in the arm with his free hand, then drew Samantha closer. "I'm so glad you came, Sam. Although my wife is now depressed, wants to grow six inches and lose twenty pounds."

She wrapped an arm around him as he hugged her. "I thought she was beautiful. And so thoughtful! Thanks to her and Veronica and all the ladies here, Zack and I are living in comfort."

"They're very excited that you've come. Their life's ambition is to fix Shea up with someone."

"But I'm only here—" she began to explain.

He interrupted her with a shake of his head. "No matter. There's a woman in proximity to him and that means I won't have to listen to a rundown of other women we should invite to dinner when he comes over."

He smiled winningly at Shea. "If you get orange juice to go with the doughnuts, then I can tell Colette I had a 'mostly healthy' breakfast."

Shea started for the kitchen, but Samantha caught his arm. He turned to her and she saw a reaction flare in his eyes.

For an instant they simply stood there, her hand on his bare forearm, the warm muscle under her fingertips a vivid reminder of other times. He remained still, his arm held out to her without resistance, his eyes reading hers.

"Yes?" he asked, his voice a little raspy.

"I'll get the juice," she said. "You sit with Tate and Zack." She headed off to the kitchen, aware that her pulse had quickened and her breath grown shallow.

How could she respond sexually, she wondered, to a man she could cheerfully murder?

CHAPTER FIVE

"YOU LOOKED LIKE THIS when you were born," Tate said to Shea as they sat on the sofa, a cushion's width between them. Tate laid the baby along his thighs and supported Zachary's head with his hands. Zachary continued to stare at him and smile.

"You remember?" Shea asked in disbelief.

"Yeah, I do. I had just turned six and was trying to get over Mike's being such an intrusion in my life, when you came along." He turned to grin at him. "Mike, at least, was shaped like a sandbag and fussed all the time, so while he got a lot of attention, I didn't really think he'd take the crown from me. But you...you were cute. Everybody said so. I came really close to having my own personal garage sale, with you going at a very reasonable price."

"What changed your mind?"

"Mom offered me a dollar to watch you while she ran muffins next door to old Mrs. McGinty."

Shea laughed. "And the money was more important to you than being without competition?"

Tate shrugged, playing with Zachary's fingers. "Although watching you for those five minutes was the perfect opportunity to do you in, I'd have had to get rid of Mike, too, to really regain my only-child status, and even at six years of age, I knew I'd never pass that off. But if I could earn a dollar watching you for five minutes, the opportunities seemed limitless, so I opted to let you live."

"Thank you," Shea said gravely. "I appreciate that."

"Sure. As soon as you learned to cook, I knew I'd made the right decision." He turned to look at Shea. "Samantha's very beautiful. Everybody likes her."

Shea couldn't deny that. "She's very likable. She's just not wild about me at the moment."

"Well, we'll just have to teach her to tolerate you anyway, the way we all do."

Shea opened his mouth to return a barb, when another knock sounded on the door.

Shea went to answer it, as Tate pretended to nibble on the baby's fingers. It was Felicia Ferryman, the mayor of French River. She wore a dark blue coat with a fur collar, and a matching hat with a little brim set at a jaunty angle on dark blond curls.

Shea planted himself squarely in the doorway. Felicia struck terror into his heart. She'd been determined to land one of the Delancey brothers since they'd arrived in town last January. Tate and Mike had each had brushes with her, and now that they were married, Shea was Felicia's final chance.

She gave him a sweet smile; then, clipboard in hand, elbowed her way past him with all the style of a football coach in a locker room. "Good morning, Shea," she said.

"Good morning, Felicia," he replied with a polite smile, resisting the impulse to courteously help her off with her coat, hoping she didn't intend to stay that long. "What brings you to Delancey Vineyards?"

But she was already taking it off herself. He had no choice but to assist her.

"The council and I brainstormed last night after everyone else left the meeting," she said, "and I think we got a really terrific idea. Oh, hi...Tate." She moved toward him with great caution as Shea put her coat in the closet. "Who's that?"

"It's my nephew." Tate patted the sofa cushion beside him. "Come and sit down and you can hold him." She started toward him, then put her hands behind her back and shook her head. "No," she said. "No, I couldn't. But...thanks." She looked a little nervously from one brother to the other, then smiled to dispel the awkward moment. "It's... Mike's baby?"

"No," Shea said, realizing that therein lay the instrument of his release from the bondage of Felicia's attentions. "He's my son."

"You're *kidding!*" Felicia gasped quietly. She did come around to sit near Tate, but she remained stiffly on the edge of the sofa and leaned over the baby as though her glance alone might hurt it.

"Here we are!" Samantha breezed into the room with a tray bearing three glasses of orange juice and three napkins. Then she noticed Felicia as she set the tray down on the coffee table.

"Oh," she said, smiling uncertainly at Shea. "I thought I'd met all the women in your life." She offered her hand to Felicia with an open friendliness he instantly resented. He'd been hoping for jealousy. "Hi! I'm Samantha Haskell."

Felicia stared at her. "Yes," she said, taking her hand. "I saw you on the news."

Samantha rolled her eyes. "Right. Who hasn't?"

"Felicia's mayor of French River," Shea said. "And Sam is Zachary's mother."

Felicia looked stricken. Her thoughts could not have

been read more clearly had there been words written in eyebrow pencil on her face: *Oh, no! Don't tell me I've lost you, as well, before I even had a chance!*

Samantha read the look, too—and did just what Shea was warning her not to do, if she'd taken the trouble to read *his* face.

"Oh, but Shea and I aren't together," she assured Felicia quickly. "We're just here for the holidays so Zack can meet his family. Are you two…?" She waggled her index finger as she looked from Shea to Felicia.

Felicia smiled brightly. "We're trying to be!"

"Well, go for it." Samantha spread both arms to indicate support. "Shea is as free as you are. Hold on. I'll get one more juice."

Shea read the amusement in Tate's eyes as he excused himself to follow Samantha into the kitchen.

"What do you think you're doing?" he demanded as she reached into the refrigerator.

"Pouring juice." She looked at him in surprise as she drew out the pitcher and closed the door. "Why? What's the matter?"

"We are not…!" He said, repeating her gesture with her fingers. "And where do you get off throwing the father of your son at another woman?"

She raised an eyebrow and set the juice on the counter. "But you are free."

"No," he said with aggravated patience, "I am not. I'm committed to Zachary, and he belongs to you."

She opened the overhead cupboard for a glass. "Oh, is that all? Well, we can work that out. People do it all the time."

"I am not interested in Felicia!"

"Well, you'd better explain that to her. She seems

to have another impression entirely.'' The juice poured, she put the pitcher back in the refrigerator, then walked off with the glass.

Samantha wasn't sure what she felt. Automatic jealousy had reared up at the sight of the pretty blonde, who was clearly fascinated by Shea, but she dismissed it as unreasonable. She'd cared once; what she felt now was probably just some kind of heart memory that lingered despite intelligent proof that what they had was over.

She handed Felicia the glass of juice and decided there was no reason the woman shouldn't have a clear field if she intended to pursue Shea. Samantha thought wickedly that Shea's displeasure over Felicia's attentions was just a bonus.

Felicia sat down in the chair at a right angle to the sofa, tugging at the short snug skirt that matched the blue coat. She'd left her hat on, giving the room a tea-party atmosphere. The juice she balanced on her clipboard.

Samantha seated herself in the middle of the sofa. Tate had Zachary's tiny hands in his big ones, the baby gripping his uncle's thumbs.

"Tate's probably already told you," Felicia said to Shea as he leaned against the fireplace, "that he's volunteered to design the new seniors facility....''

When they all turned to him in surprise, he pretended to take a modest bow. Felicia went on. "Well, he did. We got promises of clothes, furniture and pharmaceuticals last night. And you guys have promised food, which was greatly appreciated. But Margie McGowan—you know her? Margie's Dress Shop? She also came up with a great idea for a fund-raiser that should make a lot of money for the seniors.''

"And you're going to need our brilliant input," Tate guessed with a grin.

She shook her head. "I'm going to need your brilliant chef."

Shea gave his brother a superior look. "To do what?" he asked Felicia.

"To create a holiday dinner that will be so sumptuous and so beautifully presented we'll be able to charge a fortune and turn most of the money over to the seniors." She smiled a little stiffly. "That means you have to be willing to donate your skills. We'll buy the groceries, of course, but your only remuneration will be the satisfaction of service and probably some excellent public relations."

"How many people are we talking about?" Shea asked.

She shrugged. "However many people Delancey's can hold. Do you suppose you could close on a Saturday night just for us?"

Shea met Tate's eyes across the room. "What do you think?"

"Sure. It's not a problem for me. But we should let Mike put in his two cents' worth. I called him this morning and he was going to come by when Rachel finished serving breakfast at the B and B."

Felicia nodded. "Fair enough. We were thinking something really killer elegant so we can charge one hundred dollars a plate and people will feel they got their money's worth, even though it's for a charitable cause." Her smile at Shea was distinctly seductive. "I know you can do that."

Another rap on the door announced Mike's arrival. He let himself in, apologized quickly for being late and came to take the far end of the sofa. After greeting

Samantha with a warm smile, he leaned over her to catch Zachary's hand.

Tate pushed him away. "You had him last night. Today he's mine."

"He isn't yours," Mike scoffed. "He doesn't even like you. Look at the tension on his face. Come on, Zack. Come and see Uncle Mike."

"Tension? He's smiling!"

"He's kicking!"

"That's an expression of happiness."

"Seems to me he's trying to get away from you. Come on, Zack. You want to come to Uncle Mike?"

Tate handed him carefully over Samantha. "All right, here. But don't scare him."

Samantha helped the transfer, then glanced up at Shea and saw a fond smile on his face. He watched with pride as his brothers fought over his son's attention.

Zachary took the change without protest, as interested in Mike as he had been in Tate. Sam experienced a little flicker of warmth deep inside her at her clear conviction that bringing Zachary to French River had been a good thing.

Felicia shook her head over the whole situation. "Shall we continue?" she asked finally. "Mike, I was explaining to Shea and Tate..." She repeated most of what she'd already said, then told him his brothers needed his approval before they could go ahead with the plan.

"Of course I approve," he said immediately. "But, Shea, won't you have to hire help?"

Shea shook his head. "No, I'll just pay my staff for that night, though I'll need to see if they'll be willing to work without tips. Then I can employ all of you, also."

Mike and Tate looked at each other.

"Us," Tate said flatly. "But you've always said we're worse than no help at all."

"There'll be a lot to do besides cook. We'll have to make centerpieces, set tables—all kinds of chores. I think we can make it work."

"Terrific!" Felicia scribbled something on her clipboard. "I'll take care of sending out invitations and printing tickets. And, Tate, I think it'd be great if we got your plans for the new place mounted somewhere so everyone can see them. Even if they're just rough plans."

Tate nodded. "We can do that."

"Wonderful." She looked up at Shea. "Is there anything else I can do for you?"

Samantha didn't know whether it was her own latent jealousy at work, but the question sounded rife with innuendo.

Shea shifted his weight, and she guessed that he'd noticed, too. He shook his head and replied amiably, "Nothing that I can think of at the moment, but if something comes up, I'll have Sam call you."

Felicia gazed into his eyes as though to tell him that he could be as difficult as he wanted to be, but now that she had Samantha's okay, she would continue her pursuit.

"Shall we pick a date?" she asked.

While they all munched on doughnuts, they compared and coordinated schedules. The last Saturday before Christmas was finally agreed upon.

"Good," Felicia said. "That's deep enough into the season for people to really be in the spirit but not close enough to Christmas Day to get in the way. Any thoughts on a theme for tickets and advertising, or do you just want to leave that to me?'' She glanced from one brother to the other.

Shea thought a minute, then shrugged. ''I've got nothing.''

Tate and Mike both shook their heads.

''All right, then.'' She clipped her pen onto the top of her clipboard. ''Father Wolff's my cochairman. Maybe he'll have an idea.'' She stood. ''I guess that's it for now. Call me with any ideas or suggestions, and I'll be in touch with you.''

All the men stood, also. Shea walked her to the door, beckoning for Samantha to follow.

She intended to ignore him, but Mike pushed gently on her shoulder and Tate moved to allow her past him. ''Go,'' he said quietly. ''He needs a bodyguard. And I mean that literally.''

Samantha went rather than argue. Shea looked relieved. Felicia smiled wryly as the three stood together on the porch.

''Have you met the llama yet?'' she asked Samantha.

''No.'' They walked down the stairs, then down the small slope to Felicia's little imported car. ''I saw her last night when we drove in, but we haven't formally met.''

Felicia unlocked her car door with the remote. ''She was my first introduction to the Delancey Vineyards,'' she said, opening the door and smiling at Shea and Samantha over it. ''I came to pay a courtesy call because I heard there were three gorgeous new bachelors in town and I wanted to welcome them to French River. But I met Victoria instead. Be careful. She French-kisses.''

Samantha made a face.

"That was my reaction." Felicia turned limpid blue eyes on Shea. "Can you settle on a menu in a couple of days and bring it to me so I can put it in the advertising?"

He smiled. "I'll fax it to you."

With a glance that chided him for the futility of his efforts to escape her, she slid gracefully into the car.

Shea pushed her door closed, then drew Samantha back with him out of the way as Felicia drove off.

Samantha smiled after her. "She has the hots for you big-time."

"No, she doesn't," he insisted as they walked back up the slope and the steps. "She wanted one of us, and terrorized Tate, then Mike, before she got to me."

"They got married before she could land them, huh?"

"They did their best to evade her, too. Now I'm her last chance."

"She's very beautiful."

He pushed the door open for her. "That seems to be Felicia's stock-in-trade. The rumor is she's capitalized on that to get what she wants from the council."

"She seems to be taking a responsible hand in getting the seniors facility funded," Mike said as they walked back into the room. Zachary had started to cry and he handed him to Tate.

"It allows her to work with Shea," Tate said, putting the baby to his shoulder with visible skill and experience. He grinned at his youngest brother. "You were getting some pretty powerful looks there, bro."

Shea groaned. "I'm glad you're all so amused, but I seem to remember you each singing a different tune when it was one of *you* she was after."

Mike patted his shoulder as he went to the door.
"We live to harass you, Shea. You know that. I've
gotta run. Veronica says we're still invited to dinner
tomorrow?"

"Yeah. Sunday dinner. As usual."

Tate handed him the baby, who hadn't stopped crying. "Don't you want a little time to yourself?"

Shea made a rueful face at Samantha. "As Sam
keeps reminding me, she brought Zack here to get acquainted with his family, not for her to spend time with
me. So—Sunday dinner as usual."

"But he pined for you," Tate said to Samantha, "all
the time you were apart. He was this lost and angry
soul."

Shea could have killed Tate for revealing him like
that, but Samantha looked as though the words had
thrown her off balance. He liked that.

She glanced at Shea, then looked away in consternation. "I'd love to see you all at Sunday dinner," she
said with a smile, clearly eager to change the subject—
or at least shift its focus. "Have you ever had his caramel flan?"

Tate and Mike frowned at each other, then at him.
"You been holding out on us?" Tate asked.

"It won the San Francisco Gastronomic Society
award," she added.

It took Shea a minute to figure out why she was
heaping praise on him. Then he understood. It turned
their attention from her to him.

"He used to make it at Chez Shea on Sundays. I'll
see that he makes it for you."

"You'd better be on your toes," Mike warned Shea
as he opened the door. "Sam's watching out for us."

Shea sighed with forbearance. "You need someone

with a butterfly net watching out for you. And don't leave these doughnuts here. I have no conscience when it comes to apple fritters.''

As Tate reached for the doughnuts, certain Megan and Katie would love them, Samantha snatched a glazed old-fashioned from the box. She smiled self-deprecatingly. ''These are my weakness.''

''Don't tell Colette,'' Tate advised as he prepared to follow Mike out the door. ''If she knew you stayed that slender while eating those, she'd be suicidal.''

''That's ridiculous,'' she said, ''because Colette is beautiful. But the doughnuts will be our secret.''

When the door closed behind Tate and Mike, Shea held the baby up to look into his face. It was scrunched up, his eyes shut tightly and his little mouth opened wide with the vehemence of his distress.

''Good Lord,'' he said to Samantha. ''What could be that upsetting when you're two months old?''

She took the baby from him, held him high on her shoulder so she could lean her cheek into him, and rocked from side to side. ''Probably not being able to communicate what's upsetting you,'' she replied. ''I mean, I usually figure out when he's hungry or wet or has colic. But imagine what it must be like to be scared and not be able to say, 'Hold me! Somebody hold me!' Or to wake up and not see anybody and wonder where everbody is. You can't even yoo-hoo.''

Shea smiled. Not at the scared scenario, because he'd been there himself, and not that long ago, but at the thought that Zachary might someday turn to him and yoo-hoo.

''Why don't you bundle him into that snowsuit thing,'' Shea suggested, ''and we'll take a walk around the vineyard.''

She looked out at the gray day, then back at him, tempted. "Don't you have to go to work?"

"I've got a couple of hours." They used to walk together in the rain in San Francisco, he remembered. She'd liked fog and blustery days and moody clouds. Although he worked late into the night at the restaurant, he'd wake up early to spend time with her on Fisherman's Wharf or downtown, just walking and looking and enjoying being arm in arm.

"I'd love that," she said, still rocking the baby. "Give me a couple of minutes to get him changed and dressed, and we'll be right down."

He carried their juice glasses into the kitchen and puttered around, letting his mind work on a menu for Felicia's dinner that would fit all her specifications.

Elegant. For almost a hundred people. Fish or lamb would be more interesting to prepare, but the average person preferred chicken or beef two to one. Chicken, probably, for the health-conscious.

Potatoes would be easier to deal with than pasta in those numbers. Garlic potatoes. And salad rather than soup. It wouldn't take up burner space those last critical minutes. Green beans, maybe, plus the hazelnut vinaigrette he'd been experimenting with.

Beautiful presentation. That wouldn't be a problem. Good food itself was beautiful, and he knew all the tricks to show it off.

Centerpieces. Something that could be taken home as a reminder of a particularly special night.

Gingerbread houses? he wondered. They always smelled wonderful, but they were a lot of work. He'd have to give that more thought.

He looked up from wiping off the counter and saw Samantha standing in the doorway, the baby in a front carrier tied around her hip-length red wool jacket. She'd spread a lightweight, colorful blanket over him.

"We're ready," she said, pulling on a pair of gloves.

"Why don't I carry him!" he said.

She shook her head. "I'm fine. If I get tired, we'll trade off."

"All right." He noticed her bare head. "Do you have a hat?" he asked.

"If it rains, I have a hood."

"The wind whips down the valley as though someone left a giant refrigerator open in Canada."

He went out into the hallway to grab his jacket and dug a black watch cap out of the pocket. He twirled it on the index finger of his right hand and eyed her hair doubtfully. "Can we mess that up?" he asked.

She laughed lightly and reached up to unpin it. He wasn't sure what the joke was, but he liked the girlish sound.

Her hair fell to her shoulders, platinum and silky and stick straight. He placed the cap gently on her. "How's that?" he teased when the cuff rested over her eyes.

She laughed again. "If it comes with radar, perfect!"

He widened the cuff and tipped it backward slightly so she could see again. Then he fluffed her bangs awkwardly. "Better?"

"Much. Do I look dweebie?"

He turned her toward the front door. "You couldn't look dweebie if you tried."

THE DAY WAS OVERCAST and cold for Oregon, somewhere in the high thirties. She stopped at the foot of the porch steps, uttering a soft cry and dragging in a deep breath of air. She closed her eyes and did it again.

"I swear," she said after a moment, opening her

eyes to look at him, "that the air is so fresh I can smell sandalwood in Hong Kong and waffles on a griddle somewhere in Bavaria."

He put an arm around her shoulders and led her off. "You'll have to compare notes with Tate. After a year, he still raves about the air. Come on. We'll start in the vineyard, then I'll show you around the compound on our way back."

"Okay." She settled into long graceful strides, heading for the road he'd pointed to that led off the compound and into the vineyard. She looked back over her shoulder at the B and B, then looked at the restaurant as they passed it.

But a wicker turned her attention toward Rachel's pen and the woolly white llama watching them with big-eyed interest and a clear invitation to come over and say good-morning.

Samantha took off for the pen, talking to Zachary. "Look, Zack!" she said. "That's Victoria! Isn't she wonderful? This is a first for us!"

Reaching the fence, she raised a cautious hand to Victoria's long neck. "Do you like to be petted?" she asked, holding the baby to her with one hand while patting gently with the other.

Victoria responded by sniffing Samantha's hat, then her face, then offering her approval with a broad, rubbery kiss.

"Well, thank you." Samantha wiped her face with the back of a gloved hand and turned sideways so Zachary could see one of nature's more whimsical creations. "Look, sweetie! Right here in your own backyard!"

Shea noted Samantha's delight and his son's wide-eyed, openmouthed attempt to evaluate what he saw. It made Shea ridiculously happy.

Samantha faced him, her smile still wide. "I can't believe how beautiful those eyes are. She's just looking for friends."

Recognizing Shea, Victoria leaned over the fence to snuffle his hair. He stroked her and told her she was beautiful.

"Rachel rescued her and brought her here, and she seems to want to make it clear that she's grateful. We don't have many visitors through the winter, but when tours come through in the spring, summer and fall, the children find her endlessly fascinating."

As they talked, a pair of geese strolled over to the fence to get acquainted, along with a doe, which usually roamed near the lake but always returned home for dinner.

Shea pointed to a small shelter in the back. "A couple of raccoons live here, too. Rachel keeps them well fed, so they just run around being clowns and charming the visitors. She also has a couple of dogs in the house, a few cats and a white mouse."

"Good morning!" Rachel stepped out on the porch of the cottage beside the pen and the dogs bounded out with her, eager to investigate the newcomers.

"This big shaggy one," Shea said, scratching between the ears of a sheepdog-Saint Bernard cross, "is Moose, and the three-legged beagle is Snoopy. They're both very gentle."

They sniffed Samantha's hand, then the baby's feet, until Rachel called them back to her side.

"Did you sleep well?" Rachel asked. "How's Zachary this morning?"

"We slept very well, thank you," Samantha said,

moving down the fence to Rachel. "Zack and I both love your animals."

Rachel nodded. "Of course. They're our connection to the earth. Are you on a tour of the compound?"

Shea nodded. "We were headed for the vineyard, but Sam got distracted by Victoria."

"Well, have a good time. And come and see me, Samantha, if you want company while Shea's working."

"I will, thank you, Rachel."

THEY WALKED SIDE BY SIDE down the road that led into the vineyard. Shoulder-high vines in their winter nakedness followed the curve of the hill and stretched over it to the left and right and all the way down the slope.

"You'd think there's nothing to look at in the winter," Shea said, stopping her where the hill was terraced and a narrow road ran across it. "But isn't this a beautiful sight? Like black lace strewn across the hills. It's splendid in the spring when the leaves first come out, and in the fall when the vines are heavy with grapes, but I like this, too, when the vines are just...waiting, anticipating the right temperature, the right conditions, to burst out and let us take over from there."

Samantha remembered that as a chef preparing the earth's bounty, Shea had respected and appreciated nature's largesse. But she didn't recall his being quite this philosophical about it.

"Tate's developed such a sense of responsibility to this place," he said, taking her hand and leading her along the crossroad so they could look down on the rows upon rows of vines. "And Colette has a degree in horticulture. Though she's only been here three years now, she's trying to absorb all her father's knowledge and experience. You haven't met Armand yet, have you?"

"No."

"He was a winemaker in France, before coming to work for Uncle Jack. He kept the vines going when Jack disappeared, except he sold the grapes to other wineries rather than attempting to make wine on his own. That's a pretty big job, and he had no idea what had happened to Jack or when and if he was coming back. So he supported the winery by selling the grapes. Rachel was a signatory on the checking account, so she could pay Armand and the bills and together they kept things going."

Samantha frowned at him as Zachary lolled sleepily against her. "Colette and Veronica were telling me about that last night. They said you have some kind of investigation under way?"

He nodded. "We're beginning to suspect Jack may have disappeared deliberately."

"But why?"

He smiled. "What gets all men into trouble?"

"Pride," she replied, knowing that wasn't the answer he was looking for.

She was surprised when he laughed. "Besides that."

"Oh, let's see. Shortsightedness, a tendency to be narrow-minded, selfish…"

"Okay, okay." He stopped her, amusedly defensive. "I meant women. A woman seems to be at the root of his disappearance."

"The one Colette and Veronica told me about? She was in a train wreck or something, only you suspect she didn't really die."

"Right. We're not sure, of course. We know Jack was involved with a woman who'd left her husband, then went back to him when he fell ill. In the meantime, though, she'd become pregnant with Jack's baby."

Clearly aware of certain similarities to their situation, Samantha looked at him with a furrowed brow. "How is that her fault? Or do you mean he disappeared to evade her?"

"I mean," he said patiently, "that she was presumed dead in a wreck where there wasn't much evidence left. And in those days they didn't have the technology to read ashes and test DNA. But we think she might have escaped the fire, decided it was a way to flee her life, and got word to Jack."

"That's why Mike has a detective looking into things."

"Right. He put us on the trail of a man who bought the car Jack was driving when he disappeared. This guy got it from a junkyard."

"But...why would he do that?"

"He just had a real affection for it. I think he abandoned it, then bought it back under an assumed name."

She shook her head in confusion. "How do you know it was Jack under an assumed name?"

"Because the name is a term used in vineyard work. 'Girdling.' It's a cut made in the vine to improve fruit set. The guy who bought the Caddy was named Al Girdling."

"And that's too odd a name to be coincidence?"

"We think so."

She sighed. "Would he do that to his family? I mean, cause you that kind of pain? Not to mention simply abandoning his livelihood."

"I think he loved Tess enough to give up everything. Even to hurt us in the interest of finally having her."

"Wow," she said quietly, staring out over the horizon. "It's hard to imagine a love that enduring."

"Is it?" he asked. They'd certainly mishandled their relationship, but he thought she was missing a detail here.

"Yes," she replied. Her voice was quiet, sad. "You were able to just give up ours because you presumed I'd be unhappy without my luxuries. We'd spent all that time together, we'd made love a hundred times, and you were that wrong about me."

He shook his head. "It wasn't that I didn't think you could live without them. It was that I didn't want you to have to."

She looked into his eyes a moment, then groaned. "Well, whatever it was, the result was the same. Our love lasted a measly eight months."

"Maybe for you," he said, walking on. "For me it's still going at—let's see—nineteen months."

CHAPTER SIX

"I DON'T THINK IT'S LOVE," she challenged, following him up a wide road that led to the one to the compound. "I think this situation is just more comfortable for you."

He stopped and waited for her to catch up. "Comfortable?" he asked.

"Yes." She came to within inches of him, then turned down a narrow row between the vines. "You've made the restaurant a big success, you're settled comfortably with your brothers in a really going operation and *I'm* the one who's lost everything. You're willing to have a relationship because you're the one in the superior position."

He smiled wickedly. "I'd have a relationship in any position."

She didn't smile. "I'm serious."

"So am I." He raised both hands in surrender when she tried to walk around him.

"You're right, sort of," he said, turning her around so that he could reach the hook for the baby carrier. "But for the wrong reason. Hold on to Zack. I'm going to take the carrier."

"I'm all right."

"You're breathless, and I know it's not that I'm affecting your heartbeat." He turned her around again to slip the padded shoulder straps off while she held the baby to her. Then he tucked the baby against his chest and let her help him slip on the carrier. She walked around him to hook it in the back.

"Hang on a minute," she said. "I have to lengthen this strap. So, you're saying I'm right but wrong? How very male."

"I am more at ease with the way things are than I was when I left," he said, standing still as her fingers worked against his back. "Not because I'm in any way superior, but because I've finally gotten past feeling like an idiot."

He felt a tug as she tightened the strap. She walked around him to frown up into his face. "You didn't lose the money and therefore the restaurant. Marty Hirsch did."

"But I let it happen because I wasn't watching the details."

"You were shopping, cooking, trying new things all the time. The business end of the place was his responsibility."

"My name was on the restaurant. I should have been more careful."

"You trusted him."

"Yeah," he said with a mirthless laugh. "I've used that as an excuse a lot. But the more I think about it, the more I realize that—" he took her hand and started up the slope again "—maybe I was just ignoring the part of the business I didn't like so that all I had to deal with was the part I enjoyed. Not very mature."

"But very human. I used to spend a lot more time overseeing the family and metro news than I did the national stuff, simply because I found it more interesting." The wind caught her hair and whipped it around her face. She held it down with a gloved hand. "My father saw his world crumbling and hid out with a showgirl rather than do anything about it.''

''Maybe he just didn't know what to do.''

She shook her head. ''He always knew what to do. It's pretty clear he just didn't care anymore—about me or Zack or anyone.''

''That doesn't sound like your father.''

''Then where is he?''

''I don't know. But he loved you very much. That doesn't stop.''

She reached up to adjust the blanket over Zachary. ''He loved my mother and *that* stopped. You loved me and *that* stopped.''

''No.'' He pulled her to a halt and took hold of her shoulder, his thumbs biting through her coat. ''I left because at that point in time I couldn't be all the things I wanted to be for you. I didn't know how to fix that, so I left to try to work on it in my own way. But as I said before, I never stopped loving you.''

Anger erupted in her despite her tolerance of a moment ago. Her pinched cheeks grew rosy, her gray eyes smoky. ''I called to tell you I was having your baby, and you wouldn't take the phone!''

''You didn't say that was why you were calling,'' he reminded her.

''If you loved me that much, you'd have wanted to talk to me for whatever reason I called!''

''When I left,'' he said, still mildly, ''you told me you wouldn't wait for me to resolve my financial problems. And you told me to go to hell. I thought I was just going to be hearing more of that and I'd already had a particularly rough day.''

''Yeah, well, I was having a particularly rough day myself.''

"I'm sorry, Sam."

"Yeah," she replied stiffly. "Me, too. So, let's just not talk about love anymore, all right? We're supposed to be talking about grapes." She stopped at the top of the hill and turned to look down the slope, pointing to the expanse of vines below. "Are these all the same?"

"No." He sighed away his frustration over the seemingly unsolvable argument and pointed to her right. "Those are chardonnay. On this side of the road the grapes are pinot noir. So far, those are the only two wines we're trying to produce. The white won't be ready for another year and a half. The red will take longer. If we do well with those, we might do a little experimenting."

"Well." She started back along the road to the compound. You'll have to send me a bottle of chardonnay when it's ready."

He watched her stride ahead of him, nose in the air as she reminded him that her presence here was temporary.

"Maybe I'll just be there to pour it for you!" he called after her.

She pretended not to hear him.

Armand was working at a small desk in the back when they walked into the winery. The building was barnlike in structure and smelled of yeast and oak; the pungent aroma of fermented grapes hung in the air. He came to greet them, average in height with wiry gray hair. Gnarled hands and a slow gait attested to rheumatoid arthritis but his shoulders were well-muscled and his back still straight.

"You must be Samantha," he said, offering her his hand and a warm smile. "I'm Armand, Colette's father."

"I've heard about you." Samantha took his hand gently but noted it was strong despite the affliction. "Everyone has glowing praise for your skill as a wine-maker."

"That remains to be seen." He winked. "I intend to be sunning myself in Tahiti when they sample this batch, just in case they're wrong. I'm sorry we haven't better weather for you."

"I'm from San Francisco," she said with a laugh. "It's like this a lot of the time, though a little warmer. Would you like to meet my son?"

Armand lifted his gaze to Shea, who removed the blanket that covered the sleeping baby and drew closer.

"Handsome little devil, isn't he?" Shea asked, running a knuckle tenderly over the baby's pink cheek.

Armand stroked the woolly blue cap on Zachary's head. "He certainly is. He has your coloring, but I'd say his good looks come from his mother."

Shea disapproved that appraisal. "No, they don't. At least not all of them."

Armand studied the baby again, then looked up at Shea with a smile. "Yes. They do. But perhaps he's inherited your artistry with food."

"He has inherited his eagerness to eat it," she said. She looked around at the open stainless vats in the middle of the large room, the tall tanks against the wall and the stairs at the side that led to a second floor. Everything, she noticed, was spotless.

"Open vats for the red wine," Shea said, pointing, "covered vats for the whites. The stairs go up to our offices. This is the tasting room."

He walked her into a soft white room with an oak bar running the width of it and a few small tables and chairs arranged in the middle.

Behind the bar was a painting of the Delancey logo, a shield bearing a cluster of grapes backed by three lances.

"That's going to be our label," Shea said, "when we finally bottle the wine."

The far end of the room held shelves filled with souvenirs—wineglasses that could be purchased plain or etched with the Delancey shield, decorative corks, coasters, napkins and packaged cake and cookie mixes from the restaurant.

"Nothing much to see upstairs," he said, leading her out of the room again, "but you might enjoy the cellar. It looks like something out of a movie."

It did, she thought, with its low ceiling and shadowy corners. Rows upon rows of barrels lined both sides of the room, and it smelled like a wine cellar should—as though it had been painted with the product.

The barrels appeared new.

"Limousin oak," Shea said, running a hand proprietarily over one of them. "Colette insists it's the best for ageing because it imparts a flavor the wine doesn't get from stainless steel."

Samantha nodded and pointed to a newly built wine rack at the rear of the room. It was the very traditional crisscross kind, enabling a wine bottle to be stored on it's side. Several floor-to-ceiling racks had been made and stood new and empty under the dim light of one bare bulb.

"I see you're preparing to store an impressive stock," Samantha said.

Shea nodded. "Yes, we are. We all helped make the decisions that got us this far, and we all have a lot of faith in one another." He smiled broadly, sincerely. "I fully expect we'll be winning ribbons in a couple of years."

Given what she knew of everyone here, she liked to think that would be true. "I hope so."

After another handshake and a renewed welcome from Armand, Samantha followed Shea across the compound to the Green Acres Day Care Canter, but the door was locked.

"No kids on a Saturday," he said, "so they're probably out partying or something. Want to see the restaurant?"

"Is there a double-tall mocha in it for me?" she asked, almost salivating at the memory of how wonderfully he made those for her in San Francisco.

"Absolutely. Come on. We'll go in through the dining room."

Shea led Samantha to a building with a western flavor. Whereas the winery had looked like a barn, this reminded her of a nineteenth-century saloon, except for the tall carved double doors. Planters with giant winter cabbages and ivy decorated the front.

"Actually, I think it was a bunkhouse," Shea said when she shared that thought with him. "It had a big fireplace at the back, in what had been the kitchen, and that's what sold me."

Shea pushed the doors and let Samantha pass before him into a large dining room that held several dozen round tables, already dressed for lunch in dark blue tablecloths. High-backed chairs upholstered in a pink-and-blue fabric stood ready for patrons.

The walls were a soft gray-blue, and a deep wallpaper border of acanthus leaves trimmed them just below the ceiling, where crystal chandeliers sprang to life when Shea flipped a switch.

The room was warm and elegant all at once. He'd always had a gift for that, she remembered. Chez Shea had had an elegant French atmosphere but had been just as warm and inviting.

"It's beautiful," she praised. "What a perfect spot to enjoy one of your meals."

He turned the lights off, but not before she caught the surprised arch of his eyebrow.

"I could work you over with brass knuckles," she said, noting *his* surprise at her compliment, "but I'm open-minded enough to give credit where credit is due. You're the finest chef west of the Mississippi and I know that."

He smiled. "Only west?"

She patted his shoulder consolingly. "Sorry. Paul Prudhomme is east."

"True. Come into the kitchen."

She followed him as he wound his way through the sea of tables to the spacious, brightly lit commercial kitchen, with its large appliances, open grills, central work space stretching the length of the room and pots and pans hanging from an overhead laticework rack.

A deep fieldstone fireplace was built into the back wall. "Not up to code to cook on, I'm afraid, but sometimes I light it when I'm doing the books or planning banquets."

Everything was pristine at the moment.

Shea checked his watch. "Charlie will be in in half an hour to get things under way for lunch. Great guy. I found him behind the counter in a little spot downtown. We got to talking about being newcomers here, he said he'd come from this place in Galveston where he'd worked in fine dining and wanted to do that again, so I hired him on the spot."

He opened the refrigerator door and scanned the shelves. "We have a kitchen staff of five," he went on, apparently pleased with the contents. "I was afraid it would up my costs too much, but you know how I am about having anybody wait too long. As it turned out, we've been swamped most of the time, so having a large staff pays for itself several times over each week."

"That's great," she said, leaning against the long worktable that took up the middle of the room. "And I'm sure it's comforting to know your brothers aren't going to gamble away your profits."

"Yes, it is."

"What's new with Marty Hirsch? Do you ever hear from him?"

Shea shook his head. "Not a word. I'm sure the fact that I helped convict him of fraud and put him away for a couple of years hasn't made him miss me a whole lot."

"You supported him for three years."

He rolled his eyes. "In a manner to which his bookie grew to be accustomed. Mostly, I've put all that away, though I'm trying to pay everybody back little by little."

He remembered belatedly that his insistence on repaying his creditors *without* her help was partially responsible for her telling him to go to hell just before he'd left San Francisco. He expected a snide remark.

Instead, she said with a grim smile, "Fortunately, all I have are my Visa bill and my account at F.A.O. Schwarz. But unless I win the lottery, they're going to take my entire lifetime to pay off."

He returned her smile. "Come work for me. My waitresses make good tips."

She knew he was teasing, but she recalled helping out one night when Chez Shea had hosted a banquet and been short a waitress. Samantha had leaped into the breach with a well-bred rich girl's curiosity and emerged four hours later with singed fingers, an aching back and very sore feet.

Though most people had been polite and considerate, some had been rude, and a surprising number had treated her as though she were either invisible or a vegetable.

She'd also emerged with a sincere appreciation for the unfailing courtesy and good humor of the other waitresses.

"Thanks, but I'm not sure I'm sweet enough for the work. One wrong word to me on the wrong day and your patron might end up with his soup in his pocket. You'd get sued and there you'd be—more debts to pay off."

She also recalled, though, with a sudden quickening of her pulse, that Shea had raised her self-esteem after the banquet in a very creative way.

"Does this mean you're not going to help me with the fund-raiser Christmas dinner?" he asked.

HE REMEMBERED how willingly she'd helped him out of a staffing bind once in San Francisco. She'd been thrilled with her thirty dollars in tips but disgusted by the way waitresses were treated by some patrons.

He remembered in brilliant detail how he'd consoled her—hugs and kisses, long loving strokes of scented oil, lovemaking that had gone on and on.

He knew when her gray eyes locked with his and lost focus that she was remembering, too. He took advantage of the moment and drew her to him, pulling

her around the baby and into his arms. He kissed her
as he had that night, with tenderness and gratitude and
all the affection her eagerness inspired in him.

She leaned into him, opened her mouth to him—but
after one delicious moment, stiffened and drew back.
She looked hurt and angry, as though he'd somehow
betrayed her.

"Stop it!" she said. "We've already had this out."

He'd always had trouble keeping up with her when
she was angry. Her brain often dug up old grievances
he'd completely forgotten. "What?" he asked, clue-
less.

She waved the back of her hand at him. "This…this
sweet protective thing you do."

Sweet? Not really the word he wanted applied to his
attempts at seduction. "I'm sorry," he said. "I didn't
mean to be sweet." No. That wasn't going to help.

"I told you last night not to do that." The baby's
blanket had fallen when she'd drawn away and she
snatched it up off the floor. Zachary's cheek lay against
Shea's stomach and her face softened at the sight.

"I didn't kiss you last night," he pointed out.

She refocused on him, her jaw firming. "Don't be
sweet to me, don't put your arm around me, don't *kiss*
me. I'm not falling for your line again, Dalancey. 'Fool
me twice, shame on me!'" she quoted loudly. "I'm
here for Zachary. That's it. So don't try your gentle-
man-charmer stuff on me, all right? Just…keep you
distance."

The woman had a head of English oak. Fortunately,
so did he. He took the blanket from her and dropped
it on the worktable. Then he cupped an arm around the
baby as he started to slip off the carrier's shoulder
straps. "So you're not interested in helping with the

gingerbread houses?'' he asked absently, pretending total absorption in his task.

The Christmas they'd been together, he'd made gingerbread houses for the pediatrics ward at one of the city hospitals and she'd had more fun than anyone applying the candies that stood in for architectural detail.

He'd teased her about how expensive her help became when she ate as many candies as she applied.

"What gingerbread houses?" She walked around him to unhook the back strap, reluctance in her voice, but he knew he had her interest.

"Felicia wanted me to do something special for centerpieces," he explained, patting the baby through the blanket. The carrier released, he laid the baby in an old barrel chair in the corner, which he or Charlie usually fell into for a few minutes after the dinner rush.

He pointed to the blanket and Samantha handed it to him. Then he untied the baby's hood and unzipped the snowsuit. "I was thinking gingerbread houses would be nice. Something simple and elegant, since we have to do so many. Maybe just white icing trim and gold or silver dragées."

She seemed to be considering that. "It would look beautiful," she finally conceded, "but the dragées are no fun to eat. They taste like buckshot."

He laughed. "All right. We'll find something you could enjoy eating that'll still look classy."

"I'll help," she promised. "Just don't think you're going to use this as an element in seduction, because this is only for the holidays, remember. On January 2 I go back home and find a job."

He ignored that and went to the cappuccino maker in the corner of the counter.

She'd been studying him, probably expecting an argument, but when she spotted the ornate brass contraption, with its decorative eagle at the top and all sorts of knobs and valves—the only thing he'd been able to salvage from Chez Shea—she forgot herself and joined him with a wide smile.

"You still have it! That's great!" She patted the machine affectionately. "This thing made the best mochas I've ever had anywhere. Do you have caramel and vanilla syrup?"

He opened the overhead cupboard to reveal a collection of several dozen flavored syrups. "I have died and gone to heaven," she said with heartfelt sincerity. Then she called herself back to their previous discussion.

"It just isn't like you to be so amenable," she said suspiciously as she watched him work all the strange knobs and spigots.

"I made you mochas all the time," he protested.

"I mean, amenable about nothing going on between us. What's up your sleeve?"

He held his arm out to her. "Want to see for yourself?"

She gave it a punitive but gentle swat. "You're doing it again! Just get to work on my mocha."

He knew it was perfect when he handed it to her several moments later. He'd used the best coffee roasted by the Astoria Coffee Company about one hundred and thirty miles away, syrups imported from Italy and cream that he bought from a small local dairy.

The best ingredients prepared with the utmost care and attention delivered the best results.

"Ooh." Samantha put a hand to her heart after the first sip and closed her eyes to relish it. "I haven't had mocha this wonderful since..."

He knew why she hesitated. He'd made one for her

the night before he'd left. The evening had begun with both of them angry, though trying to be rational, but emotion had soon outdistanced reason and had ended in shouts, tears and recriminations.

She'd thrown her glass mug at him and stormed off, consigning him to hell.

But he didn't want her to think about that now. "Before the restaurant opened, when Tate and Mike and I shared the house, we used to have this in the breakfast nook and I spent most of my life making cappuccinos for them. It was a long cold winter."

"They don't get them anymore?" she asked empathetically.

He sipped at his own, flavored with amaretto. "Sure they do. They just haunt the restaurant kitchen now. We'll have to get a small machine for the house and teach you how to make your own."

She shook her head. "It'd never be the same." She wandered toward the chair to check on the baby, who slept on in apparent contentment.

Shea pulled two stools out from under the counter and leaned a hip on one, while she put down her mocha and climbed onto the other. She reclaimed her drink and took a deep sip.

"I'm glad your dream finally came true," she said. It sounded as though that admission had taken a small toll on her. "When you left, I have to admit that I imagined everything falling apart on you and you returning to San Francisco, looking me up and begging me to take you back and find you a job."

He had to smile at her candor. "At which point you'd have thrown me out on my ear?" he guessed.

"I'd have had my husband, the senator, do it." She swung a leg back and forth, taking pleasure in her little scenario. "In front of the fifty or so friends at our little soirée."

He toasted her with his mug. "I've always admired your ability to be compassionate."

She seemed to consider her vengeful imaginings as her due. "I wanted you to be as miserable as you'd made me. Particularly when I found out I was pregnant. It was a time we should have shared in happy anticipation, whether we had a dime or not, but..." A wave of her hand suggested that his pride had swept away that possibility.

She took another pull on her glass. "But I got mine, didn't I? It's too bad *you're* not married to a senator. You could have had her throw me out on my ear. Felicia looked as though she wanted to do it."

"I never had a reason to plot revenge," he said. He met her eyes, wanting to see through the attempts at humor and the pretense that what they had together no longer mattered. "I didn't understand your attitude or your anger, but that never diminished my feelings for you. I missed you every minute."

She opened her mouth to reply, but he held a hand up to stop her. "I know. It brings us back to the phone call. I thought that if I heard your voice, I'd forget everything I wanted to accomplish and rush back to San Francisco. Believe it or not, I thought *not* taking your call was the best thing for both of us." He sighed, a bur in his chest he'd probably feel for the rest of his life. "Of course, I didn't know you were about to deliver our baby."

He expected her to jump right in, agreeing that it was all his fault. Instead, she studied the milky contents of her glass, then looked up at him, her eyes regretful. "I should have told you. I should have told you the day I found out. But I was still too angry with you to want to share anything. Then Zachary grew inside me and became real to me, half you and half me. I knew I had to tell you. I guess we'd just lost our ability to make anything good out of what we had.'' She shook her head and added wistfully, ''And we had so much.''

''We have Zachary,'' he reminded her. They'd connected there for a moment, but he felt she was slipping away again. He desperately tried to draw her back. ''I'm sorry I wasn't there when you delivered him, but I'm here now. And I promise to make that fact worth something.''

She couldn't throw that declaration back in his face. During the past year he seemed to have maintained all the attributes she remembered in him, while acquiring maturity and confidence. It was as if she'd been presented with the new and improved model of the man she'd once loved so much.

He would be good for their son, but he wouldn't be good for her. Love didn't last forever, no matter how wonderful it was. Her parents' love had been wonderful, and now they lived on separate continents.

''All right, then.'' She rinsed her glass mug under the hot water and placed it on the counter. ''I'll help with the centerpieces and the dinner, and we'll find a way to be friends so that you can be a father to Zack. That's all I can promise.''

He scooped the baby up off the chair and cradled him in his arm. ''That's good enough for now.'' He glanced at his watch. ''The guests might still be having breakfast at the B and B, so I'll take you through there another time, all right?''

''Yes. Of course.''

''I have to get changed for work, but the station wagon in the driveway is yours to use if you want to. Mike said he would switch the infant seat from his van to my car. Town's only a couple of miles away, if you want to go exploring.''

He flipped off the lights, opened the back door and held it for her.

"Maybe in a day or two," she said, walking through, "but I have to unpack our things, try to keep Zack on some kind of routine, write a few letters, make a few calls."

He locked the door behind them, then turned toward the house. "Okay. But if you feel the need for company while I'm at the restaurant, remember Rachel's offer. And I'm sure Colette or Veronica or the girls would come over or take off with you to look around."

"Thanks." She raised her hand to cover a yawn. "Today, at least, I think I'll just do my small chores, putter around, have a nap."

"Good. I'll send lunch over."

"Oh, don't bother. You'll be busy, and I usually skip lunch, anyway."

He looked into her eyes and she knew he saw beyond the smile she offered to that place inside where she hid all her fears.

"Why would you do that," he asked, "when you have so much to deal with on so little sleep? I know you have a lot to worry about, but if you don't take care of yourself, you won't be able to handle it."

She held both hands up to indicate emptiness. "There's nothing to handle except Zack, and he's fun despite the terrible hours he keeps. No family, no job, no bank account, pretty soon no house…"

He put an arm around her shoulders as they walked. "That's scary," he said for her.

It was easy to nod agreement. "But I'm working on it. I'll be fine."

"I'm sure you will, but not if you don't take better

care of yourself." They walked up the porch steps and she pushed the door open. "And even though your life is missing all those things at the moment, there's still something in it that requires you to be at peak performance."

She nodded, taking the baby from him as they stood just inside the living room. "Zachary."

"No," he said, turning her toward him again as soon as she started for the sofa. He pointed a thumb at his chest. "Me. You let your guard slip due to weariness or loss of focus and I'll get you back, Sammie. I'll teach you to want me all over again."

She smiled amiably. "Never...happen," she said slowly, clearly.

"Oh, yeah?" he challenged.

"Yeah," she confirmed.

"I guess we'll see."

"I guess we will."

Shea hurried upstairs, then was back in ten minutes in spotless kitchen whites, the short cut of the jacket accentuating the breadth of his shoulders, the crisp white cotton dramatizing the darkness of his features.

She'd placed the still-sleeping baby in his carrier on the sofa and was on her hands and knees, adding a log to the fire. She pretended not to notice all she'd observed.

He leaned over the sofa to touch Zachary's hand, then came to lean over her.

"I probably won't get back until after ten tonight," he said. "But if you need me, the kitchen phone has the compound's numbers on it."

She nodded, already familiar with the long workdays a restaurant required. "Thanks. I'll be fine."

"I think you should kiss me goodbye," he said.

She looked up to see that his eyes laughed, though

his lips were still and steady. "And why would that be?"

"Zack's listening."

"Zack is asleep."

"Adults learn in their sleep. I'm sure babies do, too. We're supposed to be cultivating a sense of family in him."

She pushed herself to her feet, fascinated by his laughing eyes as he straightened with her. God, she'd missed those eyes. He'd been so much fun to be with when she'd first known him, before the pressures of betrayal and loss had taken their toll.

"How about if he just hears me walk you to the door?"

"He's probably thinking that that's pretty stingy, but if it's the best you can do..."

"It's all you're going to get," she said, walking him to the door and holding it open for him. She smiled innocuously. "I'm not yet weary or losing focus, so don't think you can skate anything by me."

He looked heavenward in supplication. "There is nothing in this world as challenging to a man's romantic inclinations as a vigilant woman."

She leaned in the doorway as he stepped out onto the porch. "It pays to be vigilant."

He looked back at her. "Vigilance keeps you safe, but it also prevents you from experiencing all kinds of adventure."

"Maybe I don't need adventure."

"Maybe you're just afraid of it." He kissed her cheek and ran lightly down the steps.

CHAPTER SEVEN

SAMANTHA HUNG UP HER clothes and put the baby's things away in the dresser. She fed him again and played with him, then rocked him to sleep.

At noon a pretty young woman in beautifully fitted tuxedo-style pants, jacket, shirt and tie appeared at the door with a covered tray in her hands. Her dark hair was short and curly, her smile was friendly and her silver badge with the Delancey logo on it was engraved with the name June. Behind her, commotion reigned as restaurant patrons greeted one another and streamed in in groups.

"Lunch, Mrs.—" June stopped herself, a frown marring her sweet face. "Miss? Um…"

"Sam," Samantha said, taking the tray and offering her hand. "Hi, June. Thank you. I'm sorry you had to walk this over when you're obviously busy."

"Not a problem," the young woman replied. "Shea makes the best crab cakes in the whole world. And I love the sweet-potato straws." She lifted the edge of the napkin so Samantha could see the beautifully arranged, nestlike mound of fried sweet-potato strips.

The crab cakes were lightly breaded and drizzled with a purplish sauce that smelled like raspberry. Next to them was a small salad of exotic greens.

"I have to get back," June said with a little wave. "Welcome to Oregon, Mrs.… um…Sam."

"Thank you, June."

Samantha made a cup of tea to accompany her lunch, then sat on the floor in front of the fire and feasted. She stretched out and napped for an hour, then awoke to the ring of the telephone.

"Hello?" she said, wondering how she would transfer the call, certain it had to be for Shea or one of the other Delanceys.

"Oh, I woke you, didn't I?" Colette asked in self-disgust. "I'm sorry. I called Shea and he said you just wanted to hang around and get some things done today, but I thought I'd check and make sure you hadn't changed your mind about that. I'm sorry. I imagine you're not getting much sleep with such a young baby."

"Not much," Samantha agreed, "but nothing different from what every other mother goes through. And it was time for me to be up, anyway. Zack will be awake any minute."

"Veronica and the girls and I are going shopping," Colette went on. "Wouldn't you like to come? There are lots of us to carry the baby."

"Uh…"

"Right! I know funds are short, but I have magic plastic. If you find something you can't live without, we'll charge it and worry about it later."

Samantha laughed. "Thank you. I was hesitating, though, because I'd love to come, but I'd also love to take a long nap and just kind of collect myself. I hope you'll invite me again. I love to go shopping, even when all I can do is look."

"You bet we will. Is there anything we can bring back for you?"

"I can't think of a thing. Thank you, though."

"All right. If you need anything and Shea's too busy, Mike and Tate are in the winery office. The number's on your kitchen phone."

"Right."

Zachary began to scream.

"Okay. I hear your little angel. See you at dinner tomorrow."

She remembered the talk last night about the weekly Sunday dinner. "Bye. And thanks again."

The rest of Samantha's afternoon revolved around Zachary until she gave him his bottle and he fell asleep again.

She tidied up the morning and lunch dishes, then went to the door to find that Shea had sent dinner, this time with a cheerful, stocky young man named Dean. He, too, was in a tux.

"Prawns sautéed in butter, lime and chili pepper, with couscous and baby carrots. Shea says he'll bring dessert with him when he comes home."

Samantha stared at him a moment in disbelief, then thanked him and took the tray from him. She'd already eaten more than she usually consumed in a day.

But the aroma of the shrimps was so tantalizing that she sat at the table to try one, and thirty minutes later stared at an empty plate.

She put the plate right in the dishwasher in an attempt to remove all evidence of her old appetite. When she'd been seeing Shea, she'd tested everything he prepared and often had dessert with him when he finished work late at night.

But she'd been a little younger then, and the Blimp Baby hadn't misshapen her body. She'd had a job that kept her running, a membership in a health club and a metabolism like a tennis player's.

This had to stop. She would talk to him about it tonight.

She changed into her old belted pink chenille robe, watched television and wrote a letter to Hannah.

Shea was not home by ten. Having difficulty keeping her eyes open, Samantha lay down on the sofa to rest, determined to see the end of the news.

SHEA WALKED into the living room just before eleven, thinking that if Delancey's became any more popular, they would have to put seating upstairs. But it was a problem he was happy to deal with.

Sort of like Samantha.

He saw Zack asleep in his carrier on the coffee table, and Samantha stretched out on the sofa beside him. Shea smiled at the sight of her.

She always slept as if in the middle of a *grand jeté,* arms and legs flung out. Now one leg was pointed, fully extended, the other leg hanging off the sofa. One arm was flung back over her head, the other toward the baby.

The movements that had placed her in that position had disturbed the robe, and though the belt remained tied, the robe had slipped open and he caught a glimpse of midriff and navel, and the floral silk of pink-and-white bikini panties.

Shea put the special treat he'd brought her on the coffee table, checked his sleeping son, then leaned over her to close the robe, afraid she'd get chilled in the drafty house.

And that was when he saw the scar. It was five or six inches wide and just above the line of her panties.

The sight of it caused a cold horror in the pit of his stomach. Not that he considered it unsightly, but that it had happened to her. He remembered the satin touch of her under his hands and was horrified that her delicate flesh had been insulted in that way.

He sat down beside her on the edge of the sofa.

She awoke suddenly, sleepily confused. Then she focused on him, apparently considered him too close and tried to sit up. But his hand was on her stomach.

She looked indignant, then disappointed. He didn't bother to analyze what that all meant.

He stilled her with the hand he held to the scar. "Is this from...did you have cesarean?" he asked.

She propped herself up on her elbows, her body still tense, and rubbed at her eyes with one hand, then gazed at him, seeming less upset by his closeness and more confused by his concern. "Yes. I was bleeding and tests showed that the placenta was blocking the birth canal. So they decided to take him a week early to eliminate any problems."

He didn't know why that made him angry, but it did. "You didn't tell me that, either," he accused.

He expected an angry retort, but she simply pulled her robe together and sat up in the corner of the sofa, her legs still trapped behind him.

"Well...it just didn't come up," she said quietly. "Zachary's fine. I'm fine. It was really no big deal. Women have cesareans every day. Some have several in a lifetime. They even make the cut a little lower now so that you can still wear a bikini." She shot him an "Oh, well" lift of her eyebrows. "But my doctor was older and probably never gave that a thought."

He knew it hadn't been as easy as she made it sound. He remembered the night she phoned, remembered himself seated self-righteously at the dinner table, refusing to take the call Colette had answered, certain he knew what was best for Sam—and easiest for him.

Forgetting that she'd told him only that morning to keep his distance, he moved closer to take her into his arms. "I can't believe you and Zack were in danger and I didn't even answer the phone to ask what you were calling about."

He felt her hesitation, then—miraculously—her fingertips stroking his back. "Shea, it's all right. I didn't know I was going to have a cesarean then, anyway. I wanted you there not because of my health but just to share the arrival of our baby."

"I'm sorry," he said again.

"I know. That's all right. It's all over." She drew back slightly and, to his surprise, smiled into his eyes. "The way I look at it, the cesarean saved me several ugly hours of labor."

He felt now that he had to know every detail. "Was anyone with you?"

"No."

"Where was your father?"

"On business in Boston."

"Where was Hannah?"

"At a spa in the Seychelles. She was supposed to be my Lamaze coach, but…well, I didn't need one after all."

Guilt ground his innards in its big cold hand.

"Why didn't you call me again?" he demanded, then realized that had the situation been reversed, that was the last thing *he'd* have done. "Of course you wouldn't. God. Here I've been teasing you about getting back together and you must hate me with every cell in your body."

"I thought I did when you left," she said honestly,

"then I learned I was expecting Zack, and since he was half you, loving him helped me get over that." She smiled weakly. "I could have still killed you, but I no longer hated you."

He ran a hand over his face and tried to think. Self-flagellation wasn't going to serve any purpose here. He had to do something constructive.

He had to make her love him again so that he could make up to her and Zack for all he'd put them through. He could be a good husband and father; he was sure of it.

The problem would be convincing her after the evidence she had so far.

He would have to be subtle.

She gave his shoulder a gentle shove. "Will you lighten up?" she teased. "I thought we were going to give Zachary a happy Christmas, and we can't do that if you're going to wear that face."

There was a sudden squeal from the carrier, followed by a scream. Samantha tucked her legs up to swing them around Shea to reach for the baby. But he got him first and instinctively started pacing.

"He'll go right back to sleep again," she assured him. "We probably just got a little loud."

"Why don't you go to bed," he said, "and I'll rock him for a while."

"But you just got off work."

"It's all right. I'm so happy to have him."

"Well...if you're sure." She didn't look as certain.

He suddenly remembered what he'd brought home for her and pointed to the bag on the coffee table. "That's for you. Get a spoon and take it up to bed with you."

She opened the bag greedily, then extracted the carryout cup and pulled off the lid. "What is it?"

She gasped, stuck her index finger inside, pulled out a dollup of flan with caramel sauce and licked it off.

"Oh!" she groaned. "You did it! You actually did it! I thought you were going to just torture me with promises, but you did it!"

She jabbered all the way into the kitchen to retrieve a spoon, then spoke more slowly as she came out again, eating.

"After I devoured every bite of the dinner you sent over," she said, accusation in her tone, "I swore I wasn't going to eat again until Tuesday and look!" She waved the spoon at him menacingly, as if it were all his fault. "I'm eating flan! I can't believe it. Call Colette so she can witness my body's destruction."

He sat in the big chair by the fireplace with Zachary. "She'll be over tomorrow. As I remember, you react pretty much the same way to roast and vegetables and apple pie."

"Because they're so all-American." She sat down near him on the raised hearth. "We didn't make a big thing of Sunday dinners when I lived at home since everyone was too busy and we usually went away for Christmas—to Paris or Stockholm or sometimes Tahiti if Mom was feeling the cold. I mean, we loved each other then—it wasn't that. We just never did the traditional things everyone else did. I missed that."

Shea patted Zachary's back, his large hand covering the baby from his neck to the bottom of his spine. "You might be very tired of tradition by the time you leave here," he said. "We're all helping to hang garlands and lights on Monday. Then the following Monday, we're going to get Christmas trees. We figured we need four—one for each house. Unfortunately, we have to get artificial trees for the tasting room, the B and B, the restaurant and the day care to comply with safety rules.''

''But those look so good now. We have—had,'' she amended, averting her eyes, ''a big one in the lobby of the Haskell Media building. It looked beautiful.''

''Why don't you try to call your dad again?'' Shea asked. ''Maybe he'd like to come and spend Christmas here.''

She shook her head adamantly. ''I'm sure he's spending it with Legs somewhere.''

''What about your mom?''

''She's angry at me. I told you that.''

''But it's going to be Christmas. No one stays mad at Christmas.''

She patted his knee, then used it to push herself to her feet. ''My parents are in a snit that can't be fixed, I think. When someone's foolish behavior in a relationship brings it crashing down, I think it's just... over.''

He wondered about that. ''Maybe, unconsciously, they were just getting rid of everything superfluous to find what they'd had in the beginning.''

She thought that over, then seemed to dismiss that possibility. ''We're not the Delanceys, who separately lose everything, then pull together to rebuild their lives. The Haskells go off and sulk and blame one another. It's easier.''

''Actually, my plan of action at the time was pretty much what you describe. And Mike was hiding from his life. It took Tate to convince us we could do this. Maybe that should be your job for the Haskells.''

She opened her mouth to dispute that, he was sure,

then apparently changed her mind and walked into the kitchen with the cup and spoon.

When she returned, she leaned over him to kiss the top of Zachary's head. He'd drifted off again. "Good night, baby," she said. She turned to Shea, their faces a mere inch apart. He could see the silver flecks in her eyes, and the concern for all that had happened to her family, which she couldn't fix.

She focused on him. That close to her, he felt her attention as though he'd been shaken.

She looked into his eyes, a little frown between her eyebrows, before her gaze drifted to his mouth. It was all he could do not to take control of the moment. But he made himself wait with outward quiet, while everything inside him rioted in anticipation.

As she put her lips to his gently, he became convinced this was gratitude and not the passion he'd have preferred. But he decided it didn't matter. For now, at least, he'd take what he could get.

He responded in kind without touching her, unwilling to alarm her in any way.

Then she freed his lips and rested her cheek against his for an instant. He felt her sigh.

"Thank you for the flan," she whispered.

"Sure," he replied.

He thought she might say more, but she simply straightened and said with sudden briskness, "You know he should sleep on his back, right?"

He matched her serious-parent tone. "Right. I've watched you put him to bed."

"Okay." She gave the belt of her robe a nervous tug. "I'm off, then. Good night."

"Good night. Sleep well."

"You, too."

Shea leaned his head against the back of the chair and thought he could chalk up tonight for his side. He'd gotten Zachary back to sleep and Samantha had kissed him. It had been chaste and quick, but it had been a kiss. It counted.

Upstairs, Samantha pulled off the robe and her undies and slipped into pajamas. She looked around her at the cozy little room, then turned off the light and climbed into bed.

She felt disoriented and out of place. Long-held grudges were dissolving and the sad state of her family, which she'd accepted for so long, now was completely abhorrent. And she was going to do something about it. Just what, she wasn't sure, but something.

Odd, she thought, that it took the dissolution of her own world to make her want to fix her parents'.

Or had it taken Shea, who seemed to be rebuilding his world so beautifully?

She closed her eyes, unable, unwilling to explore an answer. It was all too complicated, she was tired and Zachary would be up again in a couple of hours.

SUNDAY DINNER REMINDED Samantha of the newsroom in the middle of a national crisis—except that the atmosphere was happy. But the noise was just as loud, the opinions as strong. There was no deadline, however, and she really liked that.

Everyone arrived around two. They planned the outside Christmas decorations while Shea distributed a new broiled marinated shrimp he was testing for the restaurant.

"I was thinking that we should have a Santa at our dinner," Shea said. "In the compound, maybe on a sleigh, to greet our guests."

Mike nodded. "I like that. Bob Burgess is Santa for the kids of Rotary members at their Christmas party. I'll ask him. And he comes with a costume."

"Great!" Colette said. "Now, that's all the business we're discussing today."

The rest of the afternoon unfolded lazily. Dinner was long and leisurely and Samantha considered it fortunate that Shea was able to buy food at wholesale prices when she saw the amount consumed. A restaurant-size platter bearing a huge roast and pounds of vegetables filled the center of the table at the beginning of the meal, and was removed with nothing but crumbs of cauliflower at the end.

After dinner, the men retired to the living room, taking Zachary with them, while Colette supervised cleanup. The girls ferried in bowls from the table while Samantha put away condiments. Rachel carried the linens into the hamper in the hallway. Colette rinsed off dishes and handed them to Veronica, who loaded the dishwasher.

"The salt and pepper shakers go into the next cupboard," Colette said, pointing a wet finger as Samantha tried to put them into the one closest to the sink.

Veronica cleared her throat. "Colette," she said mildly, "maybe she wants them in *that* cupboard."

Colette made an apologetic face. "I'm sorry. I wasn't thinking. I'm so used to cleaning up this kitchen after Sunday dinners that I forgot you should be—"

"No, no." Samantha wanted to nip that thinking in the bud. "I make no power claims here. This is Shea's kitchen, not mine. I'm just here temporarily."

"So you said." Colette leaned a hand on the counter and pointed to the living room, where the men were crowded around Zachary in his carrier on the coffee table. All the women filled the doorway to look. "You think you're going to get that baby away from his uncles and stand-in grandfather without a struggle?"

She could see tiny arms and feet flailing and hear the men's laughter.

"Good heavens, she just got here," Rachel admonished, returning with fresh dish towels. "Let's not talk about goodbyes already. If you two would finish loading the dishwasher, I'll do the pots and pans." She handed a dish towel to Megan and one to Katie.

Veronica reclaimed the extra towels and pushed her gently toward the table and chairs. "No, you won't. You're going to unwrap your cookies, pick out the biggest ones for us and let the guys have what's left."

"Aunt Rachel always brings cookies on Sundays," Katie told Samantha. "Uncle Shea says she makes better cookies than he does. She makes cookies for meetings, too."

"Meetings?"

"Business meetings," Colette explained. "Every Monday morning we all get together here and plan our strategy for the week. Except during harvest, when we're too busy to talk. Then, Tate just walks up and down the rows yelling orders."

Samantha laughed. "A pressroom is a lot like that. It's wonderful you can all work together so well."

"Occasionally there's a yelling match," Colette admitted, "but usually we're able to resolve our differences and move ahead. I think the bit of success we've had has given us faith in what we're doing, so now we do it with a little more confidence."

She could remember feeling like that—proud of her work, somewhat relieved that the word in news circles was that Haskell's daughter had inherited the old man's style and daring and worked at least as hard as he did.

When she'd first come out of college, she'd been terrified that she wouldn't measure up, but she had. That was part of the reason she'd stayed to work with her father after he and her mother had divorced. She'd been angry at both of them, but she'd managed to separate the journalistic success her father was from the thoughtless husband he'd been to her mother.

Unfortunately, loyalty was everything to her mother, and she hadn't understood.

"You going to help hang garlands tomorrow?" Veronica asked, doing a final scan of the countertops before measuring detergent into the holding cup and closing the dishwasher door. "I'm taking my day-care kids on a field trip so they won't be in the way. We're going to Salem to see the capitol."

"I'd like to." Samantha put the butter dish in the refrigerator, then reached for the cream Rachel asked for. "But Zachary…"

"I'll watch him for you." Rachel filled a large, serviceable creamer with the thick white stuff. "Armand and I are in charge of grub tomorrow while you youngsters are running up and down ladders. You can trust me. I did lose three little boys on a roof once, but that involved the James brothers, so I don't think that should count against me."

Lost three little boys on a roof. While Samantha tried to make sense of that remark, Veronica groaned and began to explain.

"I care for three of the cutest, most curious little hellions you'd ever want to know," she said, setting dials and pushing buttons on the dishwasher. She turned the machine on. "Rachel was helping me and my kids make cookies and stayed with them while I ran to her place to pick up something we forgot. Well, the James brothers got away from her and went to inspect scaffolding that was left unattended on the side of her place."

Samantha could imagine what followed and closed her eyes. "Oh, no."

"Yes," Rachel said. "Scared us all to death. Now, whenever I go to help, I chain the brothers together, then to the floor of the playroom."

Veronica laughed. "No, she doesn't, but we never let them out of our sight. Their mother is coming with me to help on the field trip. I don't think I'd dare it without her."

Samantha shook her head worriedly. "I don't suppose there's any point in hoping my son doesn't grow up to be a danger to himself."

"Not a chance," Colette said. "He's a Delancey. And with what we've witnessed of his father and his uncles, you should start taking your Valium now."

Rachel put the plate of cookies, the sugar and creamer and four cups on a tray and handed it to Megan. "Is that too heavy, sweetie?"

"No. I have it."

"Good girl." Rachel gave Katie a stack of napkins and followed them into the living room with the coffeepot.

"Can you also help us with the Christmas craft fair?" Veronica asked hopefully. "Shea says you made jeweled ornaments for Chez Shea one Christmas."

She'd completely forgotten that. "Uh…yes, I suppose. If I can find the makings."

"There's a small craft shop in town that carries

beads. I don't know if they'd be what you're after. The fair is two weeks from yesterday. Not much time, I know, but we're all working on it. My kids are making things, and Colette's making grapevine wreaths, and her girls are busy, too. If you could just make a few things, it'd help.''

''Is this also for the assisted living facility for the seniors?''

''Right. Saint Jerome's is hosting it. Father Wolff is an old friend of mine and has become a friend of the family's.''

''As busy as you'll be, you're going to need spiritual help,'' Samantha said.

The kitchen tidy, Samantha, Veronica and Colette went into the living room to join the men, Rachel and the girls. Zachary, in Tate's arms again, was smiling and charming everyone.

They settled into tight little groups around the room, Veronica in Mike's lap in the big chair, Tate and Colette taking up one corner of the sofa, the girls curled up on the floor at their feet and Armand and Rachel in the other corner.

Samantha joined Shea on the floor in front of the fireplace. Rachel had poured the coffee and the adults helped themselves. They were passing around the cookie plate, when the doorbell rang.

Shea got to his feet and admitted a smiling man in the garb of a priest. He was average in height, a little paunchy, and he glowed with good cheer.

Megan and Katie ran to him and everyone else started to rise, but he gestured them to remain seated. ''Don't get up!'' he ordered, putting an arm around each child. ''I'm just here to mooch dessert. Please don't tell me I'm too late.''

Shea handed him the plate with a solitary cookie remaining. He pretended to look stricken. "This is it?" he asked plaintively.

"Rachel made it," Megan told him.

"Oh, well then." He smiled a greeting around the room and bit into the cookie with gusto. As soon as he spotted the baby in Tate's arms, he went to claim him. "You must be Zachary, whom I heard all about after mass this morning." He cradled the baby expertly in his left arm and walked over to sit on the raised hearth near Samantha.

"Father, I'd like you to meet Samantha Haskell," Shea said, "Zack's mother. Sam, this is Father Wolff. Hang in there, Father. I think I have a piece of praline cheesecake in the freezer."

The priest smiled. "Bless you, my son. And if it comes with coffee, I promise you salvation. It'll take some fast talking, but I can do it."

Shea loped off to the kitchen, laughing.

"Samantha's from San Francisco, Father," Veronica said.

The priest nodded, frowning momentarily at Samantha before turning back to coo at the baby. When Zachary smiled, the priest smiled back and put him to his shoulder. "I saw you in the news story about Haskell Media. I was impressed with your style. You reminded me of Schwarzenegger with your 'I'll be back.'" His expression grew more serious. "I'm sure it's difficult, but I hope you're thinking of what happened as a new beginning instead of a loss."

"For a while I couldn't think at all," she admitted candidly. "But this is such a beautiful place. My mind's beginning to work again. I'll find a solution."

"Good," he said. "I thought you might all like to

know that I've come up with a brilliant theme for the Christmas dinner.''

Shea reappeared with a tray holding a piece of cheesecake on a plate, a cup of coffee and a sugar bowl and creamer.

"Wait, wait!" he said, putting the tray on the hearth beside Father Wolff. He took the baby so the priest could eat. "I don't want to miss any of this. Okay, go ahead. A theme."

"Right. But can I have a bite first?"

They waited patiently while he had two bites before he remembered his promise.

"I was thinking we'd call it the 'Magi Dinner' because the wise men bore gifts to the baby Jesus and there are three of you and you're helping to give this gift to His faithful. What do you think?"

Tate, Mike and Shea looked at one another but said nothing.

The priest raised an eyebrow. "What? Everyone else likes it. Felicia's already designing the invitation."

"It's a nice theme," Tate said finally, "but please don't relate it to us in any way. I mean, a lot of people are helping, not just us."

"Yes," Mike spoke up. "And if we were ever called upon to do anything wise, the world would be a sadder place."

Father Wolff made a face at him. "Come, now. You're all very well respected here. Delancey's is now *the* place to go in the county and rapidly gaining even more widespread attention."

"And I think their good looks," Rachel added, "and what they've done with the winery have made them romantic figures. The newspaper called them the 'Beautiful Bachelor Brothers.'" She smiled around the room at the men, who might have arrived in French River alone but were now surrounded by family. "Of course, they can't do that anymore."

"I agree with Tate and Mike," Shea said. "It's a great theme, as long as nobody tries to connect it to us."

"Good." The priest pointed his fork at the last morsel of cheesecake. "I think this should be the dessert for the dinner."

"I have something else in mind, Father," Shea said.

"Felicia's wondering when she can expect a menu."

"I'll fax it to her tomorrow."

"Great. Tate, when you finish the plans for the new facility, we'll take them to the board. Any idea when that'll be?"

"End of the week maybe," Tate replied. "If the board approves them, Felicia would like to post them at the dinner."

"Excellent." He ate the last bite and put the empty plate beside him on the hearth. "Well. Thank you all. I've enjoyed this little respite." He reached out to pat Zachary's head, then traced the sign of the cross over him and blessed him. "Welcome to the world, young man." Then he put one hand to Shea's head and the other to Samantha's. "And wisdom to your parents."

Since Shea held the baby, Samantha followed the priest to the door as he waved goodbye to everyone. Acting as hostess and escorting a guest out was different from claiming power in the kitchen. This was a...responsibility she felt as the mother of the baby he'd just blessed.

"It was a pleasure meeting you, Father," she said, offering her hand as she walked him onto the porch.

He took her hand in one of his and covered it with

the other. "I'm happy you're here, Samantha. Shea has missed you."

She opened her mouth to dispute that, then changed her mind. It certainly wasn't courteous to contradict a priest—and she wasn't sure she was still convinced Shea hadn't loved her. She wondered if Father Wolff knew about them.

"No, I don't know what's gone on between you," he said with a serene smile. "Except that your beautiful boy suggests it was something very powerful. But I know that there was always loss in Shea's eyes and now there isn't. I can only presume that your presence here replaces something he was missing."

"I'm only here for the holidays, Father," she said, clinging to what she found most comfortable.

He made a so-be-it gesture with his shoulders. "I'm only telling you what I've observed, not how I think things should be. Good night, Samantha."

"Good night, Father." Samantha waited while he climbed into a silver compact that was several years old, then watched him drive away.

Behind her in the house, rich laughter sounded, making her feel blessed because everyone welcomed her into the warm Delancey circle, but also more lonely because she couldn't quite believe she belonged.

She didn't need the priest to tell her how things should be. But she probably needed God Himself to tell her how to bring it about.

CHAPTER EIGHT

SAMANTHA KNELT ON THE gravel in the middle of the compound, wrapping a fifty-foot length of outdoor twinkle lights around one of the several dozen twenty-five-foot lengths of cedar garlands the nursery had just delivered. Colette knelt beside her, holding up the greenery.

She'd borrowed Shea's hat again against the cold, and he'd lent her a pair of work gloves, but they were so large they hindered more than helped and she'd pulled them off.

The brothers were setting up ladders in front of the B and B, preparing to fasten the garland to the peak of the roof.

"There!" Samantha let the plug-in dangle from the end of the garland so it could be attached to the greenery they'd already finished. "We're done!" she shouted toward the men.

They came to gather up the garlands. "Now, look," Tate said seriously to Shea. "This family seems to have a real difficulty with rooftops, so be careful, all right?"

"Relax," Shea said, slinging an end of light-strung cedar over his shoulder. "I put up Christmas lights for Mom and Dad while you were in college. I'll be fine."

"You'd better be. You have a woman and a child to think about."

Samantha couldn't believe how often that came up.

Even the family, who understood the status of her relationship with Shea, thought of them as a couple.

She opened her mouth to protest as the men walked away with the garland, but Colette gave her a friendly elbow to the ribs. "He *has* to think about you, even if he isn't married to you, or otherwise committed to you. You're the mother of his son. And Tate worries about him. He didn't mean to offend you."

"I'm not offended." Samantha grinned and elbowed Colette back. "I guess I'm just exasperated because it is awkward and I wish it wasn't." She pointed to the roof. "When Tate said the family had a problem with roofs, was he referring to the incident with the James boys?"

Colette watched the men worriedly. "Yes. And Tate also had an accident on a roof. Now I get the willies when anyone gets up higher than the porch steps. But there's all kinds of maintenance work that requires that they climb—washing windows, cleaning gutters, getting moss off the roof. They do as much as they can of that kind of thing to keep costs down." She shook her head as Tate began to climb the ladder at one end of the roof, while Mike held the other end of the garland and climbed a second ladder at the middle of the house. "I'd just as soon we showed a little less profit and didn't take these chances."

Samantha pulled up another string of lights, getting ready to work on another cedar garland, when she saw Shea climb out of the attic window carrying a long hooked stick.

He hauled himself onto the peak of the roof with a rope already looped around the chimney.

Once on top, he straddled the peak and moved himself foward by bracing himself on his hands and scooting, one hand holding the long stick.

So *that* was why they'd cautioned him! She hadn't thought to ask just how the job would be done.

Samantha felt the breath leave her lungs, and a cold fear trickled down every one of her vertebrae.

He'll fall, she thought. It was destined. Tate had said this family had difficulty with rooftops, and it didn't matter that Shea was the youngest and probably the most agile, because fate loved to play dirty tricks. It had given him a son he adored, so that made a fall certain. And she cared about him, and fate seemed determined to snatch away everything that meant something to her.

Shea lay on his stomach on the peak and reached down for the garland with the hooked end of the stick.

"Come on." Colette caught her arm. "I can't watch. Let's start on the other...Samantha? Sam?"

Samantha heard her voice but couldn't divert her attention to make sense of the words. Maybe she could hold Shea to the roof if she thought about it hard enough. Maybe if she really didn't want him or his family, he wouldn't fall.

She put a hand to her thumping heart and watched him hook the end of the garland Mike held. When it was fastened, Tate attached his end and they shouted congratulations to each other.

Mike and Tate climbed down, then carried up the second garland. Shea attached the light string to the one already up and fastened the end in place. Mike hooked Tate's end, and the first and most difficult garland was up.

Samantha couldn't move until Shea had let himself back down the rope and through the attic window.

She felt Colette push lightly between her shoulder blades. "Come on, Sam, breathe. In, out, in…that a girl. Hey, if you're going to live out here, you got to toughen up."

When Samantha turned to her she added quickly, "Okay. I know you're only going to be here a month. But we've got to finish the garland on the B and B and do three more buildings. You'll be dead by noon if you don't relax." She gave her a restorative slap on the back and a knowing grin. "And I thought there *wasn't* anything between you and Shea."

Samantha expelled a ragged breath and got down on her knees again to yank up another string of lights and another garland. "Yeah," she said. "So did I."

SHEA WASN'T SURE what was wrong with Samantha. She wasn't hostile precisely, just…quiet. And for a woman usually filled with opinions, objections and smart remarks, it was strange behavior.

By the time they'd finished outlining the B and B and the restaurant with white lights, it was time for lunch. They stacked their jackets, hats and gloves on the sofa, and Tate, Mike and Colette headed for the fireplace, where Rachel had spread a blanket as though for a picnic.

Shea and Samantha went into the kitchen where Rachel was placing sandwiches on a tray; a big pot of soup steamed aromatically on the stove beside her.

Armand sat at the kitchen table, his big gnarled hands holding Zachary up in front of him. The old man made faces and the baby smiled, little arms waving in the air. Sterling stood on a kitchen chair at a right angle to them and protested his lack of attention.

"Well, he looks perfectly happy without me," Samantha said in pretended dismay.

Armand held the baby out to her. "He slept for several hours and woke up crying, but the moment Rachel put a bottle to his lips and handed him to me, we bonded. I've told him all about the winery, how beautiful it's going to look when you're finished out there, and that he's soon going to learn all about Santa and the magic in store for good little children."

Shea picked up Sterling in one hand and stroked his silky head. The cat purred loudly.

"This guy's been—pardon the expression—top dog around here since Colette and the girls gave him to me." He carried him close to Zachary. The cat leaned out of Shea's arms to sniff the baby and Zachary stared back in wide-eyed interest. "No need to be jealous, Sterling."

Samantha scratched the cat between the ears, ignoring Shea entirely. "I'll hold him while I'm eating, Armand," she said, "so you can enjoy your lunch."

Armand smiled and stood to take the sandwich tray from Rachel. "I was doing very well, I thought. All my old skills were coming back to me. Colette had colic as a baby and I must have walked hundreds of miles with her across our old kitchen floor."

Samantha followed him out to the living room without a glance in Shea's direction.

Rachel turned away from ladling soup to frown at him. "You two have a spat?"

He had to smile over that question. "Our relationship is an ongoing spat, Rachel." He washed his hands in the sink and dug soupspoons out of a drawer. He put them on a tray on which she'd collected mismatched soup mugs and bowls. "What kind of soup?"

"Shea-and-Samantha soup," she replied with a bland grin, turning back to the pot and ladling the rich dark broth into a mug. "You're both in it, aren't you? In the soup," she explained when he gave her a puzzled look. "Love gets so complicated."

He reached into a drawer for napkins. "I know. I'm hoping we'll figure it out."

She put another filled mug on the tray and paused to pat his back. "You're a smart boy. I have faith in you."

"I hope it isn't misplaced." He set a handful of white paper napkins on the tray. "She's a stubborn woman and I don't always understand her. In fact, most of the time—like now—I don't understand her at all."

"Love is like faith. Sometimes it requires that you practice it without having answers to your questions."

"Whoa." He prepared to pick up the tray as she filled the last bowl. "That's heavy thinking, Rachel. You have that much time on your hands?"

She filled the bowl and made room for it on the tray. "No. I have that much love in my life. It's hard to understand it very well until you actually have to do it yourself."

He picked up the tray. "Yeah, well, I'm doing it, but I just don't *get* it."

"And you're doing it, anyway. I think that means you're better at it than you realize."

After lunch, Tate and Colette sat back-to-back in front of the fire, sipping cups of coffee, while Mike stretched out on his stomach, his head pillowed on his hands.

"Wake me when you've finished the other two buildings, okay?" he asked. "You can manage without me."

"We can," Shea replied lazily, stroking the cat, which sat in his lap, "but we don't want to. We want you to be as cold and miserable as we are."

"It'd take a lot," Mike said without raising his head, "to be as miserable as you are, Shea."

Shea, leaning back against the bottom of the sofa, kicked Mike's boot with his. "Blame it on the examples I've had to follow."

Rachel sat in the big chair with the baby while Samantha carried empty plates, mugs and bowls into the kitchen. Armand had stretched out on the sofa.

"Stop that young woman." Armand pointed toward Samantha without opening his eyes. "She is entirely too industrious for such a moody afternoon."

"I've tried," Rachel complained, "but she won't listen to me."

"I'll handle it," Shea said, bravado in his voice. He put Sterling on Armand's stomach and sprang to his feet, took the empty cup at Mike's elbow and followed Samantha into the kitchen.

"Ha!" he heard Tate say. "He'll handle it. Samantha will probably send him out of the kitchen airborne."

"Or skidding on his nose," Mike suggested. "I think I'd like that better."

"The baby is listening," Rachel admonished. "Could we have fewer insults and a little more support for one another, please?"

"I don't think so," Mike replied.

"No," Tate said.

Samantha placed the stack of dishes on the counter and opened the dishwasher but, seeing Shea behind her, took the wet dish towel into the hallway to put it in the hamper—presumably to avoid speaking to him.

He trailed after her, though, and stood in the doorway, blocking her return.

"What's going on?" he asked mildly, folding his arms. "Something's bothering you."

She indicated he was blocking her path. "At the moment, you're bothering me. I'd like to put the dishes away so Rachel doesn't have to."

"Rachel loves to putter around the kitchen, and she has Armand to help her today. What's the matter with *you?*"

She looked troubled and edgy, as if she wanted nothing more at that moment than to escape him. She had nowhere to go, though, but into the breakfast room.

She went and he followed.

"Don't you have anything to do?" she demanded, turning to him impatiently, her color high, her eyes troubled. "I'm fine. Nothing is wrong. Don't we have two more buildings to string with lights?"

"In a while. Right now all I have to do is find out what's bothering you."

With a disgusted roll of her eyes, she slipped into the far side of the booth and fell onto the bench, upset and dispirited.

He was starting to worry. "Do you feel ill?" he asked.

"I do," she replied, "and it's all your fault. You go swinging around on rooftops as though you had wings, you lie on the peak of the roof on your stomach as though you were on a rubber raft in a swimming pool, and I'm supposed to just watch you and applaud when you're done?"

He'd frightened her. The revelation was a complete surprise to him. As a rule he was agile and surefooted and had no fear of heights. Well, a healthy unwillingness to fall, to be sure—but no fear of losing his balance, no vertigo.

Plus, there were so few advantages to being the youngest, that now that he and his brothers were adults, and Tate and Mike deferred to his youth when the job required flexibility and balance, he liked it and probably showed off a little.

He couldn't remember if he'd done that this morning—he'd been busy concentrating on his task.

"You were worried for me." He was happy to clarify that for her if she hadn't already grasped it herself. He sat on the bench opposite her.

She glanced at him darkly, then looked away out the window. "Yes, I got that. Thanks."

"But you don't like it," he guessed.

"No, I don't." She scooted into the corner and turned to prop her legs up on the bench. She'd tied her hair in a loose knot for convenience and straight strands hung from it at her ears and at the back. She gave him another condemning glance, this one a shade softer than the other. "I was over you—I know I was. I'd resolved to raise the baby alone and be the best, most creative single working mom there ever was." She let her head fall back against the wall. "Even after Oliver Owens took over the company and my father bailed out on me, I was still sure I could do it. I just had to have a plan."

He propped his elbows on the table and rested one hand over the other, waiting for her to blame him because that had changed on her. He had to conceal the fact that he was happy to claim responsibility.

She sighed, one arm resting on the table, her index finger tracing the tiny checks on the green checkered tablecloth. "Then you had to come to San Francisco and remind me that deep down, under the shrewd reporter and the wanna-be Wonder Mom, I'm still an idiot.''

He knew he'd hate himself for asking. "Why an idiot?"

She swung her legs off the bench and turned to him, her voice rising. "Because I still care! You throw my attempts to help you back in my face, you walk away from me so easily, then refuse to talk to me when I swallow my pride and call you—and I still care. I can't tell you how that upsets me. I can tell myself that I can resist your charm and your helpful little ways, that I'm only here for the baby, but when you danced around that roof today, all I could think about was how terrible it would be if you fell—how much Zachary would miss. How much I... Jeez!'' She put both hands to her face.

He had no idea how to approach her in this mood. Displaying any delight would be deadly, he was sure. So he maintained a serious mien.

"We share a child," he said. "Don't you think we should have some feeling for each other? If our feelings were so transient that they're already dead, then Zack shouldn't even be here."

She dropped her hands onto the table, her expression weary and concerned. "Yes, we should. And if we didn't have a history, it'd be great, but we know each other too well. I know your pride, and you know my disregard for it."

He leaned toward her urgently. "Sam. If we didn't have a history, we wouldn't have the baby. And our different approaches might not be detrimental. Maybe they'll help us strike a balance in our lives."

"I've never known you to make concessions where

your pride is involved. I can't believe I have the extreme poor judgment to…''

He wanted desperately to hear the words. ''To…?''

''To get involved with you,'' she said, sliding out of the booth.

He caught her at the edge of the table, his fingers shackling her wrist. ''You said *have* the poor judgment, not *had*. That means you're dealing with it in the present. What is it you have the poor judgment to do, Samantha?''

When she pulled against him, refusing to answer, he held fast. ''Is it that you love me?''

She swallowed. ''You know what they say. 'Love isn't love till you give it away.' So, if I don't give it to you, it simply isn't.''

He knew what he felt, and if what she felt was anything comparable, she wouldn't be able to fight it for very long.

''Hey!'' Tate shouted from the living room. ''You guys coming?''

Shea leaned down to kiss her gently on the lips. ''If you believe that,'' he said, ''I've got some swampland and some silver mines to sell you. I'll even throw in the Brooklyn Bridge.'' He tugged her after him with the wrist he still grasped. ''Come on.''

CHAPTER NINE

SAMANTHA MADE A ROYAL effort to follow the love-isn't-love-till-you-give-it-away principle for a week. It could work. She knew it could. Her mind had been stronger than her emotions *before* she met Shea Delancey, and there was no reason it couldn't be again.

Her emotions had led her here, true, but that didn't mean she had to do anything stupid just because Christmas had come to the compound with a vengeance. Her family had loved Christmas, but this year she and her parents were spending it scattered over the globe, living testimony to love's transience. But she wouldn't think about them. She had enough trouble dealing with the here and now.

The Delancey clan stood near the fountain the night they put up the lights and waited in an eager bunch while Tate went into the winery and flipped the switch that lit every building. Thousands of white lights traced the Victorian shape of the B and B and the clean but old-fashioned lines of the restaurant, the winery, and the daycare center. Everyone gasped and Megan and Katie jumped up and down. Zachary, in the front pack Shea wore, slept peacefully.

The B and B looked particularly magnificent, with a light standing on the roof's peak, thanks to Shea's careful placement of it there.

Veronica pulled into the compound with a honking

of her horn after her day at the capitol. Mike ran to welcome her home and they walked back to the group arm in arm. She focused on the B and B's cupola with an "Oh!" of wonder.

"Will you look at that!" she exclaimed. "I've never seen anything so beautiful."

"It's a good thing you weren't here when Shea put the lights up on it," Colette said. "You'd have had a stroke. Samantha almost did."

Tate patted Samantha's shoulder. "Don't worry. He's invincible. Mike and I tried to get rid of him so many times as kids, but he's still here."

"Thanks only to a watchful mother," Shea said, draping an arm around her.

A little tremor shot through her, part reaction to the chill night air, part response to her memory of him climbing to the roof on a rope.

Shea must have felt it because he held her a little closer. "Do we need to get you long underwear?" he teased. "You're shivering."

She put her hand to the back of the baby lying so trustingly against his chest. "I'm fine. Just tired, I guess."

"Sam, look what I found for you!" Veronica pulled a box out of the satchel purse slung over her shoulder. "I had a few minutes on my own while the kids were eating. I couldn't find a bead shop, but there was this secondhand store next to the restaurant, with the best old costume jewelry. This should be perfect for your ornaments!"

Samantha opened the box and found old brooches, necklaces and earrings in cut glass, plastic and paint. Sewn or glued to satin and velvet and tucked into the boughs of a Christmas tree, they would look like something precious.

"These are wonderful!" she said, delighted. "What do I owe you?"

Veronica waved away the question. "The whole thing cost me all of five dollars. You can buy me lunch in town one day."

"It's a deal. Thank you!"

"Sure."

They piled into Mike's Blazer and Tate's van, and went to town for Chinese food. In the restaurant, Samantha was grateful when Colette suggested the women sit together to plan their projects for the craft fair. Another small table was pulled up to accommodate Megan and Katie.

It was odd, but now that she'd confronted how she felt about Shea and been honest with him about it, the tension between them seemed worse instead of better. At least on her part.

She was very much aware of his nearness, remembered in vivid detail many romantic encounters with him in the past that she would have preferred to ignore, and found herself imagining scenarios in the future that she didn't want him to ever suspect she entertained.

Now that she'd told him she wouldn't give the love she felt, it was as if that love had made up its mind to escape her on its own.

As the women chatted, the men sat together, Zachary with Shea, and watched the muted television in the corner, which was tuned to a basketball game. The enthusiastic exchange of ideas and the loud laughter at the women's table made the men turn in their direction.

"If they get thrown out of here for being rowdy," Tate said, "we don't know them."

"Speaking of things we don't know..." Mike dipped a wonton in sauce and passed the appetizer plate to Armand. "I heard from Vince Rushford today."

Everyone looked at him with a sharpening of attention.

"Who is that?" Armand asked.

"The detective investigating Jack's disappearance," Shea replied. "Has he found something?"

"Well, he's been watching Danny Mullins's place for any sign of Uncle Jack or Tess." Mike faced Armand. "Danny is Jack's son—at least, we think so. And Tess is the woman Jack loved, the one who wrote the letter Tate found. Anyway..." Mike looked from face to face. "He hasn't seen them, but he's been investigating the Mullinses and discovered that Mrs. Mullins chairs a charity whose bank account shows a monthly deposit in the same amount as Robert Mullins's Social Security check."

"You joke!" Armand said, spearing a crab puff with his fork. "Does that mean that Tess's husband...what was his name?"

"Robert," Tate supplied.

"Robert Mullins," Armand went on, "is still alive? Or is he dead and they've just continued to collect his money?"

"Hard to tell," Mike said. "If the check's going to them, Robert Mullins may be living with them and doesn't need his check and is giving it to Mrs. Mullins—although that doesn't sound like the selfish man who once made Tess so miserable, according to Al Bigby." He added for Armand's benefit, "That's the grocer on the coast who told us about Tess and Danny when we first went looking for information. Or maybe

Mullins is now dead and no one's bothered to report that fact."

"So, what's our next step?" Shea asked.

Tate shook his head. "It's hard to decide. If we approach Danny Mullins about it or report him to the government, we'd have to explain to him or to them how we know what we know. Which would end up revealing Uncle Jack—something we don't want to do if he's hiding deliberately."

"Danny Mullins said he never lived in Cave Beach and wasn't the one we were looking for," Shea said. "But he has to be the right one if he's collecting Robert Mullins's check. We've been saving his share of winery money all this time on the principle that if he's Jack's son, the winery should be his. But I'm not saving a share of the winery for some guy who's bilking the government." He absently stroked the head of the baby in his arms and sighed. "On the other hand, maybe we just don't know what's going on. Whatever it is, though, he's still our link to Jack."

Mike nodded. "I agree. We have to check this out. Can the restaurant do without you one more time?"

"I'll have to make it worth Charlie's while, but yeah, probably. If we could wait till the end of the week. I've got a banquet tomorrow and one Thursday. Can the B and B do without you?"

"Rachel can handle everything. Maybe Samantha can help her out if she gets in a bind."

"I'm sure she'd want to."

"All right, then." Tate leaned back as the waitress arrived and began to serve their food. "We're agreed. We leave Friday morning for Bellevue, Washington. Mullins is working for a place called Arrow Aeronautics. Armand guards the homestead."

Armand served himself a healthy portion of fried rice. "Fine. Leave the old man with a gaggle of high-spirited women. What I do for you boys."

Tate, seated on his right, wrapped an arm around the Frenchman's shoulders. "I took Colette off your hands, Armand. You owe me."

"And I'm the one who convinced Rachel that his attentions were sincere," Mike put in. "You owe me, too."

Armand turned to Shea, waiting for his claim that the old man was in his debt.

Shea pointed to the baby in his arms. "I brought Zachary into the compound."

Armand smiled. "Well done. But I expect hazard pay for this."

SAMANTHA WAS PLEASED to learn that Shea was leaving for several days. She looked forward to time to think without her growing feelings for him crowding all logic and reason out of her mind.

Zachary, however, had somehow divined the news and was not pleased at all. For the next three days he fussed every moment he was awake—unless Shea held him.

He awoke three or four times at night rather than twice, and nothing Samantha did appeased him. Shea was usually awakened, also, and came down to the kitchen to lend moral support.

The moment Shea took Zachary from her, the baby either stared at Shea, his eyes wide, his mouth in a little O, or he snuggled into Shea's shoulder and went to sleep. But the moment Shea put him down, he was awake again.

Shea and Samantha sat side by side on the sofa at

3:12 a.m., Friday morning, she in her pink chenille robe, stocking feet propped up on the coffee table; he in graphite-colored sweats, bare feet on the table next to hers.

Exhaustion had made her forget the distance she was trying to keep, and she rested her head on his shoulder, her eyes closed after a long siege of Zachary's screaming.

Shea, who'd gotten even less sleep than she had the past four nights, rested his head atop hers, the baby asleep on his chest.

"How come he stops crying when *you* hold him?" she complained in a sleepy voice.

"Must be some primal father-son thing," Shea said drowsily. "Or he likes me better than you. I kind of go for that one."

"But I'm the one with the foot-long scar."

"Yes, but I'm the one with the bank account. Kids think about those things, you realize. He probably knows you're broke and thinks that if he ever hopes to get an allowance, he has to suck up to me."

"Where's the justice?"

"If there was such a thing, we wouldn't be sitting here semicomatose at 3:00 a.m. We'd be in that wonderful down bed I had in San Francisco."

She smiled, remembering the comfort of that plush mattress and coverlet. She was so tired that she remembered nothing sexual about the times she'd lain with him there, only how deliciously soft and warm they'd been.

"That was some bed," she murmured.

"Mmm."

"Got sold with everything else?"

"Mmm."

"Too bad. What time are you and your brothers leaving this morning?"

"Right after breakfast. Eight-thirty. Nine."

She pushed against his arm to raise her head, which felt as though it weighed three hundred pounds. "You have to get some sleep. Let me try to put Zack back to bed."

"No," he said on a sigh, his eyes still closed. "He'll only wake up. Let's just stay here. Just toss the throw over us."

She eyed his bare feet, knowing the throw wouldn't cover them. "I'll get you some socks," she said.

He caught her wrist. "Don't go upstairs. I'll be fine."

"I've got the laundry basket in the kitchen." She disengaged his hand. "Be right back."

She returned with a pair of thick white boot socks. She'd thrown his laundry in with hers that afternoon while he'd fed Zachary on a break from the restaurant.

Holding the baby to him with one hand, he raised his foot to accommodate her as she slipped a sock on it.

He made a throaty sound of approval, his eyes still closed.

She did the same with the other foot but remembered that he was ticklish and ran her index fingernail down the center of the sole as she pulled on the sock.

He jerked his foot, but she held it, laughing. Both waited to see if the action would wake the baby. The infant, though, slept on.

"Sorry," she said, smoothing the top of the sock and bringing down the ankle of his sweats. "I couldn't resist. Blame it on exhaustion."

"You wake this guy and you have to put him back to sleep," he threatened.

She snatched the throw off the big chair and opened it out over him, then came to crawl in under it. "That's what I'm going to have to do while you're gone. He'll probably scream and stay awake until you get back."

He raised his arm to draw her into his shoulder and brought the blanket up over hers. "Comfortable?"

She answered with a big sigh and rested her cheek on his chest, face-to-face with her son. Shea's hand closed over her shoulder, atop the blanket, making her feel protected and secure; he rested his other hand on Zachary.

Despite the hour and the parental agonies of the past few days and nights, Samantha felt a sense of peace fill her to the tips of her fingers and toes. For the first time since she'd learned Haskell Media had fallen to Oliver Owens, and the world as she knew it no longer existed, she felt safe.

She closed her eyes and went to sleep.

Shea was too tired to think or analyze, he simply felt. And he felt like the king of the world.

THE DELANCEY BROTHERS traveled to Bellevue in Mike's Blazer. The day was overcast, but a watery sun tried to shine through once they'd crossed into Washington.

Mike drove, Tate rode shotgun and Shea stretched out in the second seat. They passed a bag of salsa-flavored chips back and forth.

"So, we're just going to drive to Arrow Aeronautics, find Danny Mullins's car in what must be a veritable sea of them, and confront him?" Shea asked.

Mike held up the fax he'd gotten from Vince Rushford. "He's an executive. He has an assigned parking spot and I have detailed instructions on where to find it."

"This way," Tate said, reaching back for the bag Shea held forward, "we don't alarm his family. Thanks." He held the bag toward Mike. "Want some?"

Mike watched the road while he dug into the chips. "I hope he doesn't turn out to be a flake. I've grown sort of attached to him, thinking of him as Uncle Jack's son."

Tate grinned over the back seat at Shea. "How's your lady doing after a week with us? She was watching you a little worriedly when we took off this morning."

"That's only because Zack's taken to screaming every time I'm out of the room." He tried to keep the pride out of his voice, but it didn't work. Even he could hear it. Tate exchanged an amused glance with Mike. "And suddenly, I'm the only one who can get him to sleep. I think she was just concerned about having a sleepless couple of nights while I'm gone."

Tate closed the chips bag and put it on the floor at his feet. "I hope you told her to call Colette or Veronica if she needs help."

Mike found Shea's face in the rearview mirror. "I think the girls were planning a pajama party while we're gone. I'm sure Sam will have lots of help at her fingertips."

Shea nodded. "I'm not worried. Unless you consider that they'll be grumbling about us and plotting together during our absence."

"We could do the same," Mike suggested.

"Yeah," Tate and Shea agreed simultaneously. But a long silence followed.

"I can't think of anything to complain about," Tate admitted.

Shea remembered clearly the last few hours of that morning when he'd laid between sleep and wakefulness, his arms filled with his family. He'd enjoyed the sensation too much to fall completely asleep. "I can't either," he said.

"Oh, come on," Mike chided. "Have we really become that domesticated? There must be something."

"Okay," Tate challenged. "Give us a gripe against Veronica. We're listening."

Mike thought, bought a few minutes while he followed a freeway sign that took them toward the area where they would find the aeronautics plant, then cleared his throat. "How long are you going to give me?" he asked, laughter in his voice.

"Time's up," Tate said.

"Damn," Mike complained. "She loves me, she loves my motorcycle. She loves you guys... That's it!" he said, as though all had suddenly been revealed to him. "That's enough to make me distrustful of her right there!"

Tate socked his arm.

Mike gasped indignantly. "Hey! Driver of a moving vehicle here!"

IN BELLEVUE MIKE PARKED on a side street. "Okay, this is the only iffy part," he said.

Tate unbuckled his seat belt and frowned at him. "Define 'iffy.'"

"'Not without risk,'" Mike clarified.

Shea leaned forward to get the details. "What risk?

He's a fourth-degree black belt or something and you kept it from us?''

''No.'' Mike pointed up the street to where thick shrubbery concealed a fence that enclosed the aeronautical company's property. ''We're going to have to jump the fence. There's a guard station in the front, so we can't go through without authorization. Vince thought those bushes would be our best chance.''

Tate groaned. ''If we end up doing time for this, I'm not going to be happy.''

''Oh, come on,'' Shea chided as he got out of the van. He walked around to Tate's side. ''Give you a wife and more children and you turn into an old lady. Mike's got cop connections, remember?''

''Yeah, right.'' Tate stood on the sidewalk and pushed the door closed behind him. ''In case you hadn't noticed, he's making wine and running a B and B now.''

''Are you going to whine throughout this whole operation?'' Mike asked him.

Tate rolled his eyes. ''It's not an operation. We're just trying to find Daniel Mullins and I'd prefer not to commit a crime in order to accomplish that.''

''He's probably just afraid he won't be able to make it over the fence,'' Shea teased.

''Really.'' Mike led the way toward the bushes. ''I beat him in a race from the airport terminal to the car just a year ago.''

''You took the elevator!'' Tate corrected, following him.

''Brains,'' Shea said, ''are just as important as brawn.''

They stopped at the bushes to assess the situation. Fortunately, traffic was light, and no one was visible in front of what looked like storage buildings across the street.

There was an ash tree at the edge of the bushes at the farthest corner of the lot.

"This is probably the best spot," Mike suggested. "We climb the tree rather than the fence and drop from the branch hanging over the other side."

Shea turned his back to the tree and acted casual as a car drove by. Tate leaned against the tree, looking as though he'd been standing there for hours.

"Okay, go!" Shea said the moment the car was out of sight.

Tate leaped for the bottom branch, caught the trunk with his feet and walked himself up until he reached the higher branch, then let himself down the other side of the tree with an ease that put to shame their jokes.

With nothing else coming up the street, Shea, then Mike, followed, dropping beside them between a parked truck and a van, their positions sheltered from view both from the street and from the plant.

Mike checked the map in his pocket. "Okay," he said quietly. "We have to go most of the way across the parking lot and halfway back. We're looking for a burgundy Volvo."

Keeping low, they ran lightly across the lot. They stopped near a road where their presence would be exposed to the guard if they ran across.

As though written into the Delanceys' caper by a guiding hand, a young man and a woman in business suits walked along hand in hand and stopped in the middle of the road to share a passionate kiss.

"I wish I could come with you, Neil, instead of going home to my roommates."

Crouched behind a black Cadillac, the brothers exchanged an amused glance.

"Carrie wouldn't like that."

"Well, when is this divorce going to happen, anyway?"

"When I can get around to it, Lucy. Be patient, okay?"

"It's been five years. Isn't that patient enough?"

Neil didn't seem to think so. "Lucy, I'm not having this discussion again. Do you want to follow me to the Sidelines for a drink or not?"

Lucy sighed. "I'll be right behind you."

Two car doors closed. An engine sprang to life, then another, then two compact cars headed for the exit and the guard station.

"Okay," Mike said quietly. "I'll tell you when."

He waited until the cars had almost reached the station and the guard's attention was diverted to wave the drivers through, before whispering, "Let's go!"

They made it safely across the road. Mike consulted the map one more time and they then followed it—to an empty spot in the parking lot.

Mike swore.

Tate groaned. "No car. Is that map wrong, or did we just happen to pick the day he's home sick?"

Mike put a hand to his head as he appeared to think. "We've got his home address," he said after a moment, "but we don't want to approach him in front of his family."

Shea had been scanning the parking lot, hoping that Rushford's map had simply been wrong and he'd spot the burgundy Volvo in the next row or the one after that.

And that was when he noticed one on the street, left

turn signal blinking as the vehicle prepared to drive
into the parking lot.

"What're the numbers on the plate?" Shea asked.
"Quick!"

"What?" Mike and Tate faced him in puzzlement.

He pointed to the car, still waiting to make the turn.
"The numbers on the plate! What are they?"

Mike flipped his sheet of paper over. "GGS-671,"
he said.

"GGS," Shea read off the bottom of the car just
beginning to make the turn. "6...7..." The car turned,
and he couldn't make out the last number, but he didn't
have to. The likelihood that it wasn't Daniel Mullins
was pretty remote.

They followed the Volvo proceeding toward the
front of the building. Scores of men and women were
spilling out the doors, talking and laughing and shouting good-nights.

It occurred to Shea to wonder why the Volvo was
coming into the parking lot rather than leaving it, but
he didn't pursue the matter at the moment. He simply
followed his brothers, now inconspicuous in the rush
of people heading for their cars.

The Volvo pulled to a stop, obviously there to pick
up someone on his way home.

Tate caught Mike's arm to stop him when he would
have crossed to the car. "Let me do this," he said
gravely. "If there's any problem, I—"

"If there's any problem," Mike interrupted, "I'm
the one trained in self-de—"

While they argued, Shea simply walked around
them, opened the unlocked car door, reached in to
grasp an arm and pulled out the driver.

He was literally speechless when the older man grappling with him, one arm drawn back to slug him, looked into his face and stopped cold. The man blinked, then blinked again.

Shea blinked back in disbelief. "Uncle Jack?"

CHAPTER TEN

JACK DELANCEY STARED at Shea, Mike and Tate, his mouth working unsteadily. "No!" he whispered.

"Yes, Unc," Tate said, putting his hands on the man's arms. "It's us." Then, as Jack continued to stare, he asked gently, "Remember? Shea, Mike and…"

Jack threw his arms around Tate with a strength that banished whatever thoughts they'd had that he'd become a frail old man. Then he opened his arms to reach for Mike and Shea, too.

"What in the *hell* are you doing here?" Jack demanded. "I didn't think anyone…" He stopped abruptly and looked around, as though expecting a capture.

"It's all right," Tate assured him. "No one knows where you are. Or *who* you are, for that matter, Mr. *Girdling*."

Jack was a couple of inches shorter than they were, a little paunchy, but he looked enough like their father, Shea thought, that he could have picked him out of a crowd even if he'd never seen him.

He wore a blue hooded parka over brown cords, and the thick hair Shea remembered from their summers on the winery was now nothing but a little gray fringe above his ears.

He had their father's blue eyes, though, and now that

Tate had convinced him that he was safe, they sparkled with the old affection and amusement Shea remembered seeing when was a child.

Jack hugged each of them all over again. "Where did you come from? How did you find me? My God, I covered our tracks like a CIA veteran!"

Shea and Mike left Tate to explain about finding the photo and the letter, then conducting their own investigation until they located Daniel and hired Rushford to watch him.

"By then," Tate said, "we were pretty sure you'd disappeared on purpose, and we didn't want to expose you without knowing why you'd done it."

While Jack digested that information, Shea asked gently, "Did you find Tess? She didn't die in the train wreck, did she?"

Jack looked shocked anew—and suddenly emotional. "I found her. You boys should hire out as detectives."

Tate wrapped him in his arms again. "We're so glad you're all right, Jack. That's all we wanted to know."

"Did you sell the winery?" Jack asked, swiping a hand at his eyes. "I can't tell you how many times I've thought about you and hoped the property would help you get whatever you wanted out of your lives. You still an architect?" he asked Tate.

Tate shook his head and grinned. "We kept the winery," he said. "We're working it together. Mike does our PR and manages the B and B, Shea's running the hottest restaurant in the valley and we filled the cellar with chardonnay and pinot noir in the fall."

Jack laughed, then suddenly put a hand to his heart and leaned back against the car.

"What?" Tate demanded, taking hold of one arm as Mike took the other.

"Hey!" an angry voice shouted.

Shea turned just in time to intercept the headlong rush of a man wielding a briefcase as though he intended to bean them all with it.

Shea instantly recognized the Jacklike face and blue eyes. They reminded him of a slightly older, less-angular Tate. "Whoa! Daniel!" he said, catching the man's arms as he would have attacked in defense of his father. "We're your cousins. It's okay. Nobody's hurting Jack. I think we just surprised him a little."

Daniel looked confused for a moment, then broke free of Shea's grasp and reached into Jack's parka pocket for a bottle of pills. Jack opened his mouth and Daniel put one of the pills under his tongue.

Tate and Mike eased Jack onto the driver's seat.

"I'm okay, I'm okay," he kept saying. "It wasn't an attack, just a…just a flutter." He breathed deeply and smiled up at his son. "Danny, these are your cousins, Tate, Mike and Shea Delancey. Guys, my son."

They all shook hands, though Daniel remained suspicious. "What are you doing here?" he asked politely but pointedly.

Tate explained all over again.

"When we weren't sure if Jack was alive or not," Mike said, clapping Daniel on the shoulder, "but suspected you were around somewhere, we started saving you a fourth of the winery's profits. We don't mean either of you any harm, I promise."

Daniel raised an eyebrow, then narrowed his eyes. "What?"

"We figured Uncle Jack left the winery to us," Shea said, "because he couldn't leave it to you because—"

He stopped abruptly, wondering if Daniel *did* know everything they'd learned.

"Because of Robert Mullins, my stepfather," Daniel said, smiling suddenly. He looked around the group at each of them, then at his father. "I can't believe there are three more guys in the world with your principles."

Jack grinned. "They spent a couple of weeks with me every summer, and the whole summer one time. I might have rubbed off on them."

Cars lined up behind them were beginning to honk. "Climb over," Daniel directed, letting Tate help Jack around to the passenger side and urging Mike and Shea to the back. "Where's your car? How'd you get into the lot past the guard, anyway?"

"Well, there," Mike admitted, "we might have compromised your father's principles just a little."

DANIEL TOOK THEM TO THE VAN so that they could follow him home to meet Tess and Daniel's wife, Eileen. Jack had driven Daniel to work so Jack could keep the car for an afternoon appointment at the dentist's.

Tess was plump and beautiful, a woman in her late sixties who still had the sweet look of the young woman in the photograph. She embraced each of her nephews and told them that Jack had talked about them all the time, and regretted the pain and the worry his unexplained absence might have caused.

"Did he tell you what happened?" she asked.

Jack put an arm around her. "Not yet. We didn't get much beyond 'What the hell are you doing here?' Then Daniel thought they were the police or something and came in slugging."

"No, I didn't," Daniel defended himself with a laugh. "I just tried to hit them with my briefcase. When

Shea grabbed me and I looked into his face and saw Dad's features, I got really confused.''

''Well, we'll clear it all up over dinner. Are you into pizza?'' Tess asked.

''Big-time,'' Tate replied.

''All right. Daniel, you pour some drinks, Eileen and I will order up and set the table.''

The Mullinses' house was modern and palatial but somehow cozy still. It was situated on a little hill with a view of the city lights below and Puget Sound in the distance. Eileen pointed to a hallway off the living room. ''Bathroom's back there, and we have an extra bedroom for the kids if you don't mind sleeping in bunk beds. I know Jack would love it if you stayed for a few days.''

Shea called home to check in and heard Zachary screaming.

''Sorry about that,'' Samantha said over the noise. ''I haven't been able to put him down all day. How's it going?''

He recounted what had happened, pausing while Samantha sat and gave Zack a bottle in an effort to improve the quality of the conversation.

''That's wonderful!'' she said when he'd finished. ''I can't believe it worked out so well. Veronica was worried that there was some kind of criminal connection to his disappearance and that the lot of you were all in danger. She got me worried, too.''

''The most dangerous thing we did was climb a tree to get into a private parking lot.''

''What?'' she asked.

''I'll tell you more about it when I get home,'' he said. ''Everything okay?''

''Fine. Colette and Veronica dragged me out to

lunch while the girls were in school, and Rachel and
Armand insisted on staying with Zack. You know, he
doesn't cry for them either, just for me.''

"Maybe he's trying to tell you something.''

"But what?''

He didn't dare say what was on his mind. "I don't
know," he fibbed. "I'm sure you'll get it eventually.''

"I hope so, or I'm going to be deaf by the time you
get back.''

"We've been invited to stay for a few days," he
said. "We haven't talked it over yet, but we all have
to be back Sunday afternoon, so I'll see you then for
sure.''

"Okay. Enjoy your uncle.''

"I miss you," he said.

"Zachary misses you, too," she replied. "Bye,
Shea.''

Stubborn woman. He said goodbye and hung up the
phone.

"YOU KNOW THAT I MET JACK when I'd left Robert and
was determined not to go back." Tess spoke into the
soft shadows of the living room. They'd finished their
pizza and Eileen had turned out all the lamps except
for a torchière in a corner. She'd opened the drapes so
that they could see the lights and boats moving on the
Sound.

The brothers nodded.

"Well." She sighed. "I'd married Robert with such
hope, and when I heard he'd gone blind, I went back,
sure that he needed me and that he was my responsibility. And—" she smiled at Jack "—I think that in
some way I didn't feel I had a right to be as happy as
I was with Jack. I was sure that being with Robert

would be better this time, that he would need me and he'd be less complaining and critical.''

Daniel made a scornful sound.

She sent him a loving look. ''I was wrong. I soon discovered I was pregnant with Daniel and, for right or wrong, I'm still not sure, let Robert believe he was his. I thought it might give him a new lease on the life he found so difficult and unsatisfying.

''But he was only moderately interested in him, and even less so when Daniel grew up with a mind of his own. I stayed because I thought I should. In those days, physical abuse was hardly cause for divorce, much less verbal abuse, which wasn't considered abuse at all. So, with few options, I stayed. Jack sent money, which I told Robert came from my mother.''

She stared out at the Sound and shook her head. ''Robert grew even more miserable. When Daniel was thirteen, Robert told me that he knew Daniel wasn't his, even though he couldn't see him. He claimed the boy was too soft, too artistic, to bear any resemblance to the kind of man Robert had been in his youth.

''Daniel overheard and told him in a rage that he was sure he wasn't his son, that they didn't look anything alike and that he didn't want to be like him.

''Robert put two and two together about the time I'd left him, and after that our lives became purgatory.

''Daniel graduated from college on a scholarship, was hired by the aeronautical company and left. He wanted me to come with him, but I thought I'd be in his way. I guess I was doing penance for what I'd brought about on all of us.''

The silence was heavy while Tess hesitated again.

''But you didn't bring it about,'' Jack said quietly. ''Robert's misery did.''

"No," she said, "my happiness with you did. It made it impossible for me to live my other life again, though I tried.

"Eight years ago," she went on, "I was leaving to visit Daniel in Seattle, which I did a couple of times a year, but Robert was in a mood and tried to stop me. It was a simple yank on my arm as I went past him, but I shook him off and he fell against an old oak table in the corner, hit his head as he went down. I was shocked to discover he was dead."

She spread her hands helplessly. "Everyone in the neighborhood knew we hadn't gotten along for years. In my panic, I was sure I'd be accused of murder, so I called an old friend for help. He came right over and told me he'd take care of everything."

She shook her head as she explained what he'd done. "He put Robert's body in a big industrial plastic bag, then into an old barrel. He got the barrel onto his fishing boat, took it way out to sea, weighted the body and dropped it over the side."

Shea listened in disbelief. The story was more incredible than anything he'd ever seen in film or on television.

Without warning, Tate's voice came out of the silence. "Al Bigby," he said.

It was easy to tell by Jack's and Tess's expressions that he was right.

"Don't worry," he said. "The secret's safe with us. We spoke to him early in our search, and though all he did was identify you as the woman in the photo, I thought I saw something in his eyes when he talked about you."

She smiled fondly. "I dated him before I married Robert. But all Al wanted was a grocery store, and

Robert had big plans to go to California and get into the movies, and I fell for it.'' Her smile dissolved. ''We're so stupid when we're young.''

She straightened and brought herself back to her story. ''I took the train to visit Daniel as planned, but while I was in the dining car there was a terrible crash. Grease flew everywhere and a fire broke out. I was just inside the door and leapt out onto the grass just before there was another crash and the car behind the dining car slammed into it and stuck.''

Tears streamed down her face and Jack put his arm around her. ''That's enough, Tessie,'' he said gently, but she didn't hear him.

''Everything on the train was chaos,'' she went on in a strained voice, ''but somehow I saw clearly what this meant for me. Freedom. Escape!'' Then she said, her lips trembling, ''It meant I could have Jack.''

Daniel and Eileen were crying. Tate cleared his throat, and Mike got up to look out the window.

Shea felt as though he couldn't draw breath again until she finished her story.

''If Robert's body was ever found, I would never be suspected because I'd be considered dead. And Jack and I could finally have the life both of us had dreamed of for too many years. So I called him from the first phone I could find, told him what had happened and explained that if he agreed to meet me, he, too, would have to give up his life and make certain no one knew where he'd gone.'' She wrapped his hand in hers and kissed it. ''He was there in four hours. Then we called Daniel and explained everything. We assumed phony names and moved to Twin Deer, just because I'd been there once and liked it, and it was fairly remote. Then we started feeling our years and wanted to be near Daniel.''

She looked from Tate to Mike, who'd turned away from the window, and then to Shea. Her eyes were sad. "This is the first time since I made that decision on the train that I've regretted any of it. Because Jack has to be separated from you. He can never go back to French River because his disappearance was such a major mystery there and got so much attention.'' She patted his cheek. "He's balded and grown a tummy, but he'd be recognized in a minute.''

"We'll just have to come and see him," Tate said. "And we will, I promise.''

"Can you stay for a couple of days?" Jack asked hopefully. "So we can catch up a little?''

Shea and Mike nodded.

"I guess it's unanimous," Tate said. "We can stay until Sunday morning, but we promised the wives we'd be back Sunday night.''

Jack grinned broadly. "You have wives? Oh, that's right." He pointed to Tate. "Sandy, right? And two little girls.''

Tate explained about his divorce and that he now had four daughters, while Shea sat back and thought about what a miracle it was that they'd found Jack.

He was beginning to feel the Delanceys were invincible together.

There were two sets of bunk beds in the guest room. Tate and Mike claimed bottom bunks and left Shea to climb up to the one above Tate's.

"This reminds me of summer camp," Shea grumbled good-naturedly. "One good water balloon and you guys'd be sorry for all the wrongs you've done me.''

"No, I wouldn't." Tate reached up with a foot to

kick the underside of his mattress. "And stop making threats or I'll lose your ladder."

"Then he'd just step on your face," Mike warned. "Will you two pipe down and go to sleep. Jack says he's always up at five."

"No problem for me." Shea punched his pillow and turned over carefully in the small space allotted him. "I'm usually up at two, at three, at four…"

Tate laughed. "I remember. Those first couple of years with babies are such fun and such hell. How's Samantha doing with her daddy's boy?"

"He was screaming when I called," he reported, "but she'd gotten a bit of a break because she and Colette and Veronica had gone to lunch together while Rachel and Armand baby-sat. They seem to be enjoying one another's company."

"Then you've got to find a way to make her stay." Mike yawned. "My life isn't good when Veronica's unhappy."

"I've never seen her take her frustrations out on you," Tate said.

"She doesn't. I mean my life's unhappy because *I* want her to have everything she wants."

Tate laughed softly. "This from the guy who says we're getting too domesticated."

"We'll have to start yearly hunting trips or something," Shea suggested. "Except that I don't want to kill anything. We can just set up camp and drink muddy coffee and talk about women and big trucks."

"I like it." Mike yawned again. "And we'll stop by and pick up Jack when we go."

"Yeah," Tate said. "He looks good, doesn't he?"

"Yeah." Shea gazed out the bedroom window at a

frosty crescent moon. "He has to live out his life in hiding, but he seems so happy with Tess."

"I could do that with Colette," Tate said.

Mike turned over. "I could live on an ice floe with Veronica and be happy."

Shea thought about Samantha as he'd known her in San Francisco—social, elegant, spoiled, but wonderful fun. And as he knew her now in considerably reduced circumstances—fiercely loving of their son, determined, and completely uncomplaining about the modest house he'd brought her to.

Had she been the same woman in San Francisco and he simply hadn't seen it? Or had the loss of Chez Shea made him so insecure he'd had to believe she was inadequate so he could face what fortune had dealt him? He rested his cheek on his folded arms and sighed.

He felt another kick on the underside of his mattress. "Don't worry," Tate said. "She'll come around. We have faith in you."

"We do?" Mike challenged drowsily.

"We do," Tate confirmed.

Shea closed his eyes. Their faith in him had taken him a long way this year. He decided to go on trusting it.

VERONICA SAT in front of the fire in a tailored blue velour robe, painting her fingernails a bright purple. She held up her finished left hand and blew on the wet polish.

Samantha, standing behind the big chair in which Colette sat and French-braiding her hair, winced at the color. "That's quite a shade," she said.

Veronica waved her fingers in the air. "Megan and Katie gave it to me for my birthday, as well as a bottle of bright green and a bottle of electric blue. My day-care kids think the colors are wonderful.''

Colette fed Zachary, who guzzled formula as though sure it was about to be taken away. One side of her hair was a wild red mass; the other, sleek and smooth as Samantha finished the braid.

''This little guy has a good appetite,'' Colette said. ''I wonder if your problem with him at night is that he needs more substantial food. I know he's very young, but look at the size of him. He'd make two of Megan or Katie at the same age. I'd ask the doctor about it next time.''

''Right. We have an appointment on Tuesday. Someone Shea knows.'' That section of braid secure, Samantha began to work on the other side. ''Is Zachary giving you ideas about having another baby?''

''Oh...'' Colette smoothed the baby's spiky hair and sighed. ''Sometimes I think I'd like to, but Tate now has four children, and we all work so hard around here I don't know if it's even reasonable.''

Silence fell. Samantha noticed that Veronica, who usually had an opinion on everything, simply stared into the fire, a small smile on her face.

''Are you dreaming about babies, too?'' Samantha asked.

Veronica turned to them, her eyes wide with guilt. Nevertheless a blissful smile accompanied the look.

''You're pregnant!'' Colette guessed, sitting forward.

Samantha freed her hair for fear of hurting her.

Zachary continued to eat greedily.

''You can't say a word!'' Veronica warned, ''because I just found out this morning and Mike doesn't know. I didn't want to mention anything until I told him first, but…'' Her eyes brimmed with tears. "I'm so happy I can barely stand it!''

"Well, of course!'' Samantha took the baby so Colette could get to her feet.

Colette hugged Veronica fiercely. "I'm so happy for you! You're going to love being a mother.''

"I know. I just hope Mike's okay with it.''

"He will be. He's come to terms with all that.''

"I know he wants to be a father, I just wonder how he'll feel when he's faced with the reality.''

Samantha guessed they were referring to the hostage situation Mike had been involved in as a police officer. She could understand that witnessing such a thing would affect one's willingness to have children in such a cruel, unpredictable world.

Except that the world didn't seem cruel and unpredictable at the compound. It was as though they'd built their own Camelot, where arguments could be hot and frequent but were always resolved with fairness and an eye for the common good.

Veronica held Colette to her but extended her arm to include Samantha. "Come on,'' she said, "I need all the moral support I can get. Were you afraid Shea would be upset about the baby?'' Before Samantha could speak, Veronica answered her own question. "Of course you weren't, because he went ripping out of here as soon as he heard about him and brought you back.''

She looked desperate for reassurance.

"Judging by the way Mike reacts to his nieces and nephew,'' Samantha said, "I think he'll be thrilled to find out he's going to be a father. And you have all that experience caring for children. Surely he'll find that comforting.''

Veronica considered that, then nodded. "It sounds very reasonable. It's just that sometimes Mike defies reason. And this will mean no motorcycle trips for me for a while."

Colette nodded sagely. "It's winter anyway. Who wants to get wet on a motorcycle? And defying reason must be an inherited trait. Taking over the winery wasn't reasonable, yet look what the boys accomplished. So being unreasonable has its upside."

Samantha nodded. "It means you're willing to run a risk—and that's what any kind of love is, man-woman, parent-child."

A little surprised, Veronica studied her a moment, dark eyes serious. "I can't believe Shea left you in San Francisco because he thought you wouldn't be able to live without your social connections and your comforts. You sound very genuine to me."

Samantha rolled her eyes. "What Shea hadn't noticed was that I was a socialite who was also in the news business, and though I was indulged and had everything, I'd also witnessed another world firsthand and had no illusions about my possessions making me any different from anyone else."

Zachary began to whine and Samantha patted his back, she and Colette and Veronica still standing in a tight little circle in front of the fire. "It's true that losing everything was a shock, but I regret the separation from my parents and my co-workers more than I regret the loss of money or status." She smiled from one woman to the other. "The welcome you two—and everyone else—have given me, has gone a long way toward making me forget that my life is missing anything."

Zachary relieved the moment of any sentimentality by burping loudly.

They laughed, made popcorn, put one of Colette's videos in the VCR and curled up side by side on the sofa, the baby finally asleep in Veronica's arms.

She insisted she had to practice.

SHEA, MIKE AND TATE visited the Seattle waterfront with Jack and Tess and the Mullinses. They toured boats, checked the vendors at Fisherman's Wharf and had chowder and warm bread while watching the water.

Tate told Jack about their plan for a yearly men's trip. "We'll stop by for you and Daniel."

Jack nodded. "We'd really like that, wouldn't we, Danny?"

Daniel smiled. "We have a cabin in the Wallowas. Best trout fishing you ever saw."

They agreed to set a date at the first sign of spring.

After they returned home, the men talked until well after midnight. The women had gone to bed and left them to their reminiscences.

"Is there anything we can do for you before we go, Uncle Jack?" Tate asked.

Jack shook his head, his eyes resting with pride on each of his nephews in turn. "I can't tell you what it means to me that you cared enough to be so stubborn about finding me. And that you did it in a way that kept us safe."

"We remember all your kindnesses to us," Mike said. He grinned. "I think you should do something about Robert Mullins's Social Security checks, though. When he gets to be one hundred and twelve years old and is still collecting, somebody's going to get suspicious."

Jack ran a hand over his face. "I know. We just couldn't figure out how to stop them without someone asking questions. We have no body to produce. We used every dime on a charity for the homeless."

"Maybe I can make his name disappear from the Social Security databank," Mike said.

Jack raised an eyebrow. "How?"

"I was a cop. I still have some connections who owe me and can be very useful."

Jack frowned. "But...couldn't you get into trouble?"

Mike shrugged. "It could get *you* out of trouble. And the risk is minimal."

Jack embraced him. "Thank you, Mike."

"Sure."

"I wish you could come and see what we've done with the winery," Tate said. "We've buffed up the buildings, and the vineyard's in full production. We even ripped off the water-lily wallpaper in the house and repainted."

Jack shook his head wistfully. "I'd love so much to come, but it wouldn't be safe."

"Of course. We'll send you pictures, instead, and wine when it's ready. It's only fair. We've been enjoying the old Valley Winery stuff while we've waited to taste what we've produced."

"So Armand kept it all going after I left. He'll have to come on our trips to the Wallowas."

"You bet."

"And maybe we could invite Al Bigby?"

"Sure."

Shea thought the trip was beginning to sound like a convention, but he couldn't wait.

Their departure was emotional, and not just for the women. Jack wept, Daniel hugged his cousins tightly and Tate, Mike and Shea rode silently half the way home.

"I wish we could do something for Jack so he could come and see the place," Mike said moodily.

Rain fell in a torrent, drumming on the roof of the van. The windshield wipers could barely keep up.

"I'll work on it," Tate promised. "Mike, are you sure you can pull off that computer trick without putting yourself in harm's way?"

Mike nodded, his eyes on the road. "I'm sure. I know this guy. I got his daughter out of prostitution and back to school three or four years ago."

Tate shook his head. "You're full of surprises."

Mike smiled. "Aren't we all?"

CHAPTER ELEVEN

THE HOUSE WAS SILENT when Shea walked in the door just before 7:00 p.m. A fire burned in the fireplace and the aroma of sautéing garlic and onions filled the room.

He followed the smell to the kitchen, where he stopped in the doorway, unable to believe his eyes—or what the sight did to his heart.

Samantha, wearing one of his institutional aprons over jeans and a red sweater, stood at the stove, before an iron frying pan. Her hair was pinched back in some exotic braid, and a red bow secured it at the bottom.

Zachary sat in his carrier on the counter to the left of her, arms and legs moving as she sang "The Itsy Bitsy Spider" to him, dramatizing the spider's ups and downs with the help of her wooden spoon.

The table behind her was set, and a green salad sat in the center. On the counter beside her on her right was a box of Hamburger Chef. She was cooking for him, scrambling hamburger and seasonings in a pan. It was a moment before he could act casual.

"Hi!" he said, catching her shoulders from behind her and giving her a kiss on the cheek.

"Shea!" she exclaimed, and for an instant he'd have sworn he saw delight on her face. Then she, too, tried to act casual. "What was that for?"

He couldn't decide if she'd want to know the truth or not—that he'd had second thoughts while he was away about his behavior when he'd left her in San Francisco. So he simply indicated her stance before the stove.

"This scene looks very fifties. I thought it deserved a 'Hi, honey, I'm home' and a peck on the cheek. How's my boy?"

Shea leaned into the carrier and was rewarded with a gummy smile and definite recognition. He chucked Zachary's chin and nose and took one tiny hand in his. "He knows me!" he said. "I was afraid his nine-week-old memory would forget me."

"I think he's already connected to you in a way that's more than memory."

He was surprised she would admit that. "Why didn't you just pick up something from the restaurant? I told you you can go anytime and—"

"I know. But I wasn't doing anything and I thought you might come home tired."

He took a moment to wonder what had happened here. She was being so amenable—so thoughtful. "I'm glad you're cooking. I'm beat. Mike did all the driving, but I did scale a fence and evade a security guard." He added the last with a pretense of pride. "If we ever have to embark on a life of crime, I have some experience."

"Do I want to hear more about this?" she asked in a doubtful tone. She made up two plates and put them on the table, moved Zachary in his carrier to a chair at the table, then invited Shea to explain while they ate.

"I'm glad Jack's happy," she said when they finished dinner and the story, "but it's a shame he has to be cut off from his family."

"Tate says he'll work on finding a solution, and as much faith as I have in him, I can't imagine what that would be. If Jack and Tess are recognized, it'll be clear they were escaping something, and that'd bring up the subject of Robert Mullins.''

"It sounds like an episode of *Murder She Wrote*. Ice cream?''

"What flavor?'' She used to have a passion for chocolate-chip cookie dough, something he never understood. He liked clean flavors—vanilla, strawberry, coffee.

"Paul Newman's Obscene Vanilla Bean,'' she said, gathering up their plates. "And Rachel dropped off some brownies.''

"I could die a happy man.''

She took the carton out of the freezer and scooped up ice cream. "Speaking of a happy man, Tate's going to be. His ex called from Paris—what's her name?''

"Sandy.''

"Right. His daughters are arriving next Tuesday, and they can stay until December 29. She'd like them home for a millennium celebration the French government is hosting.''

"That's great.'' Tate would be delighted. Shea knew he was eager to introduce his two sets of daughters to each other. "Colette's praying that they all get along. You know how a bunch of young girls can be. Here you go.'' She handed him a coffee cup filled with ice cream and a brownie on the saucer.

"I know all the girls in question, and they're very different from one another but all sweet and fun loving. I don't imagine it'll be perfect, but I'm sure they'll get along.''

"Good.'' She sat down again with her ice cream, suddenly appearing distracted. When she looked across the table at him, he frowned in question.

"Something wrong?" he asked.

She smiled mysteriously. "Not at all. In fact, I can probably tell you if you swear to keep it to yourself."

He couldn't imagine what she'd learned that he didn't know. He leaned toward her instinctively. "What?"

"You have to promise."

"I promise," he said dutifully.

She smiled broadly. "Veronica's pregnant!"

He was shocked. He was sure Mike didn't suspect. Mike didn't always share the details of his life, but Shea felt reasonably certain Mike would have told Tate and him. However, his entire concentration had been on Jack, just as his brother's had.

Shea didn't know what to ask. He couldn't believe she knew that about his family and he didn't. Then he remembered the pajama party. The family dynamic was changing. There was now a lively sisters-in-law component. He liked knowing that Samantha was an active part of it.

"She'd just found out Saturday morning," Samantha explained, "and she was looking so dreamy that Colette guessed. So you can't say anything, because she hasn't had a chance to tell Mike."

"Right. When's she due?"

"The Fourth of July."

He laughed. "How great is that? So you probably didn't miss me at all with this gossip to exchange."

She studied him a moment, her expression amused and devilish. "Of course I did," she said. "There was no one to spell me at night with Zachary." Then, her eyes still on him, she propped an elbow on the table, rested her chin in her hand and heaved a disgruntled sigh. "Okay, I did miss you, and not because of the baby. Not only have I come to care about you all over again, but I've gotten needy about it. I hate that, but there you are."

She blurted that out as though pressure to say it had been building inside her. Now that it was out, she was quieter. "Did you miss *me?*" she asked desultorily.

He couldn't quite believe what he'd just heard. This was a night for shockers. She'd looked pleased to see him when he'd walked in the room, she'd prepared him a meal—albeit one loaded with chemicals and preservatives—he'd learned that he was going to be an uncle again and now she was admitting that she cared and actually *needed* him.

Being calm about it took concentration.

He reached across the table to take her free hand in his and twine his fingers with hers. "Every—single— moment," he said, separating the words for impact.

Something melted in her eyes.

"We have to be careful," she said urgently.

Why? he wanted to shout, but she was very single-minded when convinced of something, and he wanted to believe that eventually that narrow road would lead her to him. So he wouldn't do anything to sidetrack her.

"It isn't just us anymore," she went on. "It's Zachary, too. If we mess up, he pays, as well. So let's think this through."

Think? He was much more interested in taking action, but he'd made a decision without listening to her input before and missed her entire pregnancy and the birth of his son because of it.

"All right." He tightened his grip on her fingers. "I know how I want this to go, but we'll follow it at your pace."

She expelled a sigh of relief. "Thank you. I was afraid you'd figure I was crazy."

"I do," he teased, "but I've always considered it part of your charm. If you want to relax, I'll clean up and watch Zack. I can tell him about his great uncle."

She put her fingertip to the baby's nose. "He loves it when you talk to him."

As though to prove that, Zachary waved his arms and legs like a whirlygig.

Shea had the kitchen clean and the baby asleep in half an hour. He took him out of the carrier and held him just for the feel of him in his arms.

When he walked into the living room Samantha was dozing on the sofa in her *grand jeté* pose, and he wished desperately that he could hold her, too. But a promise was a promise.

He sat in the big chair with the baby and watched television until a particularly noisy commercial woke Samantha just after ten. She rubbed her eyes and glanced at him apologetically. "I'm great company, aren't I?"

"I'm not too-wide awake, either," he said, turning off the television with the remote. "Why don't we just call it a night. Zack's still sleeping deeply so we might get a couple of hours before he wakes up again."

She cast him an amused glance as she got to her feet and stretched. The gesture struck him as erotic and he had to turn away and pretend to bury the fire he'd allowed to die down while she slept.

"You're being optimistic," she said, turning off the porch light, then the living-room light. The hallway light on the second level guided them upstairs.

Shea put Zachary in his crib, as Samantha leaned into it from the other side.

"Megan and Katie," she said, "spent all Saturday morning here, sitting on the sofa and taking turns holding him. Megan wanted to make cookies with me, but I had to tell her I wasn't very good at it."

"That's all right," he said, turning on the musical mobile. "You make great Hamburger Chef."

They walked into the hallway, leaving the door ajar, and faced each other in the dim light.

"I'm glad you're home," she said, her eyelids heavy.

"Me, too." And just to prove to her that he was true to his word, he kissed her chastely on the cheek, said "Good night" and walked into his room.

SAMANTHA CHANGED into her nightie and her bed socks, climbed under the covers and applauded herself for her maturity and her ability to put the demands of her body second to the demands of her situation.

And her body was making demands. If she'd been aware of Shea physically before he left for Bellevue, her loneliness for him in his absence had heightened her awareness to an almost intolerable degree.

While he was gone, she'd realized how important he'd become to her in a million little ways that had nothing to do with physical contact, and that somehow caused her to want it more.

He made her laugh; he saw to a score of niceties without fuss—assuring her lunch deliveries, bringing home her favorite desserts, getting to Zack before the fussing baby woke her up, simply being around to brighten her atmosphere.

She'd turned the original plan to leap into his arms when he came home from Bellevue into the more sedate, more reasonable dinner preparation and cheerful but subdued welcome. That had been smart.

Not satisfying, but smart.

She drifted off to sleep, pleased with herself.

Not happy, but pleased.

And then she woke up.

She propped herself on her elbows, waiting to hear the wail that usually woke her at this hour, but the house was absolutely silent. She glanced at the bedside clock. It was 2:47.

She sat up, wondering what had disturbed her. And then she felt the tension. It jangled inside her, tried to pull her out of bed and push her toward Shea's room, told her there was no need for caution, that she knew the man inside out and the fact that he'd once done something that had hurt her abominably meant only that he'd been mistaken, not flawed.

It was all right to love him.

She swung her legs out of bed, stood, then sat down again, forcing herself to exert a little self-control.

But her body's memories were stronger than her mind tonight and she could feel his touch all over her, on every silken surface and in every intimate place. A sparkling sensation rode up and down inside her, out of control.

She got up again and crept into the baby's room to find him fast asleep and breathing evenly.

Then she went to Shea's room and tiptoed inside it to the edge of his bed. He slept in the middle of the bed, one arm flung over his head, the other over the blankets pulled up to his waist.

The scent of the room was familiar—part man, part Old Spice. She'd always teased him for using the traditional aftershave, and bought him one with a designer label. He'd used it for a week to humor her, then gone back to Old Spice.

She lifted the blankets and climbed in beside him, careful not to wake him. She had to lie beside him tonight or something inside her would snap.

She still loved him. Or she loved him anew—that was probably more accurate. This wasn't the thrill of discovery their relationship in San Francisco had been. This was love that had survived despite pain and loss and clamored to be acknowledged. It didn't promise anything necessarily, but it demanded to be heard.

Ant it wouldn't wait to happen at some carefully described pace that would keep her feelings safe. It was ripping the feelings out of her and demanding, "Look at these! Do something about them!"

Well, she was going to first thing in the morning.

SHEA WASN'T SURE what had awakened him. He cocked his ear for Zachary's cry, but it didn't come.

Of course. Silence had awakened him. Since his son had moved in, silence in the early-morning hours was unusual enough to wake the dead.

He glanced at the clock, read 3:12, then closed his eyes again.

And then he became aware of the hand resting on his abdomen, of every fingertip snuggled under his sweatshirt, touching the bare flesh of his middle. He felt softness against his back, knees tucked up under his backside, cotton socks against the backs of his calves.

Then very distinctly, even through the sweatshirt, he felt a kiss planted in the middle of his back. Sensation raced through him like fire finding air.

The arm around his waist tightened and a mellow voice whispered, "Hi."

He drew a breath, prayed for wisdom and raised his head slightly to look over his shoulder. Samantha's head peered around his upper arm, her hair disheveled and bright around her face, a light in his darkness.

"Hi," he replied. "Something frighten you?"

She rested her chin on his arm. "Yes. The thought of having to wait any longer to make love with you, when love *for* you is about to push the heart right out of my body."

That turned him right around to lie face-to-face with her.

"Tell me I didn't misunderstand that," he said urgently.

"I love you," she said clearly. "I'm here to *make* love with you. I was going to wait until morning because you were sleeping so soundly, but now that you're awake..."

He repeated her words to himself, then said to her, "Are you *sure* I'm awake?"

She reached over his hip to pinch his backside. "Feel that?" she asked.

He struggled to think clearly. "So...you've resolved your concerns about us?"

She sighed and met his gaze honestly. "No. I love you—I don't doubt that anymore. I only doubt that it'll be there forever. I guess this is just selfishly about needing you. Is that all right? Does it make any sense?"

He decided it didn't have to. He opened his mouth over hers, pressed her back into the pillows and kissed her until they were both breathless.

She ran her fingers into his hair, arched her body into his and made a small, familiar sound of pleasure.

"Samantha," he breathed. "It's been forever!"

THE MOMENT SHEA WRAPPED Samantha in his arms, her world came right again. She had no recollection of what she'd lost, only what she had right now—and it was everything.

He turned onto his back, pulling her over him, and reached under the hem of her nightshirt. She bent forward over him to allow him to pull it off.

He seemed mesmerized by her nakedness. His warm strong hands stroked over her thighs, met over her stomach and lightly cinched her waist, then rose to palm her breasts, the callused underside of his fingers creating a delicious friction on her nipples as he closed, then opened, his hands.

She leaned into his touch, her hands roaming over his shoulders, still covered in the sweats he wore to bed. Holding her to his chest, he sat up and helped her remove his shirt.

When he lay back again, she knelt beside him to tug the bottoms off.

He turned onto his side instantly to reclaim her, pulled her down beside him, and with lips and fingers explored every inch of her as though it was their first time together. His tender reverence had been just a memory for so long that the reality of it brought tears to her eyes.

"What?" he asked anxiously, brushing the hair back from her face. "Second thoughts?"

"No, no!" She held tightly to his neck. "It's just so...nice, that's all. So much as I remember you, yet more wonderful, more special, more…" She ran out of words and kissed his shoulder. "I love you, Shea."

"I love you, Sam. Even more than I did before, and there were times when I thought *that* would kill me. Funny thing is…" He eased her back to look into her eyes. They were tear-filled and glistened in the darkness. "This time, I'm fearless about it. I don't care who has what or doesn't have it—I just want us to be together. I'll do anything to make that happen."

"Me, too," she promised. "Me, too. What do you want? What can I do?"

His answer was one long tender caress down the middle of her back, over her hip, then a touch inside her that claimed her with sure possession.

She leaned against him with a ragged sigh, all power in the moment abdicated as she held him closer, hitched her leg a little higher to allow his touch.

She was his in an instant, gasping, quaking, fulfillment ricocheting inside her like a bird in a chimney.

She tried to reach for him, to take him with her, but he held her hands in one of his and with the other took her places she'd never ever been.

She was breathless when it was over and empowered with the knowledge that there were such pinnacles of emotion inside her.

She pushed him firmly to the pillows and climbed astride him.

SHEA LOST ALL GOOD SENSE the moment she touched him. He wanted to reach for her, to take her with him again, but she put a hand firmly to the middle of his chest and held him still as he'd held her.

He could have resisted easily, but it never occurred to him. He lay quietly and let her torture him with her tender attentions; then, when he couldn't take it another moment, he entered her. They were wrapped together when his world ignited, and even as he was mindless in his own fulfillment, he felt her tremble again in his arms and abandoned himself to the pleasure, happy to have given as well as taken.

Samantha moved to snuggle into his shoulder, her heart pounding against him, her breath coming rapidly. She collapsed against his side, an arm thrown across his waist.

"We've still got it," she said in some amazement. "I can't quite believe it was still so...magical."

"It just reflects what we feel," he said lazily. "My brothers, two serious-minded men, have been grinning from ear to ear since the day they got married. Love is magical, whether you believe in it or not."

Samantha entwined her legs with his. "I wonder how Mike reacted to Veronica's news?"

"We'll find out in the morning when we get our Christmas trees."

"She was so excited. I hope he's happy."

"I'm sure he is."

Out of the ensuing quiet came the fragile sound of Zachary's first cries upon awakening. Shea swore he could almost here a clear "Hello? I'm up. Where are you?"

When the response wasn't quick enough—as it wasn't now that his parents had to fight the languor of a sleepy aftermath, get their legs untangled, find Shea's robe and put it on Samantha—the cries rose sharply in decibel and tempo to "I want you now! *Now,* do you hear me? It's dark and nobody's here, and I'm—"

The cries stopped immediately when Samantha scooped him out of the crib and put him to her shoulder. "At least he had the grace to wait until we'd finished."

"That's true." Shea patted the baby's back and earned a smile. He had to nuzzle him in reward. "You go back to bed with him," he said to Samantha. "I'll bring up a bottle."

"Bless you," she said.

They lay side by side in the bed, the baby between them, propped on Shea's pillows, as Samantha held the bottle. Shea rested his arm on the pillow above the baby's head and absently ran his fingers through Samantha's hair.

"I want you to call your father again," he said gently. "Maybe the first message got lost. I can't believe he wouldn't return your call if he could."

"I would. You haven't seen Legs."

"Come on, Sam. Zack has no grandparents on my side. He deserves one set, don't you think? Even if we don't stay together, he still needs them."

"But *my* parents?" she asked doubtfully. "A woman who bathes in Italian fountains and a man who runs off with showgirls?"

"Have you ever talked to them about it?"

"No. Mom ran away when Dad started divorce proceedings and then Dad took off after Legs. Mom was mad at me, I was mad at Dad…" She blew air out in exasperation. "It wasn't pretty."

"Well, it's either try to find them and reestablish communications or *hire* a set of grandparents for this guy." He was holding one of the baby's bootied feet.

She looked argumentative. "I wish Jack and Tess could come and visit."

"I do, too. But I think that's a situation even Tate

can't fix. So, how about it? There's more caramel flan in it for you,'' he bribed.

"Okay.'' She did not sound enthused. "But you're lucky I'm such an easy mark. My greed for your desserts always wins over principle.''

"Maybe you're parents aren't as guilty as you think.''

"I saw what I saw,'' she insisted stubbornly.

"But you haven't discussed it with them, so you don't know what motivated what you saw.''

"Don't nag. I said I'd call.''

"Tomorrow?''

"We're going tree cutting tomorrow.''

"Not until ten. You can call right after breakfast.''

She frowned at him, but her annoyance was half-hearted. Her eyes were still filled with love and residual pleasure.

"Will you be quiet about it if I promise?''

"Will you make love with me after you put the baby back to bed?''

She rolled her eyes in pretended pain. "Is there no end to your demands?''

"Not where your body's concerned.''

She smiled and gathered up the now-sleeping baby. "I'll be right back.''

CHAPTER TWELVE

ELEVEN PEOPLE COULD NOT be expected to reach an agreement on a Christmas tree, Samantha decided. Feelings about that special symbol of the holidays were deeply rooted in childhood memory and, of course, affected by personal preference.

The compound's tree, which Tate thought should be placed beside the fountain, had brought the group to an impasse.

Colette wanted a tall blue spruce, Tate wanted a shaggy Scotch pine and Rachel preferred the stately noble fir. Samantha tended to agree with Tate, but as the newcomer, she'd stayed out of the argument.

Megan and Katie had found a thirty-foot Douglas fir that they were convinced would be perfect.

"Okay, let's just take a vote," Tate suggested diplomatically. "Who's for the blue spruce?"

He went through the list of possible trees, tallied up the votes. "Seven," he said with a frown. "Who isn't voting besides Zachary?"

Shea pointed to Mike and Veronica, who were walking off into the woods arm in arm, apparently still basking in Veronica's news. Colette exchanged a wink with Samantha.

"They want the Scotch pine," Tate said, barely withholding a grin as he added two strokes to the tally for his favorite.

"No, they don't!" Colette snatched the sheet from him. "Veronica told me just this morning that she thought a noble fir—"

"We didn't see Veronica this morning, Mom," Katie corrected innocently, "until we got here, and then she and Uncle Mike..." At her mother's pretended glare and everyone else's laughter, she realized what she'd done. "Oh," she said simply, and pointed to the thirty-foot Douglas fir. "Me and Megan like that one better, anyway."

"Katie, we'd have to cut a hole in the sky for that one," Tate said. "We need something a little smaller."

"Why don't we get the ones we want for our homes first," Colette suggested. "Then maybe we can come to an agreement about the compound's tree."

They all agreed that was a good idea and split up. The cadre of lot assistants assigned to help them peeled off to follow their chosen couple.

Shea, Samantha and Zachary acquired a tall teenage boy with braces who tried desperately not to smile and reveal them.

They had little trouble agreeing on a fat eight-foot Scotch pine. Shea held the top while the boy cut it with a chain saw. Samantha held her mittened hands over Zachary's ears, already protected from the cold by a woolen hat made to look like Winnie-the-Pooh, but nothing, she thought, could protect one from that high-pitched whine.

Tate had driven an old flatbed truck he'd bought at a police auction after the harvest had pressed into service every vehicle on the place and revealed how much they needed one.

Shea and the boy carried the tree to the truck and

Shea gave him a tip that made him smile despite himself.

Tate and Colette arrived with her favorite blue spruce, which was about six feet tall. Mike and Veronica's lot boy carried a small pine that would probably go on a tabletop in their apartment, and Armand and Rachel returned with a five-foot noble fir, just right for her cottage living room.

The lot boys helped Tate, Mike and Shea load the trees onto the truck, then the group stood around wondering what to do about the compound's tree.

"We could buy all four," Mike teased.

Everyone glared at him.

He shrank back behind Veronica. "Boy, try to be an arbitrator and see what it gets you."

"Why don't we find a fifth option," Tate suggested.

Shea frowned. "You mean find one nobody likes?" He got the same glare Mike had earned.

He held his ground and pointed to Zachary in his carrier. "No malice, please. I'm carrying a baby."

Mike came to take the baby out of the carrier and put him to his own shoulder. "Then don't subject him to foolish remarks."

Samantha watched in fascination as Mike flushed suddenly and pointed to Veronica. "Vee has something to tell you all," he said.

Mike missed all the glances exchanged as he studied Zachary. Colette had obviously told Tate, and he and Shea had apparently talked about it. Only Megan and Katie and Armand and Rachel waited curiously.

"We're going to have a baby," Veronica announced, her eyes alight with glee despite her calm delivery of the news. "My due date is the Fourth of July."

The girls squealed and jumped up and down; Armand and Rachel went to hug her, then Mike; and Tate, Colette, Shea and Samantha closed in to offer their congratulations and silently share their relief with Veronica that Mike was pleased.

"We just can't decide whether to have a girl or a boy," Mike said seriously. "There are already lots of girls—" He winked at Megan and Katie "—but they're all so special. On the other hand, there's only one boy."

"You don't get to decide," Katie began to explain. "You have to take what…" Then she saw all the smiles directed her way and sighed in self-deprecation. "I screwed up *again*."

"No, you didn't," Shea said, hugging her. "We just love to tease you because you're always looking for answers."

"But I find the wrong ones!"

"The important part is that you're looking."

"So…" the older of the lot boys asked cautiously, "which tree, Mr. Delancey?"

Samantha stepped forward. "If you can't agree, why don't we just not get a tree?"

There was instant protest. "Oh, go ahead and get the pine," Colette said. "I'd rather have that than *no* tree."

"No, I can compromise," Tate said. "Get the spruce."

"No, no, no," Rachel insisted. "In the spirit of family harmony, let's do it your way. The pine might fit the old-fashioned look of the garlands and lights, anyway."

They stared at one another, the problem still unsolved, but compromise on the table.

"The pine?" Samantha asked Shea.

"The pine," he agreed.

"The pine," she said to the boys, and they went off eagerly to cut it.

Eyes turned on Samantha with sudden suspicion.

She smiled sweetly. "They don't call me Samantha 'Solomon' Haskell for nothing."

SHEA PUSHED A SHOPPING CART in Christmas City, a huge warehouselike shop outside of McMinnville where the women had insisted they stop on their way home with the trees. The men had protested, but with two more female votes than male, they'd lost.

The couples took off in different directions, looking for different things.

Samantha stared moodily at a shelf of ball ornaments in bright colors. "A tree should be hung with old ornaments," she said. "Things from our parents, gifts from our friends, things the children have made."

She looked stricken, and he put a hand to her back and rubbed gently. "Well...your stuff's in San Francisco, I don't have any stuff and Zack's a little too young to make anything. Even old ornaments started as new ones at some point."

She put a hand to her lips and he realized she was becoming seriously emotional about something. He pulled her closer.

"What is it?"

A tear slid down her cheek. She swiped it away. "Just that my mom used to love Christmas. She made a terrible fuss and we always had this big gaudy tree with all kinds of junk that I made in school, some really pretty things she'd gotten overseas, and..." She pressed a hand to her trembling mouth.

"You left a message with her secretary. She'll get it to her."

"But Mom's mad at me."

"Nobody's mad at anybody at Christmastime."

She wrapped an arm around him and leaned into him beside Zack. The baby swung his arm in an uncoordinated arc and whacked her in the nose.

She laughed, then she started to cry again. "I want her to see Zachary."

"She will, I promise."

She looked doubtful but nodded to humor him.

If Audrey didn't respond, Shea thought as Samantha pulled red, gold, blue and purple balls off the shelf, he was sending Vince Rushford after her.

SHEA CAME HOME AT EIGHT Tuesday night for a dinner break and found the entire female contingent of the Delanceys gathered around his living-room table, over which was spread newspaper and every bead and bauble known to man. They were making Christmas ornaments for the fair.

The Christmas tree with the new ornaments Samantha considered offensive stood in the window, strewn with pearl and chain garlands but no icicles.

Colette sat at one end, hot-gluing dried flowers and other decorations to a lineup of grapevine wreaths. She had small ones, big ones and several sizes in between.

Veronica was in the middle on one side, adding small flourishes to paper ornaments her day-care children must have made, and across from her Samantha made gaudy Victorian-looking ornaments out of pearls and beads and gold-and-silver-colored chain. He thought he saw the carcass of one of the tree's garlands among her supplies.

She held up one with a long crystal that caught the light. It made a rainbow on the wall. "What do you think?" she asked.

He didn't have words for what he thought, so he simply blew her a kiss.

At the other end of the table, Rachel, Megan and Katie painted dough-art ornaments and the standing figures Rachel had made.

Shea pretended to search beneath the projects. "You didn't lose Zachary under all this, did you?" he asked Samantha.

"He's in the kitchen," she said, "having brandies with your brothers and Armand."

"Ah." He found them in the breakfast nook, Tate sketching on a napkin while they all leaned toward him, Armand holding the baby, who also looked interested. An uncoordinated little hand struck out at Tate and knocked the pencil.

Tate eyed him seriously. "I don't think we'll put a window in the refrigerator, but thank you for the suggestion."

Zachary smiled widely and Tate laughed and kissed the top of his head.

Was it safe to be this happy, Shea wondered—to create your own family and have it fit seamlessly into the family you grew up in and felt so attached to?

"What's going on?" he asked, bending over Mike to see what Tate was illustrating.

"He's designing Veronica's and my house," Mike said. "With the baby coming, we're going to need bigger digs."

"That's right. Where you going to build?"

"On the lake," Mike replied. "That meadow in the cottonwoods."

The spot was perfect. Mike was pleased he had a child coming. Shea punched his shoulder. "Congratulations on the baby. You're going to love it."

Mike smiled up at him. "Who'd have ever thought *you'd* take to it so well?"

Shea nodded ruefully. "I guess the domesticity you're so worried about has come to claim you, too."

"Yeah. We're really going to need those weekends with Jack and Daniel and Bigby." Shea went back to work, thinking life was just about perfect. Except that he and Samantha should be married.

He made the mistake of bringing up the subject the morning of the fair. Everyone else had already left— fortunately with all the ornaments—while Samantha shouted at him in the living room.

"I didn't say 'I don't think we should be married,'" she argued.

He was sure that was what he'd heard.

"I know we should be for Zachary. I…just don't have a lot of faith in it."

"Wait a minute." He put both hands up. He wasn't sure if he was feeling for the wall she'd just erected, or if he was surrendering.

No. He was too angry for surrender. And too confused.

He pointed up the stairs. "You climbed into my bed. Your heart was beating its way out of your chest for me, you said!"

"It was! It is! But love and permanence aren't the same thing!"

"The hell they aren't! You've held on to that ridiculous notion long enough. You said you wouldn't wait for me a year ago, but you just professed to love me. I walked out of your life and tried everything in me to forget you, yet I'd die for you in a minute! What do you *call* that?''

''That's now,'' she said, folding her arms and walking away from him. ''And maybe for a while. I saw my dad carry my mother seven miles off a mountain when she broke her leg on a camping trip.'' She turned around to face him, her eyes tearful. ''I've seen her walk by his side through a mob of angry protesters objecting to his support of the gay rights initiative.'' Her pause was significant. ''But where are my parents today?''

''Sam, it's not—''

''Yes, it *is* the same thing! It's the very same thing. And I don't ever want Zachary to feel about his family the way I feel about mine now. Lost to it. Alienated.''

He didn't know how to fight this, but he was determined to try. ''So you'd rather he grew up in one that wasn't committed to its existence?''

''I'm committed to you!'' she said emphatically, making a gesture from her heart to his. ''I'm…just not sure what to do about it.''

''Sam,'' he said reasonably, ''your parents lived their lives the way they chose. But you're an adult. You're connected but separate from them. You can't make your decisions based on their failures and successes.''

She considered that, looked as though she might think it made sense. Then he saw in her eyes that she rejected it as dangerous to her point of view. ''This is all your fault!'' she accused.

Now, that threw him completely. ''Pardon me?'' he asked, too surprised to shout.

''You're the one who brought us here into this bastion of familial perfection, of everyone working for the common good, of tempers and quarrels that clear the air instead of clearing the marriage or the family. I want that for us!''

He shifted his weight and drew a breath. ''Okay. Think that through. How do you expect to get that when you're afraid to marry me because twenty years down the road you might feel differently? That's *your* fault, sweetheart, not mine.''

She glowered at him and stormed away.

''Zack and I will be in the car!'' he shouted after her.

AT THE CHURCH, Samantha joined her cohorts in the craft booth and Shea followed his brothers and Armand around the events that had a carnival flavor—ring toss, roulette, soft pitch.

''What happened?'' Mike asked Shea as each of them calculated his move with the softball.

''To what?'' Shea asked, pitching and hitting the weighted canvas figure he'd targeted. It tottered and fell.

''You and Sam.''

Shea spared him a glance intended to tell him it was none of his business.

Mike grinned. ''Was that supposed to scare me? Come on. For a couple of days it was looking as though she might stay after all, and this morning you're both smiling a lot but not at each other. You haven't exchanged a word or even glanced at each other since you got here.''

Shea leaned a hand on the booth, watched the old woman behind the narrow counter watch them and wondered if their conversation would be reported at the next altar society meeting. "Would you throw the ball?" Shea asked.

"Oh. Sure." Mike took a minute, stretched his arm back and let go with an ease in the shot Shea could never quite muster. Three bottles in a row tumbled.

He won a two-foot doll with a red-and-white crocheted hat and dress. He carried it with no visible embarrassment as they walked toward the popcorn-and-soft-drinks booth, where Tate and Armand were already paying for their purchases.

"Her family," Shea said, "seems to be getting in the way of our being a family. She says she loves me, but she's just not sure marriage is a good idea right now."

"Even for Zack?"

"Especially for Zack. She doesn't want him to feel the way she felt when her family broke up after so long."

Mike stopped him a small distance from their companions and said with a frown, "But that doesn't make sense. That was them and this is you."

"That's what I said. And she hasn't spoken to me since."

"Uh…what is *that*?" Tate asked as he and Armand joined Mike and Shea. He pointed to the very conspicuous doll.

"My winnings from the soft pitch booth," Mike said.

Tate winced at it. "You intending to carry it around?"

Mike raised an eyebrow. "I won it."

"They didn't have, like, a Barbie you could put in your pocket?"

"You're telling me your masculinity is offended by this?"

"I'm telling you that if you intend to walk around with that thing all day, you're not walking with me."

Mike gave him a pitying look. "I didn't realize your perception of your manhood was so fragile," he said. "I happen to know that someone in this auditorium was pining for just this particular—"

"Uncle Mike!" Katie appeared at Mike's elbow, her eyes wide with disbelief, her arms raised up toward the doll. "You did it! You said you could, but so did Grandpa and he couldn't! Oh, Uncle Mike! I'll love you forever and ever!"

Mike put the doll in her arms, leaned down for her noisy kiss on his cheek, then watched her scamper away, shouting, "Mom! Aunt Vee! Aunt Samantha! Look what Uncle Mike got me!" Mike, hands in his pockets, gave his companions a very superior lift of his eyebrow and walked off into the crowd.

"You know what this means," Tate said.

Shea nodded. "He's going to be insufferable all day long."

Tate indicated with a tilt of his head that that went without saying. "It means *you* have to win one for Megan or there'll be hell to pay."

MEGAN, FORTUNATELY, WAS appeased with a brown teddy bear wearing a brimmed denim hat with a red silk flower. Shea won it at the same booth, but for the downing of only two bottles, and delivered it to the cubicle festooned with ornaments, where Megan helped her mother and her aunts. Everyone fussed over it except Samantha, who was busy with a customer.

"Shea! Shea? Over here!" Shea turned at the sound

of his name but could see nothing except the throngs of families moving from booth to booth. Then he spotted Father Wolff waving at him from across the room.

The priest made an urgent beckoning gesture and Shea obeyed it.

The man was confined in a booth that appeared to have been constructed out of a refrigerator box. A barred window had been cut in it to resemble a jail, and the priest sat on one of two stools.

"What on earth…" Shea began.

The priest stood and put his hands around two cardboard "bars." "You have to get me out," he pleaded, "before I break into 'Unchained Melody'!"

"How did you get *in?*"

"It's a moneymaker," he said. "Give the jailer—" he pointed to an older woman talking to Tate; she wore a ring of old keys on the belt of her floral shirtwaist "—five dollars and she'll put anyone you want in jail for ten minutes. You can get them out for ten dollars or add to their time. Shea! I'm scheduled to man the cakewalk booth in five minutes. If I'm not there, Henry Woodson will volunteer to take care of it and he'll eat everything we have for sale. The Knights of Columbus sausage booth had to send out for more sausage after he lent them a hand."

"I don't know." Shea pretended to think about it. "I kind of like seeing you in there. It makes up for the volleyball fiasco at the barbecue last summer."

The priest reached out to take his arm, a grave expression on his face. "Son. Holding a grudge this long isn't healthy. Please. Have mercy."

Shea rolled his eyes and went to get the jailer. He handed her a ten and she followed him back to the makeshift jail, where she released the priest—then pushed Shea inside.

The priest handed her a ten-dollar bill.

"Hey!" Shea complained.

"Relax, son," the priest said, apparently waiting for something. He held on to the door and scanned the room. "Think of it as inexpensive counseling."

"Counseling for what?" The question was answered for him a moment later when he saw his brothers emerge from the crowd, each holding one of Samantha's arms. She was laughing as she let herself be led to the "jail," but her expression changed when she saw Shea already inside.

The priest opened the door and Tate pushed her gently in to join Shea.

"We want your problem at least discussed," he said, "in the ten minutes allotted. If you're still not speaking at the end of that time, we'll give Mrs. McCreedy another ten."

Mike peered at them through the bars. "We don't expect you to solve it, necessarily, just talk about it."

"Father Wolff," Samantha said, nearly falling over one of the stools as she backed in. Shea reached out instinctively to steady her and got a glare for his efforts.

He removed his hands from her and held them up to indicate that he'd intended no harm. He kicked the stool out of her way and sat down, resigned to his fate.

"This is not funny!" she told the priest and Shea's brothers. "This is...meddling!"

"Well, yeah," Tate said. "I thought you understood that that was what the Delanceys are all about. See you in ten."

She watched in disbelief as they walked away.

Shea moved the other stool back into place and patted it. "You may as well sit down," he said. "They're not coming back for ten minutes and if we don't have something to tell them, we'll be here for another ten. So, think of something."

"They're *your* brothers," she grumbled, trying to pace the small area, then giving up when she couldn't move more than one step in any direction. She sat down. "You should have to think of something."

"You're the one who wants the perfect family." He leaned his elbows on his knees and bumped his head against the side of the box. He straightened up again. "This is how the machinery works. You get a lot of love, but it's often at the expense of your peace and privacy."

Her shoulder was less than an inch from his, but she'd folded her arms so that she wouldn't touch him. She sent him an emotional glance across the small space. "I thought you wanted the perfect family, too."

"I want a family," he corrected. "Nothing's perfect."

"Mine was close," she insisted stubbornly.

"Yeah, well, close is probably the best you get. They were human, Sam. They must have had problems they kept from you, then just couldn't hide them anymore. Maybe they trusted you to understand and forgive."

"You can't understand what they don't explain to you or forgive them when they don't answer your calls!"

He sighed. "You're absolutely right."

"What do you mean?" she asked aggressively.

He turned to her impatiently. "I mean that you're right! I just don't understand how that has anything to

do with us. We're two different people in completely
different circumstances, and pardon me for pointing
this out, but you'd never be one to let a problem fester
until it got too big to deal with. You'd be all over me
about it all the time.''

"Thanks," she said dryly. She stood as though she
needed to move, and when she couldn't, she turned to
Shea looking as though she would explode. "I can't
stand this another minute!"

He smiled, caught her hand and pulled her down
onto his lap. "Sure you can. If you sit on me, you can
look out through the bars and see the crowd. You won't
feel so claustrophobic.''

He was a little surprised when she sat calmly, an
arm around his shoulder and one over her eyes.

"And this might even convince them that we've
solved things," he said. "So they'll let us out, instead
of sending us up for another ten minutes.''

"I think," she said, lowering her hand and staring
at the door, apparently missing his reassurance that
they might be freed soon, "that I admired both of them
so much. And I took pride in the part of me that was
a newsperson like my father and the part that was interested in everything like my mother. So, if I'm like
them—" she turned to him, her genuine concern a dark
shadow in her eyes "—how do I know I won't just
give up the way they did?''

He rubbed gently in the middle of her back, his hand
across her knees holding her close. "Maybe they didn't
give up," he said. "Maybe they just don't know what
to do next.''

She looped her other arm around his neck. "I'm
sorry I yelled at you this morning," she said contritely.
"I just didn't expect you to propose.''

"You said you loved me."

"I do. But my life is so uncertain, and I'm...confused."

Hardly the answer wished for by a man hoping to become a groom, but she had admitted she loved him. And pinning her down to a firm yes would alleviate his fear that he could still lose her at the end of the holidays, but if she said it under duress, it wouldn't come from her heart. And that was what they needed for the relationship to work.

"All right," he said finally. "We'll just think about enjoying the holidays, about working on the Magi Dinner and trying to understand what we want from each other. That good for you?"

Samantha couldn't believe he could be this generous. She wasn't sure she could have been, given the same circumstances.

So she kissed him. Not as a thank-you or a reward, but because she felt she needed intimate contact with the soul that could make such a concession.

She held tightly to him and gave it all she had, trying to draw out his strength and generosity and take some for herself.

He wrapped his arms around her, seemingly willing to accept what she offered and give her everything she asked for.

Absently, Samantha heard Tate say, "Jeez! It worked."

"Yes," Father Wolff said. "Get them out of there before this turns into a conjugal visit."

CHAPTER THIRTEEN

A ROTUND SANTA with a real beard posed with children in his regal chair in Margie's Dress Shop while a photographer took pictures. Margie had made space for him by moving all the shoes into the lingerie department.

"Bras and high heels," Shea whispered as he and Samantha waited their turn with Zachary. "This is a lonely bachelor's dream."

"Behave yourself!" she admonished, elbowing him in the ribs. She indicated Katie and Megan, who'd accompanied them because Tate and Colette were housecleaning in preparation for Susan and Sarah's visit.

She shifted Zachary in her arms. He wore a red one-piece with a bow tie for the occasion. "It's Christmas. You're going to end up on the coal-in-your-stocking list."

"You're going to be on the nice list," Katie assured him. "Daddy says your dinner's going to make lots and lots of money for the assisted living place because you're such a great chef."

"A great chef," Samantha said with a teasing wink, "and a good boy are entirely different things."

Megan patted his back reassuringly. "He's good. He won that bear for me at the Christmas fair. Mom said your booth made the most money. Father Wolff was really happy."

"What's going to happen," Katie asked, suddenly serious, "if Susan and Sarah don't like us? We're going to the airport to pick them up tomorrow."

Shea put a hand to Katie's head and rubbed gently. "I can't imagine that would happen. I've known both of them since the day they were born, and I think they'll think they're really lucky to have such great younger sisters."

Megan put a hand on Katie's shoulder. "She's afraid that if they don't like us," she said, her own concern showing in her eyes, "Daddy will have to give us up because he had them first."

Shea shook his head over the horrifying thoughts that went on in children's minds. "No, no. He'd never do that. First of all, they're going to love you. And second, even if they don't, he's married to your mom. He can't give you up. You're all part of his family. And they live in Paris, anyway. Say you don't like them—and I can't imagine that happening, either—you only have to put up with them for a couple of weeks."

The girls looked up at Samantha, whom they'd grown very fond of because she let them play with her makeup—and because she'd grown very fond of *them*.

"Does he know what he's talking about?" Megan asked.

Samantha cast him a glance that told him he'd owe her big for this one. "Always. He's the smartest man I know."

"Daddy," Katie said loyally, "is the smartest man we know. So we don't want to lose him."

"You're not going to lose him," Shea assured them, pushing them forward in line as Santa finished with a

gap-toothed little boy. "All that's going to happen is
that the family's getting two more girls."

"Wow," Katie said. "That makes thirteen people in
our family!" Megan narrowed her eyes and calculated.
"That's right," she finally confirmed. "And when
Uncle Mike and Aunt Vee's baby comes, that'll be
fourteen. This family's getting big!"

"Yes, it is," Shea said, putting an arm around
Samantha and Zack and letting the girls crowd in on
the other side as they held their place between the red
ropes.

And to think that a little less than a year ago, there'd
been only three Delanceys. It proved the adage that
love didn't divide, it multiplied.

The photographer shot pictures of Zack in Santa's
lap; Zack looking into Santa's face, taken from the side
because his serious expression was priceless; Zack with
his cousins in Santa's lap; and—for Tate and Colette—
each girl sitting alone with Santa, then together.

The photographer promised that the photos would be
delivered in a week.

They went for burgers afterward at the French River
Café.

"Is it hard for you to eat hamburgers?" Katie asked
in a whisper, looking around to make sure she didn't
hurt anyone's feelings. "You know, 'cause it isn't
gourmet?"

"Delancey's has a hamburger on the lunch menu,"
Megan answered for him. "A hamburger can be gourmet if it's done right. Right, Uncle Shea?"

"Right."

"What you cook doesn't make it gourmet. It's how
you prepare it. As long as you use the finest and fresh-

est ingredients in the first place.'' She glanced up, waiting for his confirmation.

"Right again,'' he said.

Samantha raised an eyebrow in surprise.

Shea tipped his head in Megan's direction. "When she grows up, she's going to the Culinary Institute of America, then she's going to be my partner.''

Megan beamed with pride.

Samantha, looking through the restaurant window to the bus station across the street, was distracted from their discussion of Megan's future by the sight of a rangy man in jeans and a photojournalist's jacket. He walked out of the station with a single small suitcase and turned away from her, taking in every detail of tiny, rural French River.

The breath caught in her throat as rare sunlight glinted off graying blond hair.

"Oh—my—God,'' she said as she recognized her father.

"What?'' Shea asked.

She ignored his question as she shooed Katie out of the booth. "Let Auntie out, sweetie. Thanks.'' Then she shot out of the restaurant and across the street.

"Daddy!'' she shouted as French River's only cab pulled up beside him and the driver leaned out to speak to him. She waved her arms. "Dad! Adam Haskell!''

He swiveled his head sharply in her direction and he smiled and opened his free arm to catch her as she launched herself at him.

"You came!'' she exclaimed, momentarily forgetting that she was furious with him and had intended to kill him the next time she saw him. "I'm so glad to see you! Daddy!''

"Of course I came,'' he returned in the querulous

manner that used to terrify newcomers to Haskell media. "Where the hell have *you* been?"

That ended the moment of forgetting.

"Where have *I* been?" she asked indignantly. "Where have *you* been. And why aren't you there now? Oh, no!" she said, a horrible possibility suddenly occurring to her. "You didn't bring Legs with you, did you?"

"I've asked you not to call her that," he said. "And no, I didn't bring her with me. She's gone home for Christmas, thank you very much." He looked around him in mild concern. "Where am I, anyway? And what are *you* doing here?"

You're in the Willamette Valley, Dad." She caught his arm and pulled him out of the middle of the street. "And I'm here because Shea's here."

"Why is he here?" he asked.

"Because he and his brothers inherited a winery. You remember. I told you all about it when…when he left. He's built a restaurant there."

"I thought that was in the Sonoma Valley."

"No, it's here. If you listened when you're reporting the news the way you listen when I talk to you, you'd be out of business."

He smiled wryly. "I *am* out of business."
They reached the sidewalk and stepped up. She squared off to face him, hands in the pockets of her coat. She no longer cared about the loss of the business, except for all the employees it had put out of work.

But she did resent that the same problem that had destroyed the business had destroyed her family.

"Yeah. I noticed. And I'm sure the people out of work have noticed it, too."

He took that salvo with a little bow in her direction.

"Thank you. Like that hasn't kept me awake nights for the past month. I appreciate your pointing it out." She was instantly sorry. He'd once been a man who'd stood up for the little guy, the persecuted, the underprivileged.

She knew he would never take his responsibility for the loss of jobs lightly.

But she'd wanted to hurt him for all the pain he'd caused her.

"Adam!" Shea said with enthusiasm as he appeared at Samantha's side with the baby in his arms and Megan and Katie trailing him. He shook hands with her father, then took his suitcase and handed him the baby. "I imagine your grandson's grown a little since the last time you saw him."

"Well, my goodness!" Adam held Zachary tenderly in the crook of his arm. "Look at you! You must have doubled in size."

"These are our nieces." Shea drew the girls forward. "Megan and Katie. Girls, this is Aunt Sam's dad, Mr. Haskell."

"Hello, ladies." He smiled at the girls, the querelous man of a few moments ago completely gone as he held his grandson with awe and devotion.

Samantha felt her hostility slip just a little.

Shea put an arm around her shoulders and, while Adam and the girls talked about the baby, whispered in her ear, "I told you he'd come. Be nice, now. You invited him to celebrate Christmas with us, not to rake him over the coals."

"I know perfectly well..."

"We'll move you into my room and let him have yours."

She'd been sleeping in Shea's room anyway for the

past week. It wouldn't be much of a change. But he looked pleased about it.

"Fine. Then you have to give me half your closet."

"I only have stuff in half of it anyhow."

They drove home with Megan in the back with Adam and the baby, and Katie in the front between Shea and Samantha.

"Heard anything from your mother?" Adam asked Samantha an hour later as she moved her things out of the closet to make room for his.

"No!" Samantha shouted from the hallway as she took her things to Shea's room. She laid them on the bed, and returned an instant later and stood in the doorway. "She never forgave me for staying with you after the divorce."

"I'm sorry." He carried clothes to the closet and hung them up. "She's always been like that. She can forgive anything but betrayal."

"Betrayal," Samantha said, going to the dresser, "is a pretty major thing."

"Yes, it is. But she did it to me first, if you remember."

"Because she wanted you to work less and have more time for her, but you wouldn't listen. That's a sort of betrayal, too."

"That was because keeping the business healthy ate up every waking moment." He went back to the suitcase and pulled socks out of a pocket. "You saw what happens when you slip for just an instant."

Samantha walked away with her underwear, dropped it on Shea's bed, then returned to add as though there'd been no interruption, "So you let the company go because of Legs, but you wouldn't do it for Mom?"

"It was more complicated than that."

"I was a good reporter. I'd be able to sort it out if you'd like to explain."

For a moment she thought he would, then he simply dropped the socks in the drawer she'd vacated and went back to his suitcase. "Actually, I've come with an important piece of news."

"Oh?" She stacked sweaters from the second drawer. "What's that?"

"I've found you a job."

She gathered up the sweaters and stopped halfway toward the door to look at him in surprise. "You're starting over?" she asked. "With what?"

He shook his head. "Your job is with Condor News. You begin January 2 if you want it. News director out of the San Francisco office. You know the town, have all the connections. You were an easy sell."

"But Haskell Media and Condor News have been competitors since—"

"Doesn't matter. I heard Owens had stolen their news director away. Bailey said he's always liked your style and would have tried to get you away from me but didn't because you were my daughter. Now that I can't employ you, it doesn't matter."

"So…you *went* to him to get me this job?" she asked in disbelief.

He shrugged and put two sweaters in the drawer where hers had been. "I figured the baby has to eat. I didn't realize you and Shea were together again."

She didn't know how to explain that they were but they weren't. "Why don't you rest until dinner," she suggested. "Or maybe you'd like a tour of the winery?"

"Maybe I'll just sack out by that fire downstairs, if I won't be in the way."

"Of course not. I'll get Shea to make you some of his mulled wine. Meet you downstairs." She carried her sweaters to the other room, then ran down to the kitchen where Shea was putting short ribs and sauerkraut in the oven. It was her father's favorite meal.

"I had short ribs in the restaurant freezer," he explained as she stared in surprise, wondering how he'd managed that without warning. "He looks a little haggard, don't you think?"

She spread her arms and went to the counter where Zachary lay in his carrier, a distinct odor wafting from him. "Dad's lost everything."

"No," Shea said, also putting potatoes in to bake. "I mean, like, maybe it's something…physical."

She turned to him at that, sudden concern warring with her long-standing grudge. "He didn't complain of anything."

"Well, he wouldn't, would he? He knows how you feel about your mother and the showgirl, and he's a guest here."

She considered that with a worried look and picked up the carrier. "I'm going to change Zack. Save me some wine, please."

"Sure thing."

Adam walked into the kitchen as Samantha left. "What's this I heard about mulled wine?" he asked.

Shea poured him a glass mug full. "It's good for the deep-down winter chill. I'm glad you came, Adam. I know Sam's happy."

Adam nodded and leaned against the counter to sip the brew. "This is wonderful. Maybe a little different than the usual. What's in it?"

"Cranberry juice along with the spices." Shea poured himself a cup.

"Sinfully delicious." Adam grew introspective with another sip. "I thought when I came home and found Sam gone that she just didn't want anything more to do with me since I turned her into a pauper. Then I checked my messages—a little belatedly—and discovered she'd left several."

"I don't think she's upset about the business," Shea said carefully.

Adam smiled. "I know what she's upset about. She always makes that very clear. But I may have redeemed myself with the job."

"The job?"

"Didn't she tell you? With Condor News in San Francisco," Adam said. "An old competitor of mine. But the publisher has great respect for Sam and just lost his own news director."

Shea felt his mouth go dry, but he asked casually, "She taking it?"

Adam shrugged. "I can't imagine she won't." He closed his eyes suddenly and groaned softly. "Oh, no. I wasn't thinking, was I? Although, when I got her the job, I didn't know about the two of you."

Shea put his cup down. The wine suddenly tasted bitter. "Going back on January 2 has been her plan all along," he said, trying to appear casual. "She was planning to start job hunting right away, but you've saved her that step."

"But, what about…?"

"Don't worry, Adam. We're working on it. Go relax by the fire. You need something to eat?"

"No, I'm good. Thanks."

Shea stoked up the fire in the fireplace and left Adam in the big chair. Then he went back into the kitchen to wonder why Samantha hadn't told him about the job.

Did it mean she was undecided? Or that she had decided and he simply hadn't figured into the choice?

He heard Samantha come downstairs, saw her give the baby to her father. Then she came into the kitchen for her wine.

He started a fresh pot of coffee. "I'm going to the restaurant," he said, "to check my produce order for the dinner." *And to wonder what will happen to my life without you and Zack.* "You need anything?"

"I'm fine." She smiled warmly, lovingly. "Anything you need me to do to the dinner while you're gone?"

He kissed her lightly. "Yes. Don't touch it."

He ran across to Delancey's and sat at the small desk in a corner of the kitchen, where he took his notes out of the middle drawer and began to recalculate his figures. He hoped that would keep him from worrying about Samantha's job offer.

He'd barely begun when there was a knock at the kitchen door, followed by Felicia calling cheerfully, "Shea? Shea, are you in here?"

He wondered whether she'd go away if he remained silent.

That option was taken from him the next moment when she walked into the room and closed the door behind her. "Shea? Samantha told me you were in here."

She headed for the dining room, unaware of him in the corner behind the door. He considered letting her go on, then darting out the back door while she explored the front of the restaurant.

But she turned around and spotted him. "Well, why didn't you *say* something?" she scolded, heading toward him in black leggings and an oversize pink sweater.

He stood, then pulled up a stool for her beside his desk. "Hi, Felicia," he said courteously. "What's up?"

She wrapped her arms around him. "Figures you won't believe!" she said excitedly, holding him a moment too long for his comfort.

He caught her arms and pushed her away on the pretext of getting to the point of her visit. "What figures? Here, sit." He eased her onto the stool, then resumed his desk chair.

"We sold out the dinner three days ago," she said, retrieving several sheets of paper from her purse on the floor and flashing him many columns of names. "We were thrilled! Ninety-six hundred dollars."

"Great," he said, pleased. Then he felt called upon to remind her, "That's minus the food."

"French River Grocery is donating the food," she said. "The owner's mother is one of our residents."

"You're kidding."

"I'm not. But there's more."

He didn't know whether to be pleased or worried.

"More what?"

"More reservations! The families of the residents have found out, including those who don't even live here, and they want to support the venture by buying tickets and seeing the plans firsthand. We've almost enough reservations to...to..."

He saw it coming and braced himself. She couldn't quite make herself say it for fear of his reaction, so he helped her out. "To have two seatings?" he asked.

"Yes!" she told him, clearly relieved he'd said it for her. "I can only imagine how much work that'll be, but—think of it! The store is willing to donate that much—I checked. That's almost twenty thousand dollars for the seniors! Plus all the fame and applause that'll come to Delancey's for this."

"That's not why we're doing it." Well, not entirely.

"I know, but it's not going to hurt, is it?"

"No. You'll have to give me a day to talk to my volunteers about it. They're going to be run ragged."

"I know. Can you let me know tomorrow night?"

He'd call a meeting at the restaurant in the morning. "Sure."

She leaped off the stool and perched on the edge of his desk. "You can come by with your answer when you close the restaurant tomorrow."

"You intend to work that late?" He pretended to misunderstand the suggestion.

She stepped away from his desk and lowered herself unceremoniously onto his lap. "Of course not," she breathed against his ear. "Come by the house. You're free. I'm free…"

He pulled her arms from around his neck and looked into her eyes. He saw hurt there, and almost regretted that she seemed to have expected his rejection. He knew what that felt like and hated inflicting it on someone else.

"I'm not free, Felicia," he said firmly.

She held his gaze. "Samantha said…"

"I know. She's given you the impression that she isn't asking anything of me despite the baby. But I have ideas of my own on how this is all going to work out." It was entirely possible Samantha didn't share them, but that was beside the point.

"I see." She stood, picked up her purse off the floor and put it on the stool. She made a production of stuffing the list back into it. Her lips trembled and her hands shook.

"Why do you keep working on me," he asked gently, "when Henry Warren follows you everywhere and is clearly in love with you? Why do you keep behaving as though all you have to sell is your body, when you're creative and smart and a very good mayor, particularly in a crunch? You've done a wonderful job on this project with very little time."

She dug a tissue out of her purse, dabbed at her eyes, then her nose. "Everyone in town thinks I'm a joke."

"No. Everyone thinks you should hold yourself to a little higher standard than you do. I understand this town loved your father very much and expected good things from you."

She shook her head at him then, her misery clear in her eyes. "And he loved them. He just didn't like me very much."

She paced away from him, weeping.

He took a bottle of chardonnay from the shelf and poured a glass for her. She seemed surprised by the kindness, then accepted the glass with a nod and a raspy "Thank you."

He waited for her to explain about her father.

"Mom was a beauty queen from the Midwest," she said, leaning against the worktable. "She hated it here. She wasn't considered royalty the way she was at home. You know how Oregonians are. Your reputation lives or dies on how you handle your adversity. She lost a baby, my father lost a lot of money to poor investment advice and we moved from a big house on a hill to an apartment above a store."

She sighed, her eyes unfocused as the child in her remembered. "She left us, and I had the misfortune of looking just like her, so every time my father saw me, he saw her. He treated me as though I wasn't there."

Having had loving parents, having a child of his own that he could never blame for someone else's sins, Shea could only imagine her anguish.

"But I discovered at about thirteen," she went on after clearing her throat, "that my looks were appreciated by my peers. At least the male ones." Her glance told him she understood what that suggested about her. "Terrible, I know. But I was desperate for attention, for words of affection, for touch. By the time I was old enough to understand that what I'd earned was not at all what I'd set out to get, my reputation was established."

"But you got elected mayor," Shea reminded her. "People have another vision of you besides what you think they see. And they've rallied behind you in this. You've accomplished something special—you started it all by yourself, knew how to call in help to make it work, and you *did.* Everyone fell into step behind you. That's a sign of a good leader. That won't go unnoticed."

"Henry won't notice," she said, pausing to sip at the wine. She swallowed, then took another long sip. "He tendered his resignation from the council last week. He's gone to Corvallis."

"I'm sorry. He seemed to really care for you."

"I guess it took me too long to catch on. Just before you and your brothers arrived in French Creek, I'd been thinking about pulling my life together, giving up the easy fixes for tough choices. And one of those choices was to find a husband the town respected so that they'd be forced to take a second look at me and reevaluate." She smiled ruefully, finished the last sip of wine and put the glass on the worktable. "And along came the Delancey brothers. *Three* of you! And you had all the qualities the town admired. Certainly I'd be able to snag one of you." She laughed and shouldered her purse. "Ah, well. I'll just have to keep a lookout at the dinner. There's bound to be someone among the out-of-towners who won't have any preconceived notions about me."

"Have you explained all this to Henry?" Shea asked, following her as she moved toward the door.

She opened it and turned to him. "I haven't told anyone," she replied. "Most people in town were friends of my father's and, deep down, I know I can't blame the choices I made on anyone but me. Call me about the two seatings, okay?"

"I will."

"Bye."

Shea watched her climb into her car and drive off, thinking that at least he wasn't feeling sorry for *himself* anymore.

CHAPTER FOURTEEN

SHEA MADE ENOUGH gingerbread dough and royal icing to replace every building on the compound with gingerbread.

In the middle of the afternoon on Tuesday, with Adam feeding Zachary by the fire and Samantha sitting across the breakfast-nook table from Shea, he studied the mock-up he'd made of a gingerbread house. It had four walls and a roof, and he'd cut out windows and scored a door.

"We have a major production problem," he said, indicating the array of candies he'd bought to decorate the model house.

"The candies that make it look so spectacular," she guessed, "take too much time to apply."

"Right. And now that the family and the staff have agreed to do two seatings, we're going to need a hundred and ninety-two of them instead of ninety-six, which would have been tough enough in the first place. We have to do something to simplify while still making them look fantastic."

"I've got it!" Samantha ran upstairs to the box of leftover beads and baubles she'd used to construct her ornaments for the fair. In the box was a craft magazine she'd bought for inspiration.

She ran back downstairs again, delighted to have the solution to Shea's problem. They were getting along well enough, and he'd been true to his promise not to push her about marriage. But there was the smallest degree of underlying tension in his dealings with her. He was never anything but kind and tolerant, still got up with her when the baby fussed, still did more than his share to help with Zachary despite the extra demands on him brought about by the Magi Dinner. She couldn't define what was wrong; she just knew something was.

She sat down opposite him, flipped through the magazine until she found the right page, then held it open for him.

Some clever artist had made a lantern in the traditional gingerbread-house shape using cookie cutters to make decoration holes in the walls and the roof sections, and placed a tea light on the bottom that could be lit with a fireplace match.

He looked across the table at her in amazement. "That's it. The cookie cutters will simplify the design part, and turning the house into a lantern makes it particularly special. You're a genius!"

She rolled her eyes heavenward. "Seems to me I've told you that repeatedly."

"I guess I'll have to start listening. I may have to go to McMinnville to find big cookie cutters."

She shook her head. "You only have to go to Rachel's. She made cookies for Veronica's kids—Santa faces, stars, angels, holly, Christmas trees, you name it."

He studied her seriously for a moment, his arms folded on the open magazine, then he smiled. "You're not a bad troubleshooter, either."

"Genius troubleshooter." She waved her hand in the air as though putting the words up in lights. "Wow.

I've come a long way from the spoiled socialite you considered incapable of living a real life.''

He stood and came around the table to lean over her, one knee on the bench, and kiss her with a fervor that made her wonder if she'd imagined that little gap between them.

"Come on," he said. "We're going to give this a try. Would you go ask Rachel if we can use her cookie cutters, while I cut out the walls and roof?''

"Sure."

He caught her arm before she could start away and reached into a lower cupboard for a shallow square container. "I'll just fill this with leftover short ribs and sauerkraut you can take her as a bribe."

More than an hour later, four walls with cut-out Christmas-tree shapes and four roofs pierced with star shapes cooled on a rack.

"I'm probably pushing this," Shea said as Samantha and Adam with Zachary stood over him, "but we'll try one to get an idea how this'll work. The pieces will have to cool longer than this."

"You don't think a lit candle will melt the icing?" Samantha asked as he used icing as a glue to hold the walls together.

"Usually, this stuff would keep real walls in place," he replied, holding up the pastry bag he'd made in a minute with a sheet of parchment paper rolled into a cone and a star tip attached to the narrow end. He squeezed the wide end with his free hand to move the icing out the tip. "But we'll test it to be sure. Do we even have a tea light?''

"There's one in that brass nativity light I bought at the craft fair." She went to the mantel to retrieve it, also snatched the fireplace matches, and brought everything to the table.

The four walls glued together, Shea applied the roof sections so that they left a small hole at the top.

"What'll we use for a base?" Samantha looked around the kitchen.

He pointed to a cutting board hanging on a hook by a leather thong. "The board," he said. "We'll just glue the tea light to it with icing so it's nothing permanent. I guess we'll have to use boards for the centerpieces. We can cover them with decorative foil or something."

He talked as he worked, gluing the little metal cup containing the candle to the cutting board, then placing the lantern over it. He then decorated all the joints, making a swirl pattern with the star tip.

When he stepped back to take a look, Samantha was amazed by how pretty it was.

"Now the test," he said, reaching for a match. He lit it, stuck it through one of the openings in the house and lit the candle.

Samantha flipped off the kitchen light.

The lantern house was beautiful, the patterns glowing brightly in the darkness.

"Well, if you two aren't the smartest pair this side of Woodward and Bernstein," Adam said. "Your guests are going to be impressed."

"They're paying one hundred bucks a pop," Shea said. "We want to make sure they get their money's worth—even if it is for charity."

Adam nodded. "I've always felt that way about the seventy-five cents invested in a newspaper. The difference is, people usually get mad when they read the news, but they're happy when you give them something wonderful to eat. Maybe *you* should employ *me*."

Shea laughed at him over the glittering gingerbread lantern house. "I'd be happy to. Can you cook?"

Adam shook his head. "Not a lick. But I did wait tables in college. What are these lanterns for?"

Samantha explained about the fire and the many fund-raising efforts to help rebuild. "Everyone's so eager to come to Shea's dinner that he's been asked to hold two seatings. His staff and his family are all volunteering their time to wait tables and bus and whatever else needs to be done."

"Including these centerpieces."

"Right."

"Well, I'm not very coordinated when it comes to something artistic like these things." He pointed to the light. "But I can wait tables."

"You're hired," Shea said, taking the baby from him. "And you didn't come here to spend all your time baby-sitting. Tomorrow Sam can introduce you to Armand Beauchamp, who used to be the winemaker here until his daughter took over. He's my oldest brother's father-in-law. He can show you around."

"Good. I'd like that." He glanced from Samantha to Shea. "I'm glad you're holding no grudges about that job offer."

For a moment Shea thought he meant the job he'd secured for Samantha, and he waited for her to look sheepish or guilty for not having mentioned it.

But she didn't.

"I never meant to offend you," Adam continued. "I thought you might enjoy cooking for the executive—"

Shea cut off his apology with a shake of his head, realizing he meant the job he'd offered him in San Francisco.

"I was flattered, not insulted by the offer. I just had

to prove to myself that although I'd lost my business and almost everything else, I still had what it took to do what I wanted to do." He caught Samantha's shoulder and pulled her to him. He smiled at Samantha. "My mistake was underestimating Sam's ability to see things through with me."

He hoped that might prompt her into realizing she had something to tell him.

It didn't.

"Yeah," Adam said moodily, staring at the flickering lights. "That was a year of mistakes all around."

SAMANTHA HANDED HER FATHER a fresh towel and washcloth that night as he prepared for bed. "Are you feeling all right?" she asked bluntly, leaning in the doorway. "I know you've dealt well with a lot of...stress, but are you sure your body's handling it well?"

He smiled directly at her. "I'm in good health. Just getting old."

"Have you had a checkup lately?"

He laughed. "Just three weeks ago, as a matter of fact. I'm fine."

"Good." She straightened and started to back away.

"Well. Good night. See you in the morning. Can I have a good-night kiss?" he asked. "You always had to have yours when you were little."

She'd been keeping her distance since her spontaneous leap into his arms in town. She wasn't sure why.

She went into his arms, hugged him and kissed his cheek. "Good night, Dad," she said, liking the way it felt to be bear-hugged again after what had seemed such a long time.

That brought instantly to mind thoughts of her

mother with her smart mouth but gentle touch. She
lingered on it a moment, let it hurt, then let it slip away.
Despite several attempts to reach her, she'd failed, always a city behind Audrey Haskell's continuous tour
of the world.

"Good night, baby," her father said.

"Do you think he is sick?" Samantha asked Shea
as they climbed into bed. "You're right. He does look
haggard. He said he had a checkup three weeks ago.
Why would he have done that if he was feeling well?
And those things aren't always accurate, you know.
You're always hearing about someone who gets a clean
bill of health and drops dead the next day of—"

Shea put a hand over her mouth to silence her. "He
does look haggard, but not as though he's at death's
door. And I imagine if he had a checkup three weeks
ago and he's been declared in good health, he probably
is."

"Maybe he's lying to me."

"That's possible."

She sat up in bed. "Maybe that's the only reason he
came. Maybe he's...dying."

Shea caught her around the waist and pulled her back
down to her pillow. "Sam, stop it. If you think he isn't
telling you the truth, just be his daughter." When she
blinked in question, he explained. "Let him know that
even though you resent what he did to your family,
you still care and you'd like to hear his side. Then he'll
be willing to confide in you."

She settled into Shea's shoulder, thinking that that
sounded like a good idea. "Thanks."

"Sure. At your service. Eighteen-hour cooking and
counseling."

She raised her head to tease. "Only eighteen?"

"To get twenty-four-hour service, you have to be my wife."

She kissed his chin. "Good night, Shea."

He kissed the top of her head, apparently following the no-pushing philosophy. "Good night, Sam."

SHEA HEARD THE QUIET when he awoke to near daylight. Daylight! The baby had slept through the night!

Panic assailed him. Zachary was too young to sleep through the night!

Shea leaped out of bed, noticing that Samantha was already up, and became convinced that something terrible had happened. He ran the small distance to the nursery, refusing to acknowledge all the horrible reasons that might have kept Zachary silent.

The bassinet was empty. Certainly Samantha would have shouted for him had the baby had a problem.

He ran downstairs, expecting to find her sitting on the sofa with the baby as she often did very early in the morning, taking an occasional sip of coffee while Zachary guzzled a bottle.

But she wasn't there. And she wasn't in the kitchen. Had she left for the job in San Francisco already?

He went to the window in the back door, checking to see if the car was still there. His search for it was momentarily distracted by the gray-blue of the early-morning sky—and the white stuff falling from it. Snow!

He stared at it for a moment in disbelief. He'd been so consumed for the past few days with Adam's arrival and plans for the Magi Dinner that he hadn't watched the news or heard a weather report.

A considerable amount of snow had collected on the

ground, and on what he could see of the B and B, and on the car—which was right where he'd left it.

With renewed worry he walked back into the living room and instinctively went to the window. Then he saw her in the garish glow of the compound lights, wearing his hat, her coat and holding the baby in his snowsuit. She was catching flakes on her mittened hands and showing them to Zack, a bright smile on her face.

Shea leaned his forehead against the window with a *thunk,* his heart softening and reshaping itself into something no longer his alone. What would he do, he wondered in barbed anguish, if she didn't stay?

Unable to answer his own question, he ran upstairs to pull on clothes, then went out to join her.

"Hi!" she exclaimed, her face wreathed in smiles. "Snow!"

He was surprised that she was so thrilled. "I thought you went to Gstaad with your parents all the time as a child."

"I did." She blinked up at the falling stuff, gasping when she caught a few flakes down her neck. "But then it was planned. I mean, it was a skiing trip. We knew there would be snow. We never get it in San Francisco, and from what Colette told me, you didn't have any in French River last year, and yet here it is—a wonderful surprise!"

Shea wiped snow off her collar, then pulled it up and fastened the tab that held it in place. Her hair, tucked into the coat, was silky against his fingers.

Shouts and squeals of laughter came from down the compound, and they turned to see Veronica running toward them, Mike in pursuit with a snowball. He threw it and hit her squarely in the back.

"Nice way to treat a pregnant woman!" she admonished laughingly.

"When our child is old enough to throw snowballs at you," he said, wrapping an arm around her as they approached Shea and Samantha and Zachary, "you'll have experience dodging them. Hi, guys! What a treat, huh?"

"Yeah," Shea replied, a few repercussions of the beautiful snow beginning to occur to him. "You hear a weather report? How long is this supposed to last?"

"Snow all day, I think," he said, "and a cold front that'll keep it on the ground for a few days. You worried about the dinner?"

Shea nodded. "People with four-wheel drives will get up our hill, but others won't. And if it rains and this turns to ice, we'll be in deep oatmeal. We'll have to be ready to reschedule or lose all the food."

"Oatmeal?" Veronica laughed.

"The chef's equivalent of the other stuff." Shea spotted movement at the far end of the compound. Six figures bundled up for the weather headed toward them. "Hey," he said, pointing in their direction. "It's Tate and Colette and all the girls. Susan and Sarah are here. Tate must be happy."

"If anyone deserves to be…" Mike said, taking Veronica's hand and starting off in their direction.

"I hope they like Megan and Katie," Samantha mused as she and Shea followed. "They were so worried."

"I think that's a moot point," he said, pointing toward the six figures. "Look. The taller one is Sarah and she seems to have Megan by the hand. And Katie's hanging on Susan."

Samantha smiled. "Thank goodness."

When they drew closer, Susan ran into Mike's arms and Sarah flung herself at Shea. As they all converged into a knot near the Christmas tree in the middle of the compound, the girls switched uncles and Tate made introductions.

"Wow!" Susan said. She had bright brown eyes under the rolled brim of a very chic all-weather hat. "We didn't have any aunts when we left for Paris and now we have two!"

Samantha accepted her hug, considering it unnecessary to correct that inaccurate detail. "And I didn't have any nieces and now I have four!"

Sarah hugged Veronica, then Samantha, and asked if she could hold the baby. Sarah also had dark eyes, but she was a little more reserved and apparently less fashion-conscious. She wore a simple red wool hat with a pom-pom and no affectation. She seemed to have no idea she was absolutely beautiful.

Katie reached up to tickle Zachary's cheek and make him smile. All the girls laughed when it worked.

"So, he's our cousin, right?" Susan asked.

"Right," Tate replied. "And Uncle Mike and Aunt Vee are about to make another one for you."

"This is *so* cool!" Susan said. "We have some really great stuff in Paris, but no relatives. Here we have tons of them."

Tate pointed to the cottage. "That's where your step-grandparents live. "We'll visit them when we're sure they're up. We're on a tour of the compound," Tate explained in an aside.

"When you're finished," Shea said, "why don't you come to the house and I'll do up Belgian waffles for everyone."

"You used to make them for us when you were in

college,'' Sarah remembered, ''and you came to visit for Christmas.''

''I can't believe you remember that. You were about six.''

She nodded. ''I remember because Mom tried to make them after that and couldn't, so I'd have them every time we went out to breakfast. But they never tasted like yours.''

''Okay, that earns you two,'' he said. ''I'll hold the baby so you can enjoy your tour.''

''Can't we keep him till we get back?'' she asked. ''We never had a cousin before.''

''We'll take good care of him,'' Tate assured Shea and Samantha. ''Don't worry. You'll get him back.''

Shea stopped by the restaurant for frozen strawberries, whipping cream and extra utensils. When he and Samantha returned to the house, Adam stood in the middle of the living room, pulling on his jacket.

''I was starting to worry about you,'' he said, looking relieved and shrugging off the jacket. ''Is everything all right?''

''We just went out to see the snow.'' Samantha reached for his jacket and hung it back in the guest closet. ''We ran into Shea's brothers, who were doing the same thing.''

Shea explained about Susan and Sarah and picking them up at the airport yesterday. ''They have your grandson and you may have to do some fast talking to get him back. Want a glass of orange juice?''

''I do, but you don't have to wait on me,'' Adam said, following him and Samantha into the kitchen.

''I have an ulterior motive.'' Shea put his burden on the counter, then reached into the cupboard for glasses.

"I'm giving you orange juice and then I'm putting you to work. They're all coming over for breakfast."

"Oh, good. A test of my table-waiting skills before the big dinner. That's probably safest."

"I can't believe you want to do this," Samantha said to Shea, carrying the cream to the stand-up mixer in the corner, "when you have to go to work in a couple of hours and you have all the details for the dinner to contend with."

"It's only waffles. And people are going to work all day making gingerbread lanterns, so I have to make sure they're properly fueled."

Samantha marveled at his attitude. He made it sound as though he were making the kind of waffles you popped into the toaster.

"Assuming my count is correct," she said, "there'll be fourteen of us if they pick up Armand and Rachel on the way. Do we have a card table or something to add on to the dining room table?"

"I'll get one. Adam, can you give me a hand?" Samantha saw her father's hesitation, followed quickly by a forced smile. "Sure," he said.

Samantha exchanged a look with Shea, thinking about his suggestion that her father was ill.

"I'll do it," she said, catching her father's arm as he would have started toward the nook.

"No," he said firmly, pulling away from her. "I'll do it. You've had a baby recently..."

Shea stood firmly in his path. "I'll wait for one of my brothers. What have *you* had, Adam?" he asked kindly. "Come on. You're among family."

Samantha held her breath while her father regarded Shea, then her, then Shea again with a sigh of resignation. He shifted his weight and leaned wearily against the counter. "Prostate surgery," he said.

Cold fear spread its wings in Samantha's stomach. "When?" she asked.

"A few weeks ago," he replied. "When the press was having such a field day with us. I was relieved to be out of the limelight, but I'm sorry you took the brunt of it."

She remembered her resentful thoughts that he'd been hiding somewhere with Legs. Guilt tore at her, biting her eyes, sanding her throat. She suddenly realized the question she should have asked first.

"Was it cancerous?"

"No," he said in apparent amazement. "It was benign. And the way things were going for me at that point, I couldn't believe it. I was prepared for the worst."

She walked up to within an inch of him, looking into his eyes. "Are you telling me the truth?"

"Yes," he replied. "I am telling you the truth. I feel good, except that trips to the bathroom are still not comfortable and I'm not supposed to lift anything." He widened his eyes in mockery of her stare. "Satisfied?"

"No." Now that her fears for his life were soothed, anger took over her emotions. "Why didn't you *tell* me?" she demanded. "You're my father, and you've left me out of every major decision you've made since Mom walked out. I suppose Legs was at your bedside?"

"Sam..." Shea cautioned.

She ignored him. "Now she stands in place of your wife *and* your daughter?"

Adam ran a hand over his face as he shook his head.

"Legs—" He closed his eyes and groaned. "Wendy has been out of my life since before I was diagnosed."

"And when was that?"

"Shortly after you had the baby."

"So when you told me to explain to the employees and you disappeared, you weren't with Legs. You were—"

"Having surgery. Right. I tried to hold it off, but I was in major misery."

"I can't *believe* you didn't tell me!"

He spread his arms helplessly. "I knew how you felt. And because of the timing, you were sort of abandoned to the wolves. It was easier to just keep it to myself."

Samantha stormed off to the linen closet in search of tablecloths, afraid of what she might say if she remained to argue.

Once the card table was set up, Colette helped Samantha spread tablecloths and distribute silverware.

Shea's waffles were heavenly, and he spent most of the time in the kitchen turning out more.

Samantha's father was warmly welcomed by everyone and appeared to enjoy himself.

Samantha, however, was coming to her wit's end as she poured coffee and carried plates back and forth.

She'd thought that reconnecting with her father would help her deal with her fear of marriage, but so far all it had done was make her feel even more alienated, as though he hadn't trusted her enough to confide a life-and-death issue.

What was worse, Shea watched her as she came and went and seemed to detect her change of mood.

He reacted to her explanation for it with impatience—clearly in a mood of his own.

"Well, he didn't tell me!" she complained while

Shea dropped a waffle onto a small pile warming in the oven. "You should be mad at him, not at me."

"Unlike you," he said, pointing to her with a spatula, "I don't react to everything with anger. I'm not mad at him and I'm not mad at you. I'm just getting really tired of your attitude."

"What attitude?" she asked, hurt.

"You think you're the only one with issues? And that they all have to be understood and met by everyone else? Okay, he should have told you, but maybe if you'd listened to his side in the first place, he might have been willing to confide in you. And you might remember that you're the one who put the wrong spin on everything without any real evidence."

"How nice of you," she said stiffly, "to try to help me feel better. You're the master of judging without evidence, so I wouldn't act so superior."

He cast her a grim glance as he spritzed the waffle iron with cooking oil, then poured more batter onto it. "Maybe he's not the only one who isn't sharing evidence."

She repeated that to herself, trying to make sense of it. She failed. "What are you talking about?"

"Why don't you just take the waffles out," he said impatiently.

Now thoroughly confused as well as angry, she exited with the plate, forcing a smile for the cheerful family around the table. With their ruddy cheeks and winter sweaters, they looked like an ad for a ski vacation.

She felt as though this morning's revelations had booted her out of their cheerful company.

And this day had had such a beautiful beginning. Right now, it couldn't get any worse.

That was when a rumble sounded in the distance and grew louder and louder with each passing second.

Avalanche! she thought. Then common sense took over. Of course not. They were at the top of the hill, and there wasn't enough snow to slide down in an angry sheet.

Tate and Mike got up from the table to investigate and Shea wandered out of the kitchen.

Samantha went to stand between the two brothers as rotating lights flashed through the window.

"It's a snowplow," Tate said in surprise. "Did you call for one?" he asked Mike.

Mike shook his head. "Wasn't me."

The snowplow stopped and the driver got out and ran around to the other side of the vehicle to open the door. He reached inside to lift down a figure in a winter-white pantsuit and low-heeled shoes.

Susan, now peering out between Samantha and Shea, said with great admiration, "Carolina Herrera!"

"Who's that?" Tate asked. "And what's she doing here?"

Susan caught Samantha's eye and smirked at her father's lack of fashion savvy. "*That's* not Carolina Herrera, Daddy. That woman is *wearing* Carolina Herrera. She's a fashion designer."

"Oh."

The driver held the woman's arm as he walked her up the slope to the foot of the porch steps.

The woman shook the driver's hand, gave him a folded bill; he tipped his cap and walked around the plow to climb back in.

The woman turned to look up at the house. She was beautiful, her highlighted blond hair none the worse for her unconventional mode of travel.

Samantha felt herself go weak with a powerful combination of happiness and trepidation.

"I'm looking for Samantha Haskell!" the woman shouted as Mike opened the door and stepped out onto the porch. "I'm her mother!"

CHAPTER FIFTEEN

"MOM!" SAMANTHA WAITED on the porch while Mike went down to help her mother up the snowy steps.

Audrey Haskell cleared the top step and opened her arms to Samantha.

"Sammie," she said, hugging her fiercely. "I thought I'd *never* get here. The cab wasn't running, but a priest happened to be at the terminal, heard my tale of woe and got me a lift on the snowplow." She drew a breath and went on. "I thought I'd have to wait until I died before you'd get in touch with me, Sam. And then, of course, I wouldn't have the opportunity to *say* anything! Like, 'How *dare* you have my grandson and not even let me know you were pregnant?'"

Samantha drew her inside. "I didn't tell you because when you left you said you didn't want anything more to do with me until I came to my senses and quit Haskell Media. But just before Zachary was born, I tried to reach you. My message is probably still chasing you across the globe."

She looked wonderful, Samantha thought, if a little pinched from the cold at the moment. "Didn't you bring a coat?"

Her mother made a self-deprecating face. "I forgot it in the cab that took me from the Portland airport to the bus terminal. But never mind about that. Where *is* my grandson? Oh, dear."

She glanced around the room to see many pairs of eyes staring at her. "What am I interrupting?"

"Just an impromptu family breakfast," Samantha said.

"Whose family?"

"Mine." Shea appeared, Zachary in his arms, and handed the baby to his grandmother. "Good to see you, Audrey."

"Shea!" Audrey took the baby gently and held him up to gaze into his face.

Zachary gazed back, his eyes wide, his little mouth working.

"Is this the most beautiful child we've ever seen?" she asked, putting the baby to her shoulder and pressing him to her. "Oh, my gosh. I'm a grandmother. What a Christmas present!" She smiled at Shea. "Yours?"

"Yes."

"Do I also have a son-in-law?"

"Not technically, no."

She turned to Samantha questioningly, then turned away. "Well, give us a hug," she ordered Shea, unwilling to loosen her hold on the baby. Shea wrapped his arms around her. "Welcome to Delancey Vineyards, Audrey," he said. "I'm so glad you're here. Come and meet my family."

Samantha waited for her mother to notice her father, but so many other faces claimed Audrey's attention and she was concentrating so hard, following along as Shea introduced the clan one by one and told her who belonged to whom.

"And I believe you know this gentleman," Shea said as they reached Adam at the far end of the table.

Adam stood, waiting a little uncertainly for her reaction.

Samantha saw her mother's face blanche, then fill with color, as she tried to maintain her equilibrium. "The face is familiar," she said after a moment. "You've been on *America's Most Wanted,* haven't you?"

Samantha put her hand to her eyes. So much for her hope that this meeting would unfold with some modicum of dignity.

She was grateful when her father reacted with a polite smile. "Hello, Audie. You're looking very well."

"Thank you," she replied, angling her chin as she studied him narrowly, as if through the lower half of bifocals. "I wish I could say the same for you. You look terrible."

"Thank *you,*" he said. "You could always be counted on for the gracious rejoinder. Can I get you some juice?"

"No, thank you." Audrey turned to Shea, who stood behind her. "Would you see if you can get the snowplow back, please? There's no way I can stay here if—"

Samantha didn't wait to hear the end of her mother's statement. She took Zachary from her and handed him to Sarah. She pointed her mother to the kitchen. "I'd like to talk to you, please."

"I don't think—" Audrey began.

"Right now, if you don't mind," she said pleasantly, but with a look that promised severe retribution if she failed to cooperate. "Dad?"

"I was very civil," he argued. "I don't see why I should—"

"Because I *said* so!" she snarled, then pulled herself

together. "Megan, Katie, would you take them to the breakfast nook, please?"

The girls were on their feet immediately, eager to do that small chore for her. And with such guides, she knew her parents wouldn't refuse to cooperate.

Samantha smiled apologetically at everyone at the tables as the four trooped into the kitchen. "I'm embarrassed that we spoiled your breakfast," she said. "They have a long-standing feud that I'm determined to work out during this holiday."

"Don't mind us," Tate said. "We're accustomed to yelling and carrying-on. We do a lot of it ourselves."

"You're just being nice." She patted his shoulder gratefully. "I've never seen it."

He patted her hand. "You just got here. Real feelings are noisy, but everybody's got them."

"Does anybody need more coffee?" she asked.

Mike stood and pushed her toward the kitchen. "Go handle your folks. I'll get the coffee."

Samantha sat down beside her mother on one side of the nook while her father took the other. Shea set the table and brought Audrey a glass of juice.

"Do you have vodka for that?" Audrey asked.

"No vodka," Samantha told Shea. Then she turned to her mother. "I want you to explain to Daddy what happened when you and Fabrizio were found in that little desert town near Palm Springs."

Her mother tried to get out of the nook. "I am not staying here. I—"

"Yes, you are," Samantha said. "We have one hundred ninety-two gingerbread lantern houses to make and we need every pair of helping hands we can get."

Even in her distress, her mother blinked in confusion. "Gingerbread what?"

"I'll explain later," Samantha said. "You were going to tell Daddy what happened the night you went missing."

Audrey retreated into a corner of the nook and glared at both of them. "He knows what happened. Fabrizio and I planned a night of wild passion."

"*Is* that what happened?" Samantha glared back. "Or is that just what it looked like?"

"Ask your father. He seemed to think they were the same thing."

"You told me that was what happened," Adam said without looking at her.

"No, I didn't!" Audrey cried, suddenly exploding. "You told *me* that was what happened."

"You're saying it wasn't?" He turned to her, his tone openly disbelieving.

Samantha made a quieting gesture with her hands.

"You probably paid the repair bill," Audrey retorted, lowering her voice only slightly. "And you're the one who insisted on keeping that ancient limo. Is a stuck thermostat usually a planned occurrence? I don't think so. Fabrizio had driven you the day before and everything was fine. Do you actually think he made the limo overheat so he could strand us in the desert and have his way with me?"

Her father's expression remained fierce, but she saw him swallow. "What are you saying?" he asked.

"What difference does it make? You haven't listened to me in the past ten years, and when I finally thought I had your attention and that you might want to talk things through, give me a little more of your time, your answer was to divorce me. I can't imagine you'll listen to me now."

"So, you didn't sleep with Fabrizio?" Samantha insisted.

Audrey groaned theatrically. "He was handsome and muscular and a good driver. But my taste in men runs toward intelligence above physical appearance." She cast a dark look at Adam. "Although sometimes you can be fooled."

Samantha felt enormously relieved to have her mother say it aloud.

Her father, apparently, didn't take quite the same comfort in the words. "Then why was he naked in your motel room when the police and I found you?" he demanded.

"He wasn't naked," her mother corrected. "He was wearing a towel—because *you* dragged him out of the bathroom!"

"Why was he showering in your room?"

"He wasn't. When you found us, I was in his room. I'd gone to get sandwiches while he showered and I'd very innocently walked in to leave his on his bedside table, when you stormed in like some nearsighted Victorian husband.

"However." She folded her arms and looked haughtily across the table. "You and Wendy Merriweather were a different story, though, weren't you? You wanted to get back at me and took up with a showgirl. That's so nineteenth century, Adam." Her mother was being offhand and above it all, but the pain in her eyes was clearly visible.

"Well, damn it all, Audie," her father said, pounding a fist on the table, "can't you just be honest instead of staging your little dramas!"

"I didn't stage anything! It was an accident!"

"Well, why didn't you tell me that?"

"Because you never listened! You just ranted and raved and left! Next thing I knew, I had divorce papers!"

"I'd have listened to that! I was devastated! I'd have taken any crumb of a suggestion that you still loved me!"

Everyone in the room was surprised that he'd spoken those words, including Adam himself. He and Audrey held each other's gaze for an interminable moment. Audrey finally lowered her eyes. "Maybe you should have told *me* that," she said. She took another sip of juice.

Samantha noticed that her hand trembled.

Shea stopped in the doorway, holding two plates with hot pads. "Is it safe to come in?" he asked.

Samantha slipped out of the nook. "Sure it is. They're about to discuss their problems like two reasonable adults."

Shea put down the plates, left the room and returned with a bowl of strawberries and one of whipped cream. "Eat while you're talking," he advised. "Good food's a soothing influence." He pointed to Samantha, who stood by. "And please remember that I have to live with the result of what you decide to do with your futures. We're going upstairs to move the baby into our room so you can have the nursery, Audrey."

He grasped Samantha's arm and drew her with him as he left the room.

She caught the molding and leaned back to say, "Tell her about your surgery, Daddy."

As she let herself be led away, she had the satisfaction of hearing her mother ask a little anxiously, "What surgery? When?"

Shea would not allow her to eavesdrop.

He commissioned Mike and Tate to bring one of the beds down from the attic. Colette had already gone in search of bedding.

"I have to go to work," Shea said. "Will you supervise the making of the lanterns? I was thinking we could use the dining-room table to roll out and cut sides, the nook table to assemble, then... Storing's going to be a problem. We have a couple of days until the dinner and the lanterns will be a little delicate. Any ideas?"

"Um..." She had to tear her mind from her parents to think. "What about the tasting room and the winery?" On second thought, she frowned. "But what would we put them on in the winery? There aren't many tables, and we wouldn't want to put them on the floor. We could place some in the empty vats, but they won't hold that many."

"That's it!" he said. "We've got some plywood sheets left over from a cubbyhole project for the day care. We can place them over the vats and they'll hold a lot more."

She buffed her nails against the shoulder of her sweater in a gesture of superiority. "Genius troubleshooter strikes again."

He put his hands to the counter on either side of her and blocked her in. "So when are you going to apply that problem-solving talent to our marriage? And don't you dare tell me that you want to wait to see what your parents do, because I am not marrying you based on their plans. I'm hopeful, but neither one of them is going to win a peace prize."

"You promised you wouldn't push," she reminded him.

"And I've kept that promise," he said. "But a relationship requires choices, Sam. I just want to remind you that the clock's ticking. I know you're worried about them, but you have to give some thought to us.''

"We've chosen each other," she said. "And I think about us all the time."

"All right." He kissed her, one hand at the middle of her back holding her firmly to him. Then he raised his head. "Keep thinking," he advised, "until you find a solution we can both live with."

"Trust me."

"I do."

BY SATURDAY MORNING of the dinner, the snow had melted, everything was in readiness for the night's two seatings at Delancey's and the air was spiced with the scent of gingerbread lanterns, which were everywhere.

Everyone had worked valiantly, the girls and Samantha's parents included. Adam and Audrey were speaking to each other, though Samantha saw no evidence that led her to believe they might reconcile. She had yet to see them touch.

Deep down, she knew that expecting them to remarry was probably outrageous, considering what they'd done to each other, but she remembered how they'd once been together and couldn't quite abandon the hope.

But watching Shea at work the past few days made her realize that it was time to take charge of her own marriage—or the absence thereof.

A plum news-industry job had been dropped in her lap, and as much as she loved the notion that her father had gotten it for her, she could drum up no enthusiasm for it. Her heart was here with Shea and their son and the rest of his family.

She was a big-city girl, born and bred, but she'd fallen in love with the vine-covered hills of French River. The day might come when she'd feel the need to take a job on the town's little weekly newspaper as a respite from her cozy life in the old four-square Victorian, but she didn't think so.

She'd seen Shea work tirelessly to make the dinner successful, marshal the people around him to help and keep them in good spirits with delicious snacks, wonderful meals and sincere appreciation.

There was a generosity in him that she'd taken for granted when they'd been together in San Francisco. He seemed blessed with the qualities required in a good husband and father.

He needled her occasionally about her reluctance to marry him, but he was always considerate and kind, and contributed as much to Zachary's care as he could, despite all the other pressures on him.

It was time she trusted all those qualities and made sure her own were as unselfishly dependable.

MIDMORNING, SHE HEARD the laundry truck rumble into the compound. The women in the family leaned over the dining-room and breakfast-nook tables, wrapping wood bases for the lanterns, in dark blue foil covered in tiny stars.

The men were in the yard, raking gravel and generally buffing up the outside. The entire compound would be turned into a parking area to accommodate the crowd.

Samantha went to her mother, who had the sleeping Zachary beside her in his carrier. ''I'm going to the restaurant to help Shea's crew set up now that the tablecloths and napkins have arrived. Why don't I take Zack with me.''

"He's fine here," Audrey answered. "If he starts to fuss, I'll give him a bottle.''

"You're sure?" Samantha asked. "What if you want to take a walk later or something?''

Audrey looked out at the cold and gloomy day. "A walk? I don't think so.''

"Even if she does…" Rachel, working across the table from her, glanced up to smile. "Say, if Adam invited her to walk through the vineyard or something, there are lots of us to take over.'' She put that idea forth in all apparent innocence.

Because of Adam and Audrey's quarrelsome meeting the day Audrey arrived, everyone on the compound knew their situation and did as much as possible to throw them together.

Samantha was touched by the knowledge that what was important to her had become important to the Delanceys.

"Okay, then.'' She kissed her mother's cheek, touched the baby's head, waved at Shea's brave band of slaves and headed for the restaurant. She stopped in the middle of the compound to sniff the damp but pure air and felt it fill every corner of her being. Marriage, she thought, seeing Shea in her mind's eye, was a wonderful idea. She pulled one of the double doors open and let herself into the restaurant.

SHEA GLANCED AT HIS WATCH, then at the skewered vegetables for the Mediterranean kabobs, and decided that things were going remarkably well. The wait staff were starting to set tables, the kitchen staff were working on the green-bean salad and Charlie was peeling pears to poach in pinot noir for dessert.

Shea pulled out of the oven a simple coffee cake that he'd made with sweet cream, covered it with a cloth and hurried out the kitchen door to take it to his lantern-making crew.

He was welcomed as enthusiastically as if he'd brought gold, though everyone kept working.

He went to the carrier to look in on his sleeping son, the hot pan held away from him. He experienced the now-familiar delight. "Where's Sam?" he asked Audrey.

Audrey frowned at him. "Didn't you see her? She went over to help you."

"Ah. Must have missed each other. You'll have to let this cool a couple of minutes," he said to Colette. "Then dish it up. Use butter, not that yogurt-whipped margarine mixture you put in the refrigerator."

"You're going to be fat in your middle age," Colette called after him as he walked into the kitchen, "and I'm going to be svelte."

"But I won't have hydrogenated oils in my body!" he shouted back.

He put the cake on the counter and helped himself to a cup of coffee. Charlie was a caffeine addict and had drained the staff pot in the restaurant kitchen.

The telephone rang and he put the cup down to answer it.

"Samantha Haskell, please?" a deep male voice said.

"She's not here at the moment," Shea replied. "May I take a message?"

"Yes," the man replied. "This is Kevin Bailey at

Condor News. I'm at my sister's for the holidays. Would you take down this number, please?''

Condor News. Shea didn't like the sound of this. But he reached for a pencil cup on the edge of the counter and a notepad beside it.

Shea dutifully recorded the number.

"Would you ask her to call me at this number and let me know when we can expect her?'' Bailey said.

The ground fell out from under Shea. The sensation was heightened by the cold dread that accompanied it. She was taking the job.

Without even telling him she'd been offered it.

After telling him she loved him and lying in his arms night after night.

Somehow, he found the voice to reply, "I'll see that she gets the message.''

"Thank you.''

"Sure.''

He hung up the phone, ripped the note off the pad and walked out the back door to the restaurant, the cold dread now replaced by hot anger.

She was walking back toward the house when he met her in the middle of the freshly raked gravel. She was all smiles, hair loose and flying out behind her as she picked up her pace toward him.

"There you are!'' she said, her voice light and warm. "I was coming to help set up, but I heard you'd headed for the house with a warm coffee...'' Her eyes roved his face as she talked, then she stopped abruptly when she reached his eyes. "What?'' she asked warily.

"This!'' he said, thrusting the note at her.

She read it, then nodded regretfully. "I was going to tell you about that, but we—''

"Oh, I know,'' he interrupted, his anger cooling,

hardening into emotional plastique. "You'd have called me from San Francisco to tell me you'd left. Just like you told me I was a father by letting me find out on the six o'clock news."

Her face paled, her eyes darkened with pain. "That isn't fair."

He pointed to the note she held. "And that is? We've been loving our son together, loving each other, sharing my family and yours, and you were going to just—"

She tried to interrupt. "I was—"

He kept talking as though she hadn't spoken, "—walk away to find your own future because you can't trust yourself to be any more responsible about holding on to love than your parents were! Have you learned nothing in the time we've spent together?" He hated that he was shouting. He'd wanted to speak his piece in a calm and controlled manner to show her that he was going to survive this.

But it was becoming clear that wasn't going to happen. Her leaving was a giant barbed thing inside him that he had to force out, and shouting seemed to help.

He made a conscious effort to lower his voice. One hundred and ninety-two people were coming to dinner tonight, and he couldn't lose it until they'd gotten what they came for.

That he was never going to get what *he* wanted didn't matter.

"Well, you know what?" he asked in a deceptively amiable tone. "I'm beginning to think you're right about yourself." He pointed to his chest. "I made mistakes, too, but they were *never* because I didn't think I could love you forever. They were because I did, and I didn't want to hurt you. So go. Enjoy your life in San Francisco. But you damn well better get a lawyer, because I'm sharing custody of Zachary whether that's part of your plan or not.''

SAMANTHA COULDN'T quite assimilate what had happened. Bailey had called the house—maybe her father had left him the number when he'd gotten her message to come?—while she was at the restaurant and Shea had taken the call.

But that didn't explain…

Shea tried to storm past her toward the restaurant, but she caught the sleeve of his chef's jacket and held on.

Confusion and hurt feelings were turning to a very lively fury and she'd be damned if she'd let him walk away before she'd spoken.

"What did Bailey say?" she demanded.

He pointed to the note. "I wrote it down!" he said, reaching for her hand to pry it off, but she tightened her grip and something in her eyes made him stop. Murder, probably.

"What did he *say?*" she screamed at him.

"That he was at his sister's for the holiday," he replied, his fingers still gripping her fist, "and you should call him there. He wanted to know when to 'expect' you."

She shook off his hand and dropped hers. "So that's what happened. He didn't get the message I left on his voice mail at the office."

Something changed in his eyes; his confidence slipped. "What message?"

Everything inside her trembled with rage, but she put her hands in her pockets and replied coolly, "That I appreciated his offer of employment, but I was getting married and staying in Oregon."

She watched Shea's sudden pallor with real pleasure and went on in the same tone. "But, all things considered, it's probably a good thing he didn't get the message, because, as you've just made clear to me…" She paused, her anger erupting in a voice several decibels louder. *"It's no longer accurate!"*

Shea closed his eyes for an instant but didn't flinch.

"I'll tell you what I learned in the time we've spent together!" she went on, still shouting. "That I will *not* spend the rest of my life with a man who has known me all this time—even made love to me!—and still hasn't a clue who I am!"

Finally finished, she felt breathless and dizzy and guessed that she was expelling far more air than she was taking in. She took a moment to gulp in a breath.

"If it wasn't for the dinner—and that I want to talk to your family first—I would be so out of here you wouldn't even see my dust. I'll stay to help, but Zack and I are gone first thing in the morning. I'd appreciate it if you'd keep of my way until then."

She walked on to the house.

CHAPTER SIXTEEN

SHEA FELT AS THOUGH HE HAD an anvil strapped to his chest. Only long experience allowed him to continue working with his customary skill, if not inspiration.

He'd just done it again—hurt her without finding out first what the true nature of the problem was. And he'd accused *her* of having learned nothing since she'd been here.

The restaurant was now a little like a military operation—controlled chaos. He finally accepted that he didn't have a moment now to focus on Samantha and Zachary, or the Magi Dinner would not come together. He pushed them to the back of his mind, trying to cheer himself with the possibility that if he threw himself on Samantha's mercy, she might listen to reason.

Then he acknowledged with a kind of fatal humor that she seldom listened to reason, even when things were *good* between them.

The kitchen door opened suddenly and Henry Warren walked in. Shea stared at him in surprise. He'd called him several days ago and shared just a little of what Felicia had told him, explaining how she'd regretted letting him go. Henry had been terse and noncommittal over the phone.

He appeared anything but now. He wore casual clothes and a very frantic look.

Shea dusted himself off on the front of his apron and held out his hand. "Hey, Henry. Good to see you."

"You, too." Henry shook his hand. "Did I thank you for calling?"

Shea thought back. "I'm not sure. I figured maybe you'd have preferred I'd butt out."

Henry sighed. "I did. But that was only because admitting that her pain was more important to me than my pain required maturity and a little time. I am glad you called. Where is…?"

As though on cue, Felicia walked into the kitchen from the dining room. She'd been gluing tea lights to lantern bases with icing since lunch and was now putting on the lanterns as they arrived.

She wore jeans and a sweatshirt with birdhouses on the front, her hair in one long disheveled braid. "Shea, do you have fireplace matches back here?" she asked. "I thought we'd light one just to make— Henry!" She stopped halfway into the room, color flooding her face.

Henry walked across the kitchen toward her, took her into his arms and kissed her so that there was no mistaking his intentions. "You're going to marry me," he said when he finally freed her.

Shea admired his style. He didn't ask the question; he made a statement.

"How come?" she asked, looking befuddled.

"Because you want to," he replied.

"But what do you want?" she asked.

"You," he replied firmly, then his features softened and he put a hand to her cheek. "I've always wanted you."

She burst into tears and threw her arms around him.

Shea wandered out into the dining room to give them a moment's privacy, feeling good about his decision to interfere. He also felt good about how the dining room looked. Large, dark blue foil bows adorned the tops of the lantern houses and the effect was dramatic against the silver-gray tablecloths.

A tall silk Chritmas tree in a corner of the room was already lit, its white lights accentuating the blue ornaments and silver stars that trimmed it. Beside it in a frame on an easel stood Tate's rendering of the new seniors facility, complete with gardens on all sides and an outside eating area.

"How does the room look, Mr. Delancey?" Dean, the backbone of his eleven-to-four shift because he went to school at night and could work afternoons, was placing silverware from a large basket.

The other seven helping out stopped in their work to hear his answer.

"I think Le Cirque would have to go a long way to beat us," he said. "I appreciate your volunteering. All of you."

"My grandmother lived there." Claudette was a senior in high school and worked the dinner shift with grace and poise. She gave him that information solemnly. "She's living with us now, but she really misses her friends."

Ginger, a gray-haired woman who worked banquets, laughed wryly. "I'll probably live there myself in a couple of years. I want to make sure it's around."

Shea pointed toward the kitchen. "Bonuses for all of you after we've cleared up tonight, just to let you know we appreciate you."

There were squeals and applause.

Shea saw Felicia and Henry come out into the dining room and go back to work assembling lanterns, every now and then looking up to gaze at each other adoringly. He went into the kitchen, relieved that he'd been able to make somebody happy.

SAMANTHA SAT ON THE FLOOR beside Shea's bed, the baby in her arms, knowing there were a million things she should be doing yet unable to muster the heart. She promised herself she would get to them in a minute, but not right now.

She'd been crying for half an hour; it hadn't helped, though. She still felt broken, crushed.

A light rap sounded on the door.

"Yes?" she asked in a high voice, a tissue pressed to her nose.

Her parents walked in, her mother leading the way. Her father closed the door behind him.

"What are you doing on the floor?" her mother asked.

"The bed is Shea's," she said. "I'm not sitting on it. I don't want anything to do with him or his things!"

Her mother sat down cross-legged on one side of her. Her father sat down on the other with a dramatic groan.

"You realize," he said, "that it's going to take a forklift to get me up again."

"Tate told us what happened," Audrey said. "He and Mike were working in the winery and the doors were open. They heard everything."

Samantha's composure crumbled again. "I can't believe he thought I'd just run off after all we've…" The last word broke on a sob.

"I can believe it," Adam said. "I did the same thing with your mother and Fabrizio." He took her hand in his two. "When you love someone very much, any threat to your being able to keep them near overloads you with feelings and you forget to think.''

"Yeah!" Samantha pointed out tearfully. "And look at what it did to you. Two great people running around like a couple of reckless oversexed sillies." She realized too late what she'd said, then glanced at each apologetically. "I'm sorry, but it's true."

"Yes," her mother admitted. "It is. But I hope what you've learned from it is that you don't want to end up like us."

"That's the truth."

"So, you're going to go to Shea after the dinner and try to straighten things out?" Adam asked.

"No!" She handed the baby to her mother and got to her feet. She dusted off her slacks and reclaimed him. "I'm leaving here in the morning before Zachary gets any more attached to him."

Her father got to his knees and used the bedroom chair to pull himself up. "But what about *your* attachment to Shea? You were miserable without him the last time. How do you think you'll feel now that you've shared this baby and his wonderful family?"

"Come on, Sam." Her mother pulled herself up, and Adam reached down to offer a helping hand. "Don't be the fool I was. Don't flounce off in anger because it's more comfortable than swallowing your hurt feelings. Give him a chance to make it right. Then if he doesn't, you haven't lost anything. Your father and I lost almost an entire year."

Samantha caught the significance of the words the moment they were spoken. She saw that her father had, too, when he stopped on his way to the door and turned to face his ex-wife.

"Are you suggesting," he asked cautiously, "that you don't want to lose any more?"

She held both hands out to him. "What would you say to that?"

He looked a little shaken. "I guess…'Will you marry me…again?' comes to mind."

"Yes, I will," her mother replied, then turned to Samantha with a smile. "See how easy that was?" She glanced at her watch. "Good grief! Five o'clock! We have to get ready."

Samantha watched in stupefaction as her parents bustled each other out the door, then forgot her promise to herself and sank onto the edge of Shea's bed.

"Did I misread that?" she asked Zachary. "Or did your grandparents just agree to remarry?"

Zachary smiled widely and flung a hand out in his excitement over her attention. It connected with her nose.

"Right," she said, catching his hand and kissing it. "There's a message for me here."

EVERYTHING READY, Shea took a last walk through the dining room. The staff, Felicia and Henry walked around the room, lighting the lanterns.

They looked as spectacular as he'd imagined. He took pride in that, but any pleasure he might have earned from it was out of reach.

He walked out the front door to check the look of the compound.

Mike and Tate, wearing tuxedos, flanked the doors, ready to greet the first arrivals, who were due at any moment. He frowned at the empty sleigh near the Christmas tree. "Where's Burgess?"

Mike shook his head. "Sorry. He got the flu. I tried

to find a replacement, but no luck. The sleigh looks pretty good, though, don't you think? Even empty."

"Yeah, looks great."

It was odd, Shea thought, how a loss from personal stupidity made you think about how lucky you were to have all the things in your life that were simply showered upon you, whether or not you deserved them.

His brothers, who'd harassed him unmercifully and still loved him back to life and financial stability; *their* families, a harbor of comfort and laughter in good times and bad; this place in this rich, sweet-smelling valley, and the purpose and knowledge working it had brought them. His staff, now good friends, who'd given up an entire day to help him.

And finding Jack. They were all so happy that he was alive, that he'd been able to make a life with Tess. Mike's friend had removed Robert Mullins's name from the Social Security files, Shea knew, so that eliminated one threat to their safety.

"The whole place looks wonderful," Shea said, then glanced from one brother to the other. "Even you guys look good. How'd you do that?"

Tate shrugged. "Everyone looks good in a tuxedo. Is this our first arrival?"

An old compact pulled into the compound, taking the corner with a squeal of tires and racing to the restaurant to brake suddenly in front with a jerk that rocked the vehicle. Its color was indistinct until it stood under the lights.

"Father Wolff!" they all said simultaneously.

Mike went to help him open his door. He had passengers with him. "Hi, Father."

He gave Mike a hug, then hugged Tate and Shea. "I'm Rudolph tonight!" he said with a wide smile.

"I've brought Santa to you. Not only Santa, but the Mrs., also!"

"Really." Tate opened the passenger door and helped out the plump Mrs. Santa, complete with dust cap, little glasses and a fluffy white wig.

He offered his hand, "Tate Delancey," he said. "Thanks for coming at the last minute like this."

"Oh, we'd have been here anyway," she said in a voice Shea found familiar but couldn't quite place. "We visit the homes of all the good boys and girls. Don't we, Santa?"

Santa stepped out of the car, a hand to his padded stomach. "Yes, we do, my dear!" he said in a big voice. "Ho! Ho! Ho! And we wouldn't miss this place...for any...thing."

They all looked at one another when Santa's voice broke. He was gazing around the compound. He pointed to the Queen Anne house, which was beautifully outlined in lights. "Is that...the B and B you told me about?" he asked.

Tate took the tip of Santa's beard and tugged. The beard and the attached mustache slid down on white elastic to reveal a very familiar face.

"Uncle Jack!" they said, again in unison.

Tate turned to Mrs. Santa. "Tess?" he asked.

"Of course," she said with a laugh. "Apparently this was Veronica's idea, though Father Wolff came for us and rented the costumes and everything. It was a way to get us here to spend Christmas with you without much risk to our discovery." She pointed to the sleigh. "If we just sit up there and wave as your guests arrive, we'll be fine. No one knows me, and Jack's unidentifiable. Then we'll just stay inside until we go home again. That'll work, won't it?"

Tate hugged her and then Jack again. "Of course it'll work."

"We'll take you on a tour first thing in the morning," Mike said, wrapping Jack in his arms. "We're so glad you're here, Jack." He moved on to Tess. "You, too. We'll keep you safe, don't worry. How's Daniel?"

"He and Eileen were going to call you and see if they could reserve a room at the B and B between Christmas and New Year's Day."

"Great! That's a quiet week for us. I'm sure that'll work."

Shea went to wrap an arm around Jack and Tess.

"Turning out to be a pretty perfect Christmas," Father Wolff said.

Shea smiled as he and Mike helped Jack and Tess onto the sleigh, and Tate closed the car door on the priest, who was heading back to town to change and return for the second seating. On one very important level it was a perfect Christmas. On another…well, changing it from bleak to perfect was up to him.

But for the next three hours, he hardly had a moment to breathe, much less track down Samantha, force her to stand still while he explained that he'd been a jerk, then convince her to forgive him.

He thought he might find time during the break between seatings, but while the staff was swamped resetting tables, putting down new lanterns, he was busy replacing two tables' worth of food dropped on the floor.

Claudette, the culprit, was beside herself. "Mr. D., I'm so sorry!" she wept, hurrying to clean up the mess. "I was trying to work too fast. I'm…"

"I'll get the extras," Charlie said, running to the fridge in the back.

"Not a problem," Shea lied while he worked. "I prepared an extra ten dinners just in case. Stay calm. When you have that cleaned up, pick two tables that look friendly and ask them if they mind waiting a few extra minutes for the food. It's all cooked. I just have to dress it up a little."

The mess disposed of, she washed her hands, smoothed her tux jacket, pasted on a smile and went out into the dining room.

Half an hour later, crisis averted, Shea poured himself a glass of wine and paced the kitchen. He'd sent Charlie out to eat with his parents and his wife, who'd bought tickets. The rest of the kitchen crew were taking a well-deserved break outside, cups of coffee in hand; a restaurant kitchen became so hot after a long day that even damp December air was a welcome relief.

Shea had seen Samantha pouring water, coffee, tea. She'd bussed in dishes during the break with only one hurt glance at him. Since then she'd come in to fill requests for more of the parsley-and-chive miniloaves, more butter, more cream, but she hadn't looked his way again.

His family had wandered into the back of the kitchen in little groups to hunt up something to eat in quiet moments, but Samantha hadn't come. He guessed that after their argument, she felt as much like eating as he did.

As soon as dessert was served, he thought, he would find her and make her listen to his apology. Until then, he would just have to wonder whether or not he'd killed his future.

Ginger bustled in. "Table twenty-one wants to see the chef, Mr. Delancey," she said.

He'd just sat down on the stool. His feet were killing him. "Do they want to compliment the chef or complain?" he asked.

She shook her head. "They didn't say, but everyone's raving about the dinner. I can't imagine they have a complaint."

"Then ask Charlie to go."

"Charlie's eating, Mr. D. And the gentlemen look important."

Shea forced himself to his feet, took off his hat and wandered out to table twenty-one. There was a smattering of applause as he passed, a few handshakes, much praise.

Nothing felt quite as good, he thought, forgetting his weariness for a moment, and his anvil of guilt, as walking out into a dining room filled with people who were eating and talking with great enjoyment, relishing the food that enhanced their conversation and camaraderie.

Distracted by that pleasure, he didn't notice who sat at table twenty-one until he was within reaching distance of one of the men wearing three-piece suits. The men were all large, all impeccably groomed, all smiling warmly. One of them caught his wrist and pulled him down into the empty chair.

These were the friends from whom Marty Hirsch had borrowed money to support the gambling debts that had finally bankrupted Chez Shea and landed him in jail.

Shea felt an oddly calm sense of having come full circle. These men had eaten at Chez Shea several times and Marty had always treated them especially well.

Shea had just presumed they were friends and never

gave their presence a second thought—except to grieve over the smallest one's request for ketchup with every meal—only to learn too late that Marty had turned over to them the business's entire budget, then paid the bank and the IRS and taken off for Mexico before the checks bounced higher than Mount McKinley.

He thought now that it should have occurred to him once Delancey's started making money that Marty's lenders might look to him for restitution. But he'd been into getting over the past, moving on—all his self-protective instincts forgotten in the adventure his life had become.

"Don't tell me," Shea said to the smallest one. "You need ketchup."

The little man opened his mouth, probably to agree, but his companions stared him down. He went back to his chicken.

The big man, whom Marty had always called "Hammer," tightened his grip on Shea's arm. He smiled for the benefit of those watching. "There's going to be red stuff all over you if you don't just shut up and listen. And it ain't going to be ketchup."

The threat bounced off Shea in light of what he might have already lost today. But on the chance that he hadn't, he thought it wise to cooperate as far as he could.

He waited for Hammer to go on.

"Good," Hammer praised, "that's good. Now, look. Hirsch went to the slammer owing us a lot of cash, and since he's not coming out anytime soon, and he's got nothin' left anyway, we think you, as his business partner, should come up with the balance. What do you think?"

Okay. He'd cooperated long enough. "I think that

your mother probably cooked with aluminum,'' Shea replied, ''and that your brain is slowly erasing itself.''

Dark color came up from the neckline of Hammer's impeccably white shirt. The middle fellow, tall and slender and somehow creepier than the other two put together, looked pleased with that answer.

Shea could only guess that it meant Hammer was going to let Creepy hurt him.

''Okay,'' Hammer said with another smile. ''We've spent a lot of effort and energy trying to find you. And we could have just shot our way in here anytime during the past couple of days, but we didn't do that.''

That was the moment when Shea began to feel fear. Up until now it had been him and them and he'd been almost more interested in what was happening than alarmed by it.

But now he was thinking about his woman, his son, his family and the unsuspecting guests who filled the room.

''No,'' Hammer went on with apparent calm sincerity. ''We showed consideration. We bought tickets to this shindig and—I gotta tell ya—we've enjoyed it. In fact, I'm thinking if the big boss could taste this, he'd probably ask you to come and cook for him to erase the debt. But he isn't here and I can't make those kinds of deals. I gotta go home with something to show for this trip, you know what I'm saying? You gotta cough it up, Delancey.''

Shea nodded. ''I understand your position,'' he said, frantically considering options. Rachel was at the house watching Zachary, and when the last guest had arrived for the second seating, Armand had taken Jack and Tess there, too.

Some guests from the first seating were touring the

winery and the tasting room, and there were guests in
the B and B. The cottage was Rachel's home, and the
daycare center was out of the question.

"Let's go for a ride into the vineyard," he said,
concentrating primarily on getting these men out of this
crowded room and away from his family. "I can probably help you out, but it's going to require some figuring."

He tried to stand, but Hammer still held his arm.
"No figuring," Hammer said. "I need a hundred grand
or I just can't leave you standing, kid."

"That may be possible," he lied. Actually, he had
almost no liquid assets—except maybe his blood. "My
checkbook's in the car."

Creepy looked doubtful. "The car? You leave a
checkbook with that kind of money in it in the car?"

Shea smiled. "I was picking up food and supplies
all morning, and you may find this hard to believe, but
there's no one in French River who'd steal anything
from anybody else. You coming?" This time he shook
off Hammer's hand and stood.

Some people turned their way, attention caught by
the movement.

"Follow me, gentlemen," Shea said, and led the
way between tables toward the dining-room door.

SAMANTHA, SUSAN AND SARAH converged at the wait
station, an area at the right side of the doors into the
kitchen. It was fitted with utensils, the coffeepots and
the bussing basins, and was shielded from the restaurant by a shoulder-high decorative wall.

Colette and Veronica were schmoozing from table
to table, Mike was conducting a tour of the winery, her
parents were talking newspapers with the publisher of

the *McMinnville News Register,* who'd bought several tables, and Megan and Katie were helping Father Wolff sell raffle tickets at a table set up at the front of the restaurant.

The wait staff were seeing to all the small demands of people enjoying their meal—more coffee, more water, the purchase of another bottle of wine.

Susan and Sarah had worked without complaint, sizing up the teenage boys accompanying their parents and meeting up during slack times to compare notes.

The evening was an unqualified success. Over the course of it, Samantha's anger vanished in the face of all Shea had accomplished here. She'd come to the conclusion that if he hadn't been so stressed, he might have given more thought to that message from Bailey, might have asked her what it meant, before he pounced on her with accusations.

If she'd explained to him in the first place that she'd been offered the job, the whole thing wouldn't have been such a surprise to him—and therefore a danger. And if she hadn't been so predisposed to believe love wouldn't last, she'd have fought harder to make him understand.

She congratulated herself on her maturity in accepting partial responsibility for their argument. And as soon as they got dessert on the table, she was going to try to explain that to him.

"Are we ready to serve dessert?" Susan asked. "I know *I'm* ready to eat one."

"Yeah." Sarah poured herself a glass of water. "Nobody makes poached pears like Uncle Shea. Did you get to taste it, Aunt Sam?"

"No, I didn't." She'd been pouting in their room when Shea had sent over the samples for the family.

"But I don't think he's capable of making anything
that isn't delicious."

She loved the way Tate's daughters, all four of them,
considered her "Aunt" Sam. They didn't understand
that she might have been ambivalent about where she
fit into Shea's life. They knew only that she shared a
house with their uncle and had his baby, so she was
Aunt Sam.

She rather liked the simplicity of it.

Samantha glanced at her watch. "We have to clear
away dinner dishes beforehand. The first tables we
served are looking finished. Maybe we should..." And
it was as she scanned the room in search of Dean to
ask him what he thought that she spotted the three men
she remembered from Chez Shea in San Francisco.

She'd seen them only a couple of times, but they'd
made her very uncomfortable, though she wouldn't
have been able to say why. Many big scary-looking
men turned out to be pussycats. She'd felt reasonably
sure those three wouldn't.

And she'd been right. They'd turned out to be the
loan sharks Marty Hirsch had been involved with.

Fear chilled her to the tips of her toes. What were
they doing here? She felt she could hazard a guess
when she saw Ginger walk out of the kitchen with Shea
and point him in the direction of their table.

She felt a sudden, desperate need to stop Shea, but
people were shaking his hand, talking to him as he
walked. When he reached the table, the biggest man
there caught his arm and pulled him down into a chair.
Despite the man's smile, she knew his intentions
couldn't be good. Marty had gone to jail owing them
a bundle. And Delancey's reputation had begun to

spread far and wide. They must have come thinking they could make Shea responsible for Marty's debt.

"Aunt Sam, what's the matter?" Sarah asked. "Are you okay?"

When everyone at the table stood, Samantha made an instant decision. She turned to Sarah. "Sweetie, please go find your dad and tell him Uncle Shea needs him."

"But what...?"

Samantha gave her a little push. "Now, Sarah, please. And hurry! Those men want to hurt your uncle!

"Susan, you go to the winery and get Uncle Mike! Tell him to come right away!"

"Okay!"

She caught the arm of the nearest waitress, asked her to call 911 and pushed her toward the kitchen. "Tell them to hurry!" she whispered after her.

She ran across the room to the aisle along the wall and intercepted the foursome halfway to the door.

"Just a minute!" she whispered harshly. While she tried to make her expression fierce, her mind hoped that Tate and Mike would be easily found. She prayed Mike hadn't wandered across the compound to show someone a dark corner of the cellar Susan might miss in her search for him. Seconds could be critical here. The big man looked upset by her interference.

She pretended not to recognize who he was. "I don't know where you think you're going with him, but these people haven't had dessert yet. He can't leave."

She braced herself for harsh words or threats from the trio, who looked like something out of *Guys and Dolls*. She was surprised when Shea caught her wrist and squeezed.

"I'll be right back," he said. His tone was gentle, though his touch was not. "Why don't you go back to the kitchen and make sure dessert's ready?"

"No, that's your job," she insisted quietly, putting her hand over his and trying to pull him along with her.

"Lady!" the big one said under his breath as he caught her arm.

Shea got between them and pushed the man away, forcing him to free her or make the scene he was trying hard to avoid.

Shea turned back to her, glancing over her shoulder at the crowded room behind her. Her heart was hammering against her ribs, but he smiled, apparently returning a greeting from someone.

"Listen to me," he said, still smiling. "I'm going to be fine. We have a dining room filled with people, so we're going *outside* to talk. I'll be back."

She understood. He was telling her he wanted them outside to minimize the risk to Delancey's guests. But she was afraid that once the three men had him beyond the door, he was fair game. She'd watched enough television to know that a loan shark's method of asking for payment was to demonstrate what would happen if terms weren't met.

She couldn't let Shea leave with them. It was an odd moment, she thought as Shea started to lead them away, to realize just how much in love with him she was. His risk, her risk. His pain, her pain. It was all the same. They were inextricably connected, and not just through their baby. What she felt now was very personal.

He belonged to her and no one was going to hurt him.

She followed them out the door and into the night lit by the compound spots and the garland lights. She was absently aware of the cold, but it blended into her fear and that was something she was determined to ignore.

"If you're taking him," she shouted, running after them, "you're taking me, too!"

The big man swung around and pointed something at her. It was poorly defined in the darkness, but one of the spotlights glinted off its surface and she concluded it was a gun.

"You take one more step—" he threatened, as Shea, caught between the other two men, kicked the gun out of his hand. It flew somewhere into the shadows.

The big man turned and punched Shea viciously in the stomach.

Samantha screamed and leaped on him, no sane plan in mind but angry retribution.

Suddenly there were shouts, scuffles and the sound of blows as she clung to the man, who bucked like a billy goat attempting to shake her off.

Then she was caught around the waist and lifted aside. Finally free of her, the big man wheeled. Shea's fists shot out, taking advantage of the man's confusion, and Hammer was nailed.

Tate and Mike emerged from the shadows, Tate half dragging the smaller man, Mike holding the other one by the back of his collar. When he let him go, he crumpled to the ground.

Shea faced Samantha, who all of a sudden was sharply aware of the cold. That must be why she didn't seem able to move. She wanted to go to him, but the spotlights were beginning to spin and...so was he.

Her knees seemed to insist on bending, though she

didn't want to kneel, and the rest of her was inclined to follow. She felt herself swept up just as she was about to hit the ground. Everything went black as the sound of a siren filled the night.

CHAPTER SEVENTEEN

WARMTH SEEPED into Samantha's frozen limbs. Even before she opened her eyes, she felt the glow of a nearby fire, the delicious comfort of strong arms wrapped around her, the hush of concerned voices in the background.

She tensed, remembering violence in the compound and Shea in danger. She sat up abruptly, shouting his name with anguish as she recalled the ugly gut punch he'd taken.

She discovered she was sitting in his lap in the corner chair, which someone had placed in front of the restaurant kitchen's fieldstone fireplace. And he was smiling at her.

She put her fingertips to a bruise on his cheek. "Are you all right?" she asked anxiously.

He smiled with the superior confidence of a man who knew himself to be loved. "I am, thank you." He smoothed the hair from her face, his eyes caressing her feature by feature. "But the next time I'm hauled away by thugs, I'd appreciate it if you'd stay back out of the way when I ask you."

His family and hers were gathered around them. She looped her arms around his neck and leaned into him without embarrassment. "Now, what kind of a wife would I be if I let someone take you away and beat you up without making some effort to stop him?"

She squeezed him tightly, so grateful for his good health that she thought she might never let him go. "Did I hear the police arrive?"

He closed his arms around her with a fervor that was almost painful. "You did," he said. "Marty's friends have been hauled away and charged with assault. I don't think we'll be seeing them for a while."

"I'm sorry about this morning," she said, tightening her grip on him.

"I know that, too. So am I. I should have told you."

There was a communal "Aah!" from the family in a stage whisper, followed by happy laughter. They began to move away to grant Shea and Samantha privacy.

Samantha straightened to catch Tate's arm and smile up at him and Mike. "Thank you for coming so quickly," she said. "I was really scared."

"That's our job," Tate said. "Mike and I to the rescue. We've been doing it since he first started walking and getting himself into trouble."

"But he's paid us back," Mike reminded him, "with the most popular restaurant in the state. I don't think we can pick on him anymore."

Tate put a hand to Mike's forehead. "Somebody get a chair. Do you feel yourself slipping?"

Mike laughed and smacked his hand away. "I know—it almost hurts to say it, but he's earned it. He's one of us." He brought his fist down lightly on Shea's head. "It was a great night, Shea. We made a bundle, everyone loved it and we may have to sell those gingerbread lantern things in the gift shop. They were a big hit. You did a remarkable job."

"That's true," Tate agreed seriously. "If you hadn't done such a great job with this place, this winter wouldn't be half as pleasant as it's been."

"And this Christmas is going to be one hell of a celebration," Mike said.

Veronica backhanded him in the stomach and pointed to the priest standing behind her. "*Heck* of a celebration," she corrected.

"Hell is fine," the priest said, nibbling on a piece of the herbed bread that had accompanied dinner. "It's a real place. He can say hell. Though it has nothing whatever to do with this place."

"That's right." Tate ushered the family toward the door to the dining room. "Come on. We've got champagne and we're going to your house, Shea. But you're not fixing anything. Rachel and the girls have collected nibblies and we're going to bask in our success."

"Great," Shea said. "We'll be right there. Who has our son, anyway?"

"That would be me." Uncle Jack, still dressed as Santa, came forward and handed over Zachary, who was wrapped in a bright yellow blanket.

As Shea's loudly laughing family walked through the dining room and across the compound, Shea sat in front of the fire with Samantha and Zachary, emotion crowding his throat.

"I'm the luckiest man on earth," he said, his voice raspy.

"How fortunate," Samantha said, kissing his jaw as she leaned into him, her arm wrapped around the baby, "that you have the luckiest woman and the luckiest child. Merry Christmas, my love."

He kissed her in reply, his heart too full for words.

IT WAS WELL AFTER MIDNIGHT when Shea saw Tate and Mike step out onto the porch. Despite the lateness of the hour and the slavish schedule of the past few days, they were all lighthearted with success and happy in one another's company. An hysterical game of charades was under way, the noise level so high it would have brought the police had the compound been any closer to town.

Sterling lay on a blanket in front of the fire, curled up to the baby, who was vigilantly watched over by all four of Tate's girls. They patted the cat and the baby.

Shea went out to join his brothers.

Tate stood at the top step right in the middle, surveying the compound like a king his kingdom. Mike and Shea stood on either side of him.

"If our wine's any good," Tate said, "then we've proven to ourselves and everyone else that we know how to do this. To maintain the level of challenge, we should maybe consider the other career we thought about when we moved here."

"You mean piracy?" Mike asked.

Tate put an arm around each of them. "Yeah. You in?"

"Sure."

Tate turned to Shea. "You?"

"Depends," Shea replied. "On what?"

"Do we have to learn to make rum?"

* * * * *

Mulled Wine

2 quarts Burgundy wine
2 quarts cranberry juice
1 cup sugar
1 whole orange peel studded with 12 cloves

(then you won't have to pick out the cloves when
you serve)
1 cinnamon stick

Simmer ingredients together until sugar dissolves,
then serve. Or put it in a crock-pot if company's
coming. Not only will it stay warm, but the aroma
will waft through the house.

Recipe thanks to Lauren Arena of Someplace
Else, a Restaurant, Astoria, Oregon.

Boiled Marinated Shrimp

12 large shrimp, shelled and deveined
1 small bottle creamy French salad dressing
1 tablespoon minced garlic
12 toast rounds
$1/2$ cup grated Cheddar cheese

Fill a medium saucepan halfway with water and
bring to a boil. Blanch shrimp just until cooked,
then drain. In a medium bowl, whisk together
French dressing and garlic. Add shrimp and stir
to cover. Refrigerate at least 2 hours or overnight.
Place shrimp on toast rounds and top each with
a little cheese. Broil until cheese is melted and
bubbly. Serve on small plates as a first course.
Serves four.

Roasted Chicken With Herbed Ricotta Stuffing

1 $2^1/2$ pound roasting chicken
salt and pepper

5 tablespoons minced fresh parsley
2 green onions, tops included, minced
1 clove garlic, minced
2 teaspoons minced fresh tarragon
$^1/_4$ teaspoon minced fresh oregano
$^1/_4$ teaspoon minced fresh thyme
1 tablespoon ricotta cheese
1 teaspoon oil
$^3/_4$ cup chicken stock

Preheat oven to 425 degrees.

Season chicken inside and out with salt and pepper. With your fingers (don't use a knife), working from the neck opening down, gently separate the skin from the breast meat, on down to the top of the drumsticks.

Combine parsley, green onions, garlic, tarragon, oregano, thyme and ricotta and make a paste with a mortar and pestle. Spread this mixture as evenly as possible on the breast and thigh meat underneath the skin. Pat the skin back in place and truss the chicken. Brush the skin lightly with 1 teaspoon oil.

Roast chicken at 425 degrees for 25 minutes. Reduce oven to 350 degrees and continue roasting for an additional 40 minutes, or until the chicken is nicely browned and the juices run clear when pierced.

Remove chicken to a warm platter and keep warm. Remove excess fat from roasting pan. Place pan on stove over medium-high heat.

Whisk in chicken stock, scraping up any browned bits. Continue to cook until reduced by half.

Cut the chicken into serving pieces and place on platter. Pour the stock reduction over the chicken and garnish with parsley.

Serves 4.

Garlic Mashed Potatoes

4 pounds baking potatoes, peeled and quartered
36 cloves garlic, peeled
9 tablespoons half-and-half
6 tablespoons butter, room temperature
Salt and freshly ground pepper to taste
Minced fresh Italian parsley

Combine potatoes and garlic in a large pot and cover with water. Bring to a boil, then reduce heat to medium and cook until potatoes are tender, about 30 minutes. Drain and mash potatoes together with garlic until smooth. Stir in half-and-half and butter. Season with salt and pepper. Garnish with minced parsley and serve.

Grilled Fresh Garden Vegetable Kabobs

1 cup soy sauce
$\frac{1}{2}$ cup Foris Vineyards Chardonnay
$\frac{1}{4}$ cup honey
3 cloves garlic, minced
1 teaspoon grated fresh ginger
2 medium yellow crookneck squash, cut into 1-inch pieces

2 medium zucchini, cut into 1-inch pieces
2 red bell peppers, cut into 1-inch pieces
$1/2$ pound medium mushrooms

Whisk together soy sauce, Foris Vineyards Chardonnay, honey, garlic and ginger in a large bowl. Place vegetables in marinade and refrigerate at least 1 hour, stirring occasionally. Thread vegetables alternately on skewers. Grill over low coals, turning frequently until vegetables are cooked and browned all over.

Serves 6.

Recipes thanks to *Recipes from the Vinyards of Oregon* by Leslie J. Whipple.

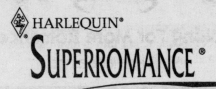

HARLEQUIN®
SUPERROMANCE®

Three childhood friends dreamed of becoming
firefighters. Now they're members of the same team
and every day they put their lives on the line.

They are

AMERICA'S BRAVEST

An exciting new trilogy by

Kathryn Shay

#871 FEEL THE HEAT
(November 1999)
#877 THE MAN WHO LOVED CHRISTMAS
(December 1999)
#882 CODE OF HONOR
(January 2000)

Available wherever Harlequin books are sold.

HARLEQUIN®
Makes any time special ™

Looking For More Romance?

Visit Romance.net

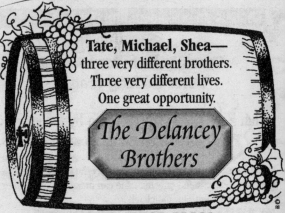

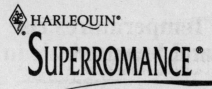